# A Fair Knight Slain

## Murder at the Renaissance Fair

Linda LeBlanc

Ama Dablam Inc

Print layout, e–book conversion, and cover design by DLD Books Editing and Self–Publishing Services
www.dldbooks.com

Published by Ama Dablam, Inc.
ISBN 978-0-9785353-3-9

1.murder mystery books, whodunit novel. 2. police procedural, police fiction, undercover.  3. Detective books, women detectives, women sleuths. 4.suspense books, suspense fiction. 5. Crime fiction, crime mystery books. 6 Bickering partners, knights, Viking, falconer.  7 Plot twist books, story with twists and turns

# Chapter 1

In the Renaissance fair village, Sara strode toward a large dragon swing suspended by heavy chains from two live oaks. Fluorescent green wings stretched along both sides, and red spikes ran down the body onto its tail. Her gut tightened as she ducked under the yellow crime scene tape. A bare-chested man in his mid-thirties lay sprawled in the belly, bloodied from his heart to the hollow of his shoulder.

She'd endured violence as a child but never grown immune to the brutality lying before her. Sara dragged her hands down over her face. *Why do people do such things to each other?*

She told the CSI team, "Don't bother dusting for fingerprints and pouring footprint molds. Hundreds of visitors have walked all over the place and climbed on the swing. Who found the body?"

An agent gestured toward a man dressed in tattered rags and broken-down shoes, his hands and face smudged with dirt. The village beggar.

"Why were you here before opening?" she asked.

"I come in early to finish picking up the grounds. He was just laying there all bloody." He shuddered. "Honestly, I didn't touch him, was too scared." He inched closer and cast a sidelong glance at the victim. "It's Gunnar the Undefeated, leader of the Knights Invincible. He bragged his name meant warrior."

"He appears to have lost this battle. Who'd want to defeat this *invincible* warrior?"

"I work the whole village, see and hear things. Many people won't mourn his death, like the knights, royal court, someone in the Roma camp, and a crazed Viking." He fingered a string around the waist of a burlap-bag pullover. "I'm supposed to be at the gate to greet visitors at opening. I have to go."

The medical examiner arrived. Lean and balding with only a gray fringe above his ears, he'd been on the job thirty-five years. He wiped his glasses before putting gloves on and leaning over the body. "I've worked some weird scenes, but death in a dragon beats it all. Somebody really had it in for this guy."

The man in charge of the fair stormed toward them shouting, "Hundreds of people with tickets are getting very impatient. I need to open the gates."

"Not until after the ME has finished," said Sara.

"And when will that be?"

The ME checked joint flexibility "Not long. After I determine time of death, we'll move the body to the morgue and you can let visitors in but not beyond the crime scene tape."

When the man was gone, Sara asked, "Cause of death?"

"To be determined at the autopsy." A quirky grin. "But let's assume something sharp."

After removing her gloves and tossing them into the trash, Sara took phone shots of the victim's face and butchered chest. Five years on the job, she'd dealt with domestic abuse cases similar to her parents and an occasional call here for a minor incident. But nothing like this had ever happened in the village. It had been a welcome part of the community for twenty years.

A reporter and cameraman approached her. "Josh Reynolds from the *Reunion Heights Sentinel*. What have you got?"

"How'd you get in here? The fair's closed."

"I have my own methods. I'm the heartbeat of the city with my ears always tuned to the police scanner. Murder in the Renaissance Village is the scoop of the year. He craned his neck to look around her. Is that a dead body in the swing?"

"No comment."

"My followers want to know. Give me something."

"The police chief will issue a statement when ready. You need to get out of here now."

A deep-throated voice from behind. "First day here, and I'm stuck with a bloody corpse."

She turned and saw a six-foot-one, beefy man with a three-day stubble. His dark-brown hair appeared to have tangled with the brush. She did not need this now.

"You must be the detective from New York I heard about."

He bowed with a flourish. "Ryker Harris. Wandering around in this strange village took me forever to find you. Nothing like it in the Big Apple, and I lived there all fifty-seven years of my shameful life. I'm a big city cop used to gang killings and drug dealers not some guy dressed up like a knight lying in a dragon's belly."

She pocketed her phone. "Then what're you doing down here in northern Florida?"

"Trying to nail that snake in the grass running for mayor against your chief of police."

Sara did a double take. "Corbin Foster?"

"AKA a drug lord with tentacles spreading throughout all of New York. NYPD has been after him for years but never made anything stick. We had him involved in the death of an influential politician and still couldn't hold him. The trial's publicity made his suppliers and buyers nervous. They dumped him. Foster and his lackeys cut bait in the middle of the night to parts unknown. Then a week ago, we got an anonymous tip he was running for mayor in Florida. What rattles my brain is why *here* in this ordinary burg of two-hundred thousand?"

"You got me. He runs a large real estate company. His face is on every bus and poster promising greater prosperity than anyone ever imagined. The chief can't compete with that."

Ryker folded his arms over his chest and skewed his mouth

left and right as if in deep deliberation. "If that shyster wins, he'll sabotage your city and turn it into a drug network. I have personal reasons for volunteering to come here. My boss and I didn't always agree on interrogation methods. I got a little heavy handed at times and am on thin ice in New York. I need to make this arrest to repair my tarnished reputation." He lit a cigarette and blew smoke.

Sara had shut the door on relationships after her husband left six years earlier. She fought to squelch the uneasiness about having to work closely with this city man so divorced from her nature soul. The chief ordered cooperation in Ryker's Foster investigation. She agreed to comply, but that was before someone dumped a murder case in her lap.

"Are you going to help me or just pursue your own agenda?" Sara asked.

"Some of both. I have to play the role of a new hire to avoid suspicion." He grinned. "My forte is this winning smile. I use it and flattery to coax information out of people. You'd be surprised the secrets they will tell." He ground the nub of his cigarette out with his heel. "Do you have an ID yet?"

*He uses words like forte?* "Yes, one of the knights, and timing's lousy. I only have nine days to find the killer before the fair closes. Eight hundred potential rennie suspects will pack up and head out to the next one."

"Eight hundred? Where do you begin?"

"The village beggar knows what's up. It may be gossip, but he claims knights, the royalty, a member of the Roma community, and a crazed Viking won't mourn the death."

"Huh, definitely not my usual lineup. We can't do anything without TOD. Your chief sent me straight here, making me miss my breakfast. I can't think on an empty stomach. The aroma from a place called Franny's Fryery beckoned as I passed by."

Might as well humor the guy. She was stuck with him. Sara took him to the Fryery. Franny fried everything in three vats one each for vegetables, meats, and desserts. Sara ordered black coffee and took a seat. Ryker joined her with coffee and two fried apple cider donuts. He plopped a pill from his shirt pocket into his mouth. "For high blood pressure and a potential heart attack. Doc says it's the stress of trying to put Foster in jail for over two decades." Three packets of sugar and creamers dropped into his cup. "He dictated a healthier diet and no more smoking and drinking."

"Yet you just had a cigarette and are about to gorge on artery–clogging, fried donuts."

"A man can't give up everything."

"Even if it means killing yourself?"

"I'm the sole person in charge of me."

Sara looked askance. "I'd fire you and hire somebody else."

She noticed a wedding ring. "Did your wife come with you?"

He closed his eyes, as if trying to drag an emotion to where he wouldn't have to feel it. "She died three years ago."

"I had no idea. I'm so sorry. You must miss her terribly."

"She was my anchor and now I'm rudderless."

A man so confident of his smile had a broken heart. She could relate to a lost love and would be more tolerant of him.

A loud boom announced opening of the castle gates. "We'd better get back there. Visitors know there was some reason they couldn't get in and will swarm all over the place to discover why."

At the crime scene, visitors clad as peasants, lords and ladies, and friars were heckling the police to breach the tape.

"What are all these people doing here?" Ryker said.

"Any secrecy attracts curious onlookers like flies to dung."

"Not just that. I mean this whole fair business."

"They come from afar to experience a different reality for the day. Fantasy rules here. You can be a king or beggar, a court jester or executioner." She opened her hand toward him. "You're free to express your true, inner self."

A whimsical grin. "You may not want to see that one."

"I'm getting a glimpse."

Her phone rang. McBride, the chief of police. He hurled angry words before she could open her mouth. "Why didn't you contain this? Breaking News on every network is showing a video of a half–naked, bloody body lying in a dragon swing. Get in here."

The damn cameraman had snuck a video while the reporter distracted her. "On our way."

When they arrived, McBride's tall, lanky body looked heavily lived in. He paced the office, scratching his forehead as if trying to rip the worry lines off. "This murder has my neck in a noose, and Foster's ready to kick the box from under me. The arrogant bastard showed up minutes ago and had the nerve to tell me to drop out of the race." The chief reached the end of the room and stopped. "If I can't solve this case, his campaign will sling enough mud to bury me. They'll paint me as a bungling, incompetent has-been who can't tell a killer from a horse's ass and is incapable of even running a police force, leastwise an entire city."

As he walked again, his fingers kept seeking places to hold onto. "*Me* who's been head of this department for twenty years. I've kept the city safe. We don't have murders here."

Sara waved her hands back and forth. "Calm down. Sit here and inhale through your nose, fill your lungs, and slowly let air escape through your mouth."

His fingers struck the desk in a series of staccato taps.

"Why are you letting him get to you like this?" Ryker said.

"I'm in the race to stop him from becoming mayor. If we don't solve this murder, I'm done. Foster will chew up and spit out the citizens I devoted my entire career to serving and protecting."

Ryker leaned across the desk. "Listen, I'm a big city cop used to dealing with thugs. It's not beyond Foster to hire an outside gun and orchestrate this whole scenario simply to defeat you."

"I don't see it," said Sara. "If your plan is to discredit a police chief, why bother killing a knight at a Renaissance fair instead of simply shooting somebody in an alley, parking lot, or field?"

"For the buzz. Think about it. Body of a homeless person in an alley isn't breaking news. But murder at the fair would stir up the masses and swing voters over to Foster."

Sara shook her head. "It had to happen after closing. Outsiders wouldn't have access to the grounds at night."

"Don't be so naïve as to think that would stop him."

"Okay, then why slash the chest? This was a crime of passion, and Foster's simply seizing the opportunity to capitalize on it. He's counting on us not being able to find the killer before the election in three weeks."

"Hate to poke a hole in your theory," Ryker said, standing back up. "Yes, you must solve the crime, but that won't be enough to win the election. Foster's a slippery snake capable of beguiling voters. He has to be taken down hard and exposed. And I'm hellbent on being the man to do it."

"And I'm hellbent on finding a murderer," said Sara. "I'm off to the ME. If you're going to help with this case, get with it and come."

Sara and Ryker drove back in separate cars and parked in the large camping area where fair workers set up living quarters. Some erected tents. Others owned trailers with awnings, lounge chairs, and outdoor grills. Signs such as *Witch Parking Only* and *Violators Will Be Toad* claimed ownership of the quintessential spots.

"It's beyond me," said Ryker, "why anyone would choose to live like this. They must be running from something."

"Nonsense. They just want the freedom to be themselves and travel their own paths. They're not hurting anything or anybody."

As they entered the village, Sara explained, "The fair's open eight themed weekends. This is the seventh Saturday and trouble's ahead. The next county warned of a biker gang heading our way for the Brew Fest theme when there's plentiful beer."

"I'd go for one." He winked at her. "To blend in with the

crowd. People are more likely to open up if they don't know you're a cop."

"You're incorrigible."

He came to an abrupt halt at a Greyhound bus trimmed like a Viking ship with sixteen oarsmen in winged helmets painted the length of each side. A red and white striped awning served as the sail. A wooden dragon prow with fiery, yellow eyes projected from the hood. "Captain of this ship is sailing in uncharted waters."

"And free to go wherever it takes him," said Sara.

She approached the ME as he zipped his bag, preparing to leave. "Time of death?"

"Between midnight and two a.m. We'll have to discuss means after the autopsy."

She thanked him and told Ryker, "Now we get to work."

"Please say you exaggerated about the number of rennies. We can't possibly question that many in nine days."

"Yep, eight hundred scattered across forty acres among food kiosks, stages, and shops."

A glazed expression on his face, he didn't seem to be listening to her. "Who's that lovely, young lass yonder?" He nodded toward a fairy with purple and blue iridescent wings four feet high and three wide. They caught the light, giving her an elfin appearance. Streaming ribbons crowned long silky hair. She posed with one hand on her right hip, the other tucked behind her head, and gave a coquettish smile.

Sara laughed. "Easy, Casanova."

"Don't worry, I have no prurient interest. She reminds me of my daughter. We haven't spoken in three years."

"Why haven't—?"

"I don't want to talk about it. Who is she?"

"A mystical spirit of the fair and part of a large cast hired to simply dress and create the atmosphere of a Renaissance village such as that other young girl coming our way."

A Native American girl pushed a cart with brilliantly colored flowers while singing, "Buy a garland for thy maid. And tonight, thou might get . . . dinner if thou art lucky."

"I'll take one of those, my pretty young miss." Ryker withdrew a dollar from his pocket and wove the rose in her hair. "You must walk throughout the village and know all the workers."

On cue, Sara whipped out Gunnar's photo. "Do you recognize this man?"

The girl studied the picture. "Is he the one everybody's talking about that got killed?"

"Yes. What do you know about him?"

"He bought an awful lot of chrysanthemums last year. This year it was roses."

Ryker's brows perked up. "Who were the roses for?"

"Don't know. Probably someone at the evening parties. I live with my parents and go home after closing." She pushed her cart on and continued singing.

The big city cop was in a foreign land. If he was going to be of any use, he needed to get a sense of how things happened around there. "Come on. We're taking a short tour." She led him down Wizard's Way, explaining the two hundred shops were limited to what would have been available during the Renaissance. In the presence of visitors, rennies could speak only Elizabethan English.

They passed The King's Dulcimer and Enchanted Glass which posted a sign *Unescorted Children Will Be Sold Into Slavery.* As they neared Thor's Treasures, she said, "I think we found the captain of that Viking bus."

Across the top of the booth, hung a steel battle axe and a 36-inch sword, its iron pommel inlaid with three silver serpents intertwined. Every item was related to Norsemen: leather boots, gauntlets, vests, scabbards, and belts—all engraved with stylized animals. On the display counter lay an array of knives and swords.

A muscular man with a red beard and wild, shoulder length

hair stood behind the counter. Over a wool tunic, he wore a leather breastplate covered with silver rivets and rings. Random bits of fur sprouted out as if a crazed animal lurked beneath. But the winged helmet was what did it, riding low over his forehead just above the eyes like the glimmering, emerald eyes of a formidable beast.

"There's something sinister and dark about him," said Ryker.

"More of your drivel. He's just part of the cast like that couple coming toward us."

A knight walked up the path in a black tunic covered by a steel breastplate. A buxom woman hung on his arm. The Viking vaulted over the counter and landed in front of them. "I can see this fair maiden doth need help, for her lungs are badly swollen." He wrapped his arm around her waist. "I wouldst have a kiss."

The knight shouted, "Unhand that most beauteous lass, thou ruttish maggot or I shall dispatch thee to thy gods."

"Nay, Warwick the Black, she is mine for truly she is the fairest lady mine eyes have yet to look upon. Stand back, thou puking, weasel, or I shall make an end of thee."

Even an audience expecting the outrageous scattered like seeds blown from a pod as the black knight struck the Viking's face. Blood sprayed from his nose. He grabbed the knight's arm and flung Warwick to the ground with a horrendous thud. Then he reached behind his shoulder, withdrew a sword from a scabbard, and held the blade at Warwick's throat. "I shall spare thee this time for thy shame is defeat enow but harken to me. Remove thyself from this place or I shall slay thee anon."

Warwick rose to his feet and brushed himself off. "We shall meet again."

A hush fell over the crowd until finally one man began to clap, and then others followed in uncertain applause. Soon everyone was whistling and calling for more.

Ryker's brows furrowed. "If that was for real, I think we just witnessed two suspects capable of drawing blood, and I intend to find out what's going on with them. Like the beggar and flower girl, the fairy must work the entire village. I'll find her and get some answers we need."

# Chapter 2

Ryker had no idea where to look for the fairy. The village was a maze of winding, shaded paths filled with visitors clad in colorful costumes eating turkey legs and cotton candy, drinking smoothies and beer. Lost, he passed the same shops and stages several times before spotting the purple and blue iridescent wings. A blushing teenage boy stood beside her for a photo op.

Smiling, Ryker sauntered over to the fairy afterward. "He'll save that picture as a memento to show his grandkids."

A pinkish hue rose in her face, and she turned her gaze away.

"You remind me of my daughter at age seventeen or eighteen. We named her Dulce, meaning sweet, since she was the sweetest thing that came into our lives."

The fairy's lips parted in silent surprise. "Is she here?"

He swallowed to keep a lump from rising in his throat. "No, I haven't seen her in three years. May I ask your name?"

"Celine."

"A pretty name for a pretty girl." He walked with her. "I'm a detective trying to discover who's responsible for a knight's death this morning. You probably know the fair better than anyone. Perhaps you've seen or heard something that could help us. Or maybe you knew him."

The muscles in her face strained.

"It's all right. You don't have to say anything that makes you uncomfortable."

"I've never told anyone."

"Told them what?"

"Two weeks ago the knight who died pinned me against a wall behind the Mail Works castle and put his hand up my skirt."

Every muscle in his body coiled with rage, but he suppressed it in his voice. "What happened then?"

"The shop owner heard me scream and ran to help. He held a dagger at the knight's throat and warned him to back off and never touch me again." A tear drop formed in the corner of her eye.

"I'm so sorry. I hope you reported it to someone."

"No, I was too ashamed thinking it must have been my fault."

"I guarantee you did nothing wrong. Get that out of your head. Undoubtedly you weren't his only victim. And knowing your story will help us do our job. Go now and keep pleasing visitors."


Sara went to her most reliable source and stood out of sight until the falconer concluded his performance. Holding a vulture on a leather gauntlet, Lazzero told the audience, "This too is a bird of prey but doesn't usually eat live animals . . . not even small children," he added with a mischievous grin. "But they do prefer fresh meat." A volunteer agreed to hold a turkey leg in the air. Lazzero released the bird. Flapping its huge wings, it went for the leg and cleaned it to the bone within seconds. The entire audience seemed to suck its breath in all at once without uttering a sound. He proclaimed, "A piranha with wings," and everyone clapped.

Sara approached him after he'd passed the tip hat. "That's quite the climax, almost as dramatic as your exit a year ago."

His finger traced the curve of her face. "Hmm, sexy as ever, my green-eyed beauty with classic high cheekbones. I didn't think you were ever going to come. Not a single word in seven weeks. It took a murder to get you here."

She recoiled. "You knew where to find me. I didn't leave

here. You did."

"I wasn't sure what to expect after the way we parted. I never stopped thinking about you all year, afraid you'd cut yourself off from others as you're prone to do. In isolation, you may lose the ability to love."

She raised her shoulders to her ears. "It simply comes down to some things can never be forgotten."

"But could be forgiven."

"Right now. I have room for only one thing in my life, solving a murder. When the fair closes, everyone will disappear and my investigation will come to a dead end. You're a people watcher. Tell me what's been going on here. You owe me that much."

He nodded acknowledgment. "I do owe you and regret what happened between us. As to Gunnar, he was universally despised by men as a pompous ass who took what he wanted with no regard for anyone but himself."

"Of those he offended, who'd want to murder him?"

"Any of the knights. He was a dictator calling all the shots."

"I need a name."

His voice lowered. "A year ago at another fair, Warwick the Black and Gunnar the Undefeated were the last two left standing in the final joust. Gunnar unhorsed Warwick, knocked him flat to the ground and rode back around to slice that scar on his face. He left him bleeding there and paraded in front of everybody, waving his arms in victory."

"In front of visitors? Why would he do something so overtly against the rules?"

"Rumor was Warwick had privately challenged him. Winner of the joust would be in sole charge of the Knights Invincible. Gunnar wasn't about to relinquish his power. Others who tried to dethrone him had paid heavily."

"What about you? Did Gunnar harm you in some way?"

Hands deep in his pockets, Lazzero pushed dirt with the toe of his shoe. "My pride and acclaim, however you want to put it.

Without provocation, he tossed three bloody, dead pigeons on my stage. It distressed the raptors and freaked out the audience. But I didn't kill him if that's what you're thinking. Sure, I hated the guy but not enough to do him in." He removed the leather gauntlet. "Be my guest at the potluck in the Scottish Camp tonight and you'll witness some of the major players in action."

Being around him again was uncomfortable, but he offered a entry to the inner workings of the rennies. She called Ryker who was tracking down another inside source. "Did you find the fairy?"

"Took half an hour but yes. Her name's Celine, and she opened up to me. Like I said, I'm good at getting people to do so. We have a new motive to pursue. Gunnar put his hand up her skirt two weeks ago. She screamed. Owner of the Mail Works rushed out and put a dagger to his throat. He threatened him to never go near her again."

"Did she turn Gunnar in?"

"Like too many women, she blamed herself. I doubt she was his only victim and would place odds that there are others whose partners would kill for them."

"We may find out at a party in the Scottish camp after closing. You don't have to come."

"I need to play my part as the new hire."

Sara searched for anyone suspicious by refusing eye contact, quickly creating distance, or having access to sharp weapons. She went to the Singing Executioners stage show. Bare chested and wearing black masks covering all but their eyes and mouths, they claimed to have invented gallows humor. One carried a heavy rope and hangman's noose. The other gripped the handle of a six-foot axe and shouted, "Welcome to the Renaissance where passions are high and penicillin's unavailable." Saying their humor had a cutting edge, they kicked their legs high and harmonized, "When we are chopping, heads are dropping. Shave and a haircut anyone?"

After they'd passed their tip hats, Sara asked if they knew any of the Knights Invincible personally.

"We have nothing to do with them. They're much too violent," said a man wielding a six-foot axe.

They seemed capable of committing humor but not murder. Seven weeks, Sara had circumvented Lazzero's stage. Seeing him aroused feelings she'd tucked into a dusty corner of her mind. She wandered on a dirt path to a forest of oak and southern magnolia surrounding a lake. From a wooden bench, she watched its placid water mirroring foliage without a ripple on its silver surface. Above her, wings hummed quietly as a tiny bird with an emerald green back and iridescent, ruby throat hovered at a red bottle bush, its long tongue licking nectar like a dog lapping water.

A year ago, a hummingbird had taken flight inside her on this same bench opening weekend. A man in skin-tight royal blue pants asked in a sonorous voice if he could share her seat. Chin length, dark hair in a casual jumble framed brown eyes that never wavered from hers. He made unmentionable parts of her anatomy awaken and tingle. She'd been lonely and needed to believe this falconer would stay. He did for six weeks before succumbing to a belly dancer. He swore it meant nothing, a single moment of drunken weakness. But once the trust was broken, there was no going back. She shut the door again, but Lazzero was chiseling at her lock.

Sara left to find Ryker and liked strolling through the fair's shady forest of gently rolling hills. Gaily colored ribbons fluttered from trees. Bright banners strung across booths whipped to their own special rhythm. Everywhere, the air was filled with the music of dulcimers, lutes, and violins plus the aroma of funnel cakes and hot baked bread, spiced meats and sugary treats.

She stopped at King Edward's Fruit Basket. Spotting Ryker on his way to the Scottish camp, she yelled, "Hey, New York, wait up. I've got something for you."

"Plying me with gifts this early in our relationship?" he said in a jaunty tone.

She handed him a bag of two large honey crisp apples.

He looked inside. "Ahhh, my precious."

"Eat those instead of artery clogging fried donuts. You might live longer and who knows? I may even like having you around."

A 20-foot, inflated Loch Ness monster and skirl of bagpipes greeted them at the Scottish camp entrance. Colorful banners with images of unicorns and castles were strung between trees and above shops such as Celtic Gourds, Treasures from the Cairn, and Cloaked in Time. A sign across Ravens Lair read *Don't mess with Scottish people. They're temperamental: half temper, half mental.* Not dressed in the clean white shirts and well-pressed, tartan kilts worn for visitors, they looked as though they'd just come from a medieval battleground. Earth-tone, plaid kilts hung loosely at their waists with sashes over the shoulders of shabby, woven tops.

Ryker squatted with his hands on his knees and tipped his head sideways to peer under the kilt of a long haired, bearded Scot who shouted at him, "Ye've got a face would melt a willy."

Ryker straightened up and opened his mouth as if ready to counter attack. "Careful," said Sara, "a man in a kilt is a man and a half. Ages ago, Scots went into battle butt naked. Sergeants used to check under kilts with a mirror tied to a stick. Now they wear dark undergarments." She smiled. "Or so I've been told."

"What, not tighty whities?"

Lazzero interrupted their banter. "Glad you came. I brought two salads for our share." He cocked an eyebrow. "And who's this?"

Ryker extended a hand. "A new hire at the station."

"I wasn't aware they were interviewing."

"You would be," said Sara, "if you'd hung around."

"Sorry. No full time falconry positions available."

A bagpipe procession cut short an awkward conversation. A man followed with a tray of what looked like very large but slightly irregular condoms with veins.

"Not on the menu at your New York deli?" she asked Ryker. "It's haggis, the national dish of Scotland. You cook a sheep's lungs, heart, and liver then mix with oatmeal, suet, onions, and spices. Pack it all in the sheep's stomach, sew it closed, and boil away."

His nose wrinkled in disgust. "I'll pass on the haggis."

Lazzero left to add their salads to the buffet. Ryker pulled Sara aside. "So what's with this guy? I sense a romantic relationship."

"A dead one he's trying to resuscitate."

"And I take it you're refusing to give CPR?"

Sara's mouth pinched tight holding back the truth she didn't want to reveal. "It's complicated."

"Maybe when you trust me more. Celine seems to have traded her fairy wings and petal skirt for shorts and a tank top. She looks lonely over there. I should keep her company."

The line of Sara's mouth tightened a fraction more. "This is a murder investigation not a social hour."

He raised his hand hushing her. "I'll simply dine and practice talking to a girl my daughter's age if I ever get that chance again."

"We're on duty. Get more out of her than idle chat."

Frustrated by not having any concrete clues, Sara had to turn her mind elsewhere. Filling her plate at the buffet table, she asked Lazzero, "Who are those two teenage girls ahead of us? One sells flowers, but I don't know the other."

"That's the Viking's daughter. On fair days, she wears a leather vest over a long dress trimmed in fur. Not a bit of skin shows. He named her Karina, meaning chaste and pure. Any man or boy who ventures too close shouldn't plan on reaching his next birthday."

"Such as our dead knight?"

He raised one shoulder. "Possible, I guess. Are you so certain the killer is among us?"

"You know I can't reveal anything regarding a case."

She carried her plate to a hay bale under the shade of a live oak. As Lazzero squeezed beside her, she inched away.

A Scot hopped onto a table. His robust frame and forceful demeanor commanded everyone's attention. "Now that ye have betaken of dinner, we've added something special. Jack Daniels is now selling a colorless, unaged whiskey similar to Prohibition moonshine. We Scots are known for our fine bevvy and have distilled our own for this special Brew Fest weekend. Bring your steins to be filled. Then let the party begin."

"Who's that?" Sara asked Lazzero.

"Balgair, head of the clan and a tough nut you wouldn't want to meet in a deserted wood on a dark night."

*Or in a dragon swing?* She texted Ryker. "Keep your eyes and ears open."

"Better keep both of yours open too," Lazzero murmured. "I think something's going down."

She leered at him. "You snooped and read my text."

From across the dining area, Warwick the Black hollered at Balgair. "What'cha got under your skirt, lassie?"

"When God was handing out chins, did ya think he said gins and ask for a double?" Balgair replied.

Lazzero whispered. "Trouble's brewing. You don't mess with Scots. After seven weeks of ridicule about their kilts and knobby knees, they're spoiling for a fight."

Warwick countered the Scot, "Didn't need to ask for a double. Every knight has twice the strength of your likes." He thrust a stein in the air. "A toast to Gunnar the Undefeated. I shall miss him."

Knights pounded their steins on a table. "Hear, hear, hear."

"Liar," shouted the Viking. "You would always be second best under him. Now that he's dead, you lust for his power and control of the almighty Knights Invincible but are too weak to get it." The Viking waved his arm toward all the knights. "Are you real men or just caricatures in tin suits of armor?"

Warwick marched over to the Viking, stood eye-to-eye, and spit on the ground. "Here's to your pagan gods."

There was a whole lot of testosterone going on here. Sara's heart rate accelerated as she reached for her phone, ready to call for backup if a Norse\Saxon war broke out.

To her relief, Balgair took command of the scene. In front of Warwick the Black, he recited loud enough for all to hear.

> *See the man in black*
> *Watch as he walks by.*
> *Black assassin*
> *Murder in disguise.*
> *Some say he's a demon*
> *A plague on the Earth.*

He separated the men. "We'll settle this with a tug-of-war."

"It's always part of the Highlander games," Lazzero told Sara. "You're only as strong as your weakest link. Judging by their size, strength, and fitness from daily training and fighting, I'd bet on the knights. Calling themselves invincible, they can't afford to lose face, especially Warwick. He has to prove himself as powerful as Gunnar or step down."

Bagpipers played a continuous hum as Balgair prepared the ground. He used flour to draw a center line, marked the midpoint of a long rope, measured about fifteen feet in each direction. Both teams lined up on their respective sides.

Shoulders squared and chest forward, Warwick strutted to the front of seven knights and planted himself directly opposite six Scots led by Balgair. He repeated louder, "What'cha got under your skirt, haggis breath? Careful, least you break a fingernail."

The Viking swaggered to the Scots and added the seventh man behind Balgair. He bent forward with hands on his thighs and cast a verbal hook at Warwick. "What he's got under there is far too large to fit in that micro-nut-cup, jock armor you're wearing."

"A final drink to the games," interrupted a chorus of Scottish lasses as they walked the line giving each competitor a fresh stein to slake his thirst. Everyone swigged it down.

Men gripped the rope with their hands tight against their hips, positioned their feet, and then leaned back with one foot in front and the heel of the other dug in.

Once the rope was taut with no slack between men, Balgair yelled, "Pull!"

Each team tried to drag the other to the ground as the rope moved an inch in one direction and then back. Cries like *pull, brake* and *now* broke down into grunts. In spite of much growling and swearing, neither side budged until the knights seemed a bit disoriented and loose hinged as if their minds and bodies had lost communication. The Viking lifted his back foot and planted it several inches behind him. The Scots pulled steadily, forcing the knights to tumble one by one. The last to give in, Warwick fell face first across the line. The entire Scottish camp and their champions cheered. They'd vanquished the knights in a humiliating rout.

Lazzero tapped Sara's knee. "Be right back. Got a hunch and need to check it out."

Sweat coursed through dust on Warwick's face. He staggered toward the Viking. "I don't know how, but you and the milk livered Scots cheated us."

"You lost because you're shameless as a liar's tongue." The Viking leaped onto the knights' table and thrust his chest forward. "A toast to the gods. I shall take a seat in the great halls of Valhalla and spend eternity feasting and fighting. Only the bravest among us are chosen to die with honor on the battlefield." He toppled a step forward. "And you, Warwick, are a coward. Do you know where those who die without courage and honor go?" He searched the crowd for an answer. "To Niflheim, a land of frozen fog, snow, and ice ruled by the goddess Hel who inflicts the hideous fate of boredom, an eternal life without challenge."

Warwick shouted, "We're not done yet. You'll pay for this," and stormed out of camp followed by several other knights.

Sara's beat returned to its normal rate as the tension eased. She glanced at Ryker and gave a reassuring nod. Lazzero returned holding a stein in each hand. Raising the corner of his mouth in a wry smile, he handed her one. "This proves how they did it. I know you don't drink but just taste it."

She took a guarded sip and rolled the liquid over her tongue. "It's just water."

"Uh-huh." He handed her the other. "Now this one."

"Aggghhh. That burned all the way down."

To soothe her throat, she grabbed the first stein and gulped too much water too fast. A little dizzy, she lost her balance and slid off the bale.

Laughing, Lazzero lifted her back up. "While Scots were only drinking water, they served the knights about hundred-seventy proof moonshine. Totally hammered, they didn't stand a chance." He brushed a kiss on her cheek. "Do I stand a chance with you?"

*Will you never let up?* She hunched her shoulders to fend him off. "I've already answered. Now go and leave me alone." Finally rid of him, she called Ryker. "Did you catch all of that or were you too busy yakking?"

"You mean those two bulls snorting at each other? Warwick's power motive is clear, but I don't get what's up with the Viking. He seems angry enough to murder someone but why Gunnar?"

"The whole scene's unfathomable," said Sara.

"We'll figure it out. Too much Scottish bevy's been consumed by angry men. Fights could break out in a dark parking lot. For safety, I'll escort Celine to her trailer."

Physically and emotionally wiped out, Sara went home and entered through the laundry room of a ten-year-old, two-bedroom house. She set her keys and revolver on the dryer, removed both shoes, and trudged into the kitchen. Her go-to comfort food, Mac 'n cheese, would take too long to boil pasta. She dumped a container of Greek yogurt, a banana, and strawberries in a food processor. Sixty seconds on high and the fruit smoothie was ready.

She sat cross legged on a leather couch and spooned it while watching the nightly news report of no progress in the hunt for the killer of a knight in the Renaissance village. In the replay of a live interview with McBride, he said the investigation was ongoing and had no further comment at present. She'd just started the next episode in a British mystery series when there was loud banging at the front door. Probably Lazzero bearing her favorite carbonated drink as he did every night last year. Couldn't he give her a few moments of peace? Her stocking feet slid in a whisper across a tile floor. She opened the door, and two broad shouldered strangers strong armed their way past into her home.

"Who the hell are you?" she demanded.

# Chapter 3

Sara wrested her arm free from a man with a long pointy nose like the possum that moved into her garage last winter. His breath smelled of rotten eggs.

"Let go of her," said his taller cohort with an unusually large mouth like the grouper fish she'd seen in the Keys. "We agreed no visible marks or bruises that would attract attention."

Possum shoved her onto the couch.

Sara hissed through clenched teeth. "Get out of my house. You have no business here."

"You'll do exactly what we tell you."

"Dimwitted goons like you don't frighten me."

Possum pulled a gun from his belt and pointed it at the center of her forehead. "Can you outrun a bullet to your skull?"

She pushed closer to the muzzle. "No visible marks? A bullet hole in my head would make a hell of a one."

"Shut up." He wrapped his finger around the trigger.

She told Grouper, "Your partner's not getting the message, so I'm asking you. Why are you here? What do you want?"

"For you to convince the police chief to resign from the race."

"Not gonna happen. It's his whole life."

"Then it's all up to you. Press your brake pedal and slow down the investigation until time runs out and the fair closes. Case goes unsolved proving your chief's incompetence. Corbin Foster wins the election."

Sara scoffed. "Now why would I do that?"

Possum lowered the gun. "To keep a headline like this from appearing in the news. *Nathaniel Lansing, father of detective Sara Lansing, convicted of insider trading.*"

"That's preposterous. My father's no criminal."

He nodded toward his partner. "Encourage her."

Grouper withdrew papers from his jacket and handed over printouts on her father's letterhead. Sara quickly scanned twelve pages detailing stock trades in advance of company earnings. "How'd you get these?"

"Those are just a trickle. We downloaded all the files from his computer onto a flash drive. Do you really believe he financed his luxury lifestyle with hard earned cash?"

Sara erupted in laughter. "Now you're living in fantasy land. There's no way you got into my father's house."

Grouper reached into the other side of his jacket and handed her a photo taken at age eight. "We also took a shot of his desktop. Check the screensaver."

It was a picture she'd drawn at nine of her father holding her in his arms—her sullen mother standing alone on the far left.

"Look at the folder titled Business. We clicked it and had to go down three layers of subfolders to find the pages we just gave you. He was hiding them. We printed them off his computer."

Possum asked, "Do you understand our agreement, detective Sarah Lansing? Solve the murder and your father goes to prison for fifteen years and pays a three million dollar fine."

"And if I don't solve it?"

"He's a free man and Foster defeats a bungling police chief. Simple as that."

With an unflinching stare, Sara said, "I can have you arrested for aggravated assault against a police officer, interference with an investigation, and possible RICO for Foster."

"NYPD went after him for years and couldn't touch him," said Grouper. "His lawyers would have us out in days. Ask yourself if you're willing to expose your father when you could have easily saved him." He snatched the papers. "I'll keep these safe."

Possum paused at the door. "We'll be watching your every move and listening to every word. Mention the slightest hint of this meeting to anyone and your dad is dead. That includes your boss, the new hire, and especially your father." He pretended to fire the gun. "*Bang, bang.* Dad's life is in your hands."

Sara's stomach seized so suddenly she barely made it to the toilet before spewing fruit smoothie in a viscous mass that burned all the way up her throat and into her nose. She bent over the bowl heaving until there was nothing left but a foul taste in her mouth. She lumbered to her room and collapsed face down on the bed, horrified that a wrong move or misspoken word would cause her father's death.

Night faded into a gray dawn Sunday morning. The early whistling and trills of mockingbirds woke Sara. Their chorus imbued the air with the less ambient noise of buzzing insects, barking dogs, and traffic. Getting up early and jogging in nature had always been her escape, a time to release tension and sorrow. As soon as she stepped outside, the neighbor's dog jumped up and down, running in circles, until he found his tennis ball. Then he stood on his back legs with front paws on the fence and dropped it into her open hand. "Oh, did you want me to throw this?" Not moving a muscle, eyes fixed on the ball, he waited for the toss. There it went. He raced across the yard, scooped it up in his mouth, and brought it back to her. Sara tossed two more times and then scratched behind his ears. "Sorry, gotta go. See you tonight." She'd never had a pet as a child, and now Ralphie, a young beagle, was her only friend.

Low on energy from lack of sleep, she started jogging slowly. The steady pounding on the dirt path was her mantra to drown out, *Mention the slightest hint of this meeting to anyone and your dad is dead.* Dead? He'd already disappeared from her life when he quit speaking to her six years ago for failing expectations. She picked up the pace to get fresh air in her lungs and blood flowing to her limbs. *Get in the zone, reduce stress, energize thinking.*

She remembered being ten years old and her father running alongside. "Keep moving."

She pumped her legs, gaining speed with each push.

"Faster," he shouted. "Faster."

Her heart throbbed in her chest. "I can't."

"You'll never be a winner if you don't try harder."

"I don't care." Her calves burned and her toes were cramped in outgrown shoes.

"Life's made up of two kinds of people—winners and losers. Quit dawdling."

Her feet flew over loose gravel trying to keep up with the punishing pace. Sweat dripping from her forehead blurred her vision. She took her eyes from the path only long enough to dry them and didn't see the rock. Her toe jammed against it and threw her headlong onto the ground. Abrasions on her hands and knees were bleeding and embedded with fine bits of sand. But she didn't dare cry in front of him. Never in front of dad.

He grabbed her shirt and yanked her up. "When you fall down in life, you have to get right back up onto your feet"

"I want to go home," she whimpered.

"Not until you run faster. You must rise above all others and come out on top, no matter what the cost."

*Come out on top, no matter what the cost* echoed in her head as Sara returned home to get ready for work. She stripped off her clothes and turned on the shower. When the temperature was right, she stepped inside and let water spill over her face in a gentle waterfall. Its white noise lulled her into a private place where she could think. Solving the murder would save her boss and perhaps make her a winner in her dad's eyes, but he'd end up in jail.

The phone rang as Sara exited the shower—McBride ordering her to get to the station immediately. She wasn't ready to face him yet. Her emotions and thoughts were strewn like broken branches after a storm. As a good cop, she should report last night's incident. But as a daughter, how could she?

When Sara arrived, Ryker was leaning against the side of the building with a sack of fries from Franny's Fryery. Sara huffed. "Those are terrible for your heart. They'll kill you."

He touched a scar just above his temple. "Somebody already tried but missed the brain. No real damage done."

*That's debatable.*

He pushed off the wall. "I wasn't going in there alone. He's already come to the front door twice looking for us and slammed it. He's got a buzzing bee up his butt." Ryker cocked his head and eyed her. "Working all those years in New York, I'm an expert at reading people. Right now, I sense all is not well. What's wrong?"

"Nothing. I just didn't get enough sleep last night and took too long an early run."

"You do that kind of nonsense every day?"

"A habit since childhood. Running calms me, clears my head."

"That endorphin thing?"

"Yeah."

His shoulders shook. "Definitely not on my daily agenda."

The officer at the front duty desk called out, "McBride wants both of you in his office right now. I'd tread lightly."

He was pacing when they entered, eyes to the floor as though tracing the wood grain. "What have you got?"

"Three probable suspects, but no hard evidence," said Sara.

McBride handed her two Ziploc bags. "The SCI found these three turquoise beads in the bottom of the swing and this single brown hair on the body."

"That's not much to go on," she said.

The veins in his forehead pulsed like blue worms inching under his scalp. He shook a paper in their faces. "Have you seen the morning news denouncing me as an oafish, incompetent fool?"

Sara grabbed it from his hand. "Foster must have something on the editor to make him to print such outrageous accusations. We've had the body less than twenty-four hours."

"Then get out there and do your jobs."

As they went to her car, she reminded Ryker, "The beggar gave us leads, but let's visit the blacksmith first. He knows the most about weapons used in the village."

They parked in the camping area. She led him down Morgan's Alley to the Well Tempered Forge. They peered inside at a six-foot-two, bearded blacksmith in a sleeveless tunic. His biceps bulging, he hammered a long piece of steel on an anvil.

Ryker's arm barred her entrance. "This is a man's job."

Blood slammed in her ears. *Excuse me, I'm perfectly capable of taking care of myself.* She marched around him. "Just act like a couple of tourists while we scout the place."

Sara perused a display of potential murder weapons: daggers, knives, swords, maces, and axes. "It's quite an array," she told the blacksmith. "Did you make all of these?"

"Yes." He pointed to a sword. "I could personalize one for your husband with runic inscriptions on the guard or an eagle pommel."

A self-conscious expression spread across Ryker's face at the husband reference. He picked up a shiny blade. "How long to make one of these?"

The muscles in the blacksmith's neck hardened like cables. "Put that down."

Ryker held his hands up in defense. "Okay, sorry, just asking."

"Days to months depending on the metal and design."

"Did any of the rennies working this fair buy one?" said Sara.

"You sure ask a lot of questions."

Enough of this dancing around the subject. She flipped open her ID. "We're investigating a murder early Saturday morning."

"What's that got to do with me?"

"A sharp weapon was used much like the ones here. It could have come from your shop. Who bought from you recently."

"None of your business," he said with the temper of a man not meant to be crossed.

"I suggest you reconsider your answer to the lady's question and show her some respect."

The blacksmith thumped his middle finger on Ryker's chest. "Get out of my shop."

Ryker grabbed the finger. "I repeat. Show her respect unless you'd rather take a little trip down to the station."

"I have no time for this crap." He turned to Sara. "I apologize. Now can I get back to work."

"Give me names," she said.

Using a tong, the blacksmith pulled a piece of glowing metal from the fire, placed it on an anvil, and turned it from side to side as he pounded. "I'm too busy to socialize and learn names. I only know them by where they work. Last week, I sold to that grubby sap from the petting zoo and two knights. One of them dresses in black pants, tunic, and gauntlets; the other, all in green."

She showed Gunnar's photo. "Know this man?"

"No." He wiped the back of his arm across sweat and ash on his forehead. "But I heard rumors that he played in the queen's bed. My daughter's a lady-in-waiting. She and the other courtiers are college kids prone to gossiping about their elders."

A clue, a real clue. "Does the king know about his wife sleeping with a knight?"

The blacksmith pounded the metal shaping it into an axe. "You figure it out."

Ryker's face flushed with rage. Sara quickly intervened and rushed him outside before he crossed a line. The chief had enough trouble without accusations of not being in control of his men. "Grabbing that finger was pretty ballsy. He could wipe the floor with you."

"Sorry, I have no tolerance for men who don't respect women. Enthusiasm tends to get the better of me. On occasion, I've charged headlong into situations and acted . . . well, let's just say, somewhat out of bounds."

"Well, you need to cool it here." She led Ryker down Toad's Lane "Let's pay the king and queen a little visit. I've seen the royalty retire at McDuff's Beans for morning brew after performing their lofty duties of greeting early visitors."

"I wonder if the king's wearing horns?"

"What are you talking about?"

"A horned cuckold as in *Much Ado About Nothing.*"

Sara shook her head, laughing. "You've got to be kidding. You read Shakespeare?"

"I'm not just a pretty face but must humbly confess my wife dragged me to the play. She explained a horned beast can't see its own horns like husbands can't see their wives are fooling around."

"She sounds like a remarkable woman."

"She'd have to be to put up with me."

They reached the coffee shop only minutes before the royal party arrived and took over three rows of tables on the far side of the court yard. The king wore a purple velvet robe lined with fur and trimmed in gold metallic cloth, his large balloon sleeves almost touching the ground. Gold, silk, and jewels adorned the women's gowns, long hooped skirts, and billowy sleeves. Young courtiers and ladies-in-waiting attended them in equal finery.

Sara cut in front of Ryker as they wound through a crowd of thirsty visitors. She displayed her badge to the king. "I'm detective Sara Lansing and this is detective Ryker Harris." She showed him the phone photo. "We're looking into the death of this man."

The king smirked. "You can't think any of us were involved."

She squeezed her lips to conceal a smile. He didn't have a clue the blacksmith had just compromised him. "I'm talking to everyone who might have seen or heard anything."

Ryker stood directly across from the king. "What was your relationship with Gunnar the Undefeated?"

"Didn't know him personally."

"Royalty living in the same village for seven weeks and you don't know your subjects?"

The king flipped a plastic stirrer back and forth between his fingers. "Only heard about him and none of it good."

"Such as him having a way with women, even married ones?"

"I need more coffee." The king shoved his paunch away from the table and used both hands to lift himself off the chair.

Sara pulled Ryker aside. "That could just be gossip."

"It's precisely why I was pushing for a reaction to see if he knows he's a cuckold."

"And your conclusion?"

"Not sure yet."

The king returned and set the cup down so hard that liquid sloshed onto the table. "I'm not interested in private affairs."

*Not even your wife's?* Sara kept quiet and decided to let them entangle their own lives for now. "When and where was the last time you saw him?" she said instead.

"From the grandstand where royalty presides over jousting matches. He and that black knight put on quite a show. There's been bad blood between them from the beginning."

"Based on what?" Ryker said.

"Not my business."

"Mine is to ask where you were between midnight and two yesterday morning."

"At home in bed with my queen. We live in town and leave the village right after closing unless we stay for the evening potluck."

Both arms resting on the table, Ryker leaned forward. "But

you could sneak in the employee entrance at night."

"I suppose but there's no reason to. We only get here in time to dress as royalty and prepare to greet visitors at opening."

"And where's your lovely queen now?" said Sara.

"Shopping, I suppose." The king stared into the depths of his coffee cup. "You should be talking to the knights who worked and traveled with Gunnar, not the royal court."

"Thank you for your time." Ryker looked at Sara. "Now to Franny's Fryery?"

She shook her head. "You're hopeless, a lost cause."

"And you think you know what's better for everybody else."

An awkward silence accompanied them. Franny kept her vats of hot oil ready to fry. Nothing was cooked ahead of time and left sitting under a heat lamp. Ryker bought coffee and stood nearby sipping it and waiting for his order of two funnel cakes.

Suddenly from the beer garden rang the boisterous sounds of men who'd already imbibed too much. When the ruckus amped into gun fire, Sara yelled, "Ryker, we've got trouble."

# Chapter 4

Ryker tossed his cup in the trash. "Sorry, Franny, gotta go."

"Hurry," Sara yelled, pushing through a group of teenagers dressed as Robin Hood's Merry Men. "Police, get out of my way."

She reached twelve bikers in their twenties guzzling beer as if they'd just emerged from eight days lost in a blazing desert.

Ryker caught up to her, huffing. "What's going on?"

"Bunch of drunken morons showing off." Her eyes narrowed. "Which one of you idiots fired the gun?"

A six-foot-three, tattooed biker came toward her clutching his crotch. "Now that would be me. What'cha gonna do about it?"

Within seconds, Ryker raised his fist to strike. "Take that back or you'll never utter another word."

Resounding in spit-laden laughs, two of the biker buddies grabbed him from behind and hurled Ryker to the ground, giving their gun-toting pal a chance to flee.

Sara helped him up. "You all right?"

He brushed himself off. "Yes, but the mook already beat it. You'll never catch him."

"Just watch." A cheetah in pursuit of a wildebeest, Sara took off. His height made him easy to spot twenty yards ahead as he blasted through a crowd, knocking down two teenage girls. He leaped over the exit turnstile and turned toward the parking lot with too great a lead to catch him before reaching his bike.

She took a short cut and climbed onto the roof of a shop that backed to the ten-foot stone wall designed to keep out freeloaders and looters. Using hand and foot holds to clamber over it required greater strength and skill than eight and nine years ago when she did such crazy things. Jagged rocks chafed her fingers. Her foot slipped twice but she made it to the top. From there, she spotted him zigzagging between rows of parked vehicles in the gravel lot. She dropped to the ground but lost sight of him. Where was he? She scurried across the end lines of cars, pickups, and RVs and saw him half way down an aisle, bent over, hands on his thighs. Lugging that beer gut had done him in, but he was still more than twice her size. To bag him, she'd gamble on surprise.

Sara stole along the adjacent row, lay on her belly, and peered underneath. Motorcycle boots about three cars ahead. She quietly climbed onto the roof of two trucks behind him, hopped across them, and jumped down, planting herself squarely in front, her gun drawn. "On the ground, sucker."

He reached for his. "Make me."

"Don't even think about it."

An incredulous expression on his face, he took a tentative step toward this crazy woman pointing a weapon at his family jewels.

"You really don't want to go there."

He tried staring her down and failed. "Okay, okay. But you'll hear from my lawyer."

She snickered and cuffed him. "Yeah, right, like you've got one at your beck and call. Discharging a firearm on the fairgrounds is illegal. Time at the pleasure of our local gendarme will give you ample opportunity to reflect on your stupidity."

Sara raked both hands through the sides of her hair to draw sweat away from her face. She phoned McBride. "Send a squad car to pick up a biker who just had to go and shoot his pistol here."

"You need to be turning over every rock to locate a murderer, not wasting time and a tight budget on minor stuff like this."

"Don't you get it? He was firing a gun in a crowd. You want to add a second death to Foster's stink?"

"No, but I need an arrest to stop his attacks on my character."

"Then get a car here for this pitiful excuse of a man so we can get back to work."

Sara had just ended the call when Ryker caught up to her breathing heavily as if there was too much air for his lungs to hold. He bent over. "You're like five foot five and he's—?"

"I'm five foot six and, yes, he's a tad bigger."

Ryker mocked the biker. "Big man taken down by a wee girly half your size. I took a photo you can proudly share with your drinking buddies."

"Shut up, fat man and you too, bitch."

"You stinking piece of shit. Don't talk to a woman like that." Ryker ran his tongue along his lips as if strangling the man seemed a pleasant option.

"Enough tough guy talk," said Sara.

"If you insist." After double checking the cuffs were secure, Ryker asked her, "How'd you do that?"

"Do what?"

"Catch him? What else could I mean?"

She leaned against a pickup, her arms crossed over her chest. "I used to compete in international adventure races."

"Running obviously."

"Also biking through knee deep mud and kayaking in rough seas and high winds."

His jaw dropped. "You're putting me on."

"To keep other teams from passing, we slept two hours out of twenty-four, lived on unknown food, and encountered dangerous wildlife like snakes, biting insects, and poison dart frogs."

"Huh, you're certainly not the woman I imagined. What race was the hardest?"

"The boiling hot Amazon rainforest. We ran in darkness using headlamps and carrying all our gear. If you can't find your way in the wilderness, you might as well not compete."

Ryker just shook his head as if still in disbelief. "How'd you get caught up in all that?"

"Coed teams of four are required to have at least one woman. I met a guy named Michael who asked me to join theirs."

"Undoubtedly for the big prize money."

Sara laughed. "All you win are bragging rights."

"I don't get it. Why punish your body for no paper?"

"To experience exotic places most people will never see. And mostly, to prove I could. My father programmed me to win."

"Then why give up all that fun to become a cop?"

"Good question. I had a degree in criminal justice when we got married. Instead of using it, I spent seven years racing in the most outlandish places on the planet." Sara bounced off the truck and strode to the end of the row and back looking for the squad car. "And then, Michael left me."

"What the—?"

The car's arrival gave her an excuse to turn away and end an unpleasant conversation. She made sure officers hefted the biker into the back seat and secured him before closing the door. "See that this lowlife is kept off the streets at least overnight."

When the car left, Ryker stared at her as if awaiting further explanation. "Sara?"

"Uh . . . uh. I need to get back to the village and question more suspects."


As they walked back through the parking lot, Ryker picked up an empty beer can, crushed it in one hand, and tossed it in a dumpster. He didn't know what to make of Sara, so unlike his wife who had a PhD in English Literature and hung out with university professors. Intellect was her realm not the physical world and certainly not Sara's inhabited by poison dart frogs. Yet the woman walking beside him who had singlehandedly taken down a man twice her size seemed alone and beyond his reach. He'd sensed vulnerability in her voice when she spoke of Michael leaving and the comment about her father programming her to win. His had unknowingly programmed him to protect women. His response to disrespectful or rough men had jeopardized his career. Sara was already onto him. He needed to gain her trust and confidence if they were going to work together.

"I couldn't have gone the places you've been or accomplished what you did. Your dad must be very proud of you."

Total silence, not even a break in her stride. His usual method of complimenting and empathizing to encourage someone to open up had failed. New plan. "You mentioned your husband, Michael. Did you keep your married name?"

"Lansing's my maiden one."

He risked the wrath of Sara the indomitable but said anyway, "I think you waver between anger and sorrow over your dad."

An irate look. "You running an internal affairs investigation?"

"I need to know who I'm working with."

Sara quickened her pace. "Here's the abridged version. For as far back as I can remember, my mother was an alcoholic and drug addict abusing me emotionally and physically. When the situation became unbearable, I ran away at sixteen and just kept on going."

"Where was your father in this saga?"

"Left when I was ten and never came back. End of story."

He'd blown the test and not the first time with women. He needed to reorganize his thoughts and try a new approach.


When they entered the village, Sara stopped in the Royal Flush. She combed shoulder length, ash blond hair behind her ears and swept long bangs to the right. As a racer, she never had time for an elaborate beauty routine and still chose the natural look with only a mere brush of mascara.

A toilet flushed behind her, and the stall door opened. Her royal highness, the queen, exited and moved to the sink. She wore a deep-red gown, cinched tight at the waist and with a voluminous, bell-shaped skirt covering layers and layers of petticoats reaching to the floor. Jewels adorned the gold embroidery on the bodice.

Sara's first thought was how could she have gotten out of all those clothes and dressed again for a quickie with Gunnar. She tapped the soap dispenser and stuck both hands under the faucet. "How long have you and the king worked the fair?"

"Excuse me?"

"How many years have you two been part of the cast?"

"Five."

"And how often with the Knights Invincible?"

The queen's mouth thinned with displeasure. "Who are you to ask all these questions?"

Sara cranked a paper towel from the holder and dried her hands to display her badge. "I'm investigating the knight's murder early Saturday morning. Know anything about it?"

"No, why would I?"

"Well, since you were intimate with Gunnar . . ."

"What? Why I never—"

Sara glanced over her shoulder. "Oh, but you were. Question is whether the king knew."

"You have no proof." The queen wadded two towels and threw them in the trash barrel.

"Got it firsthand from an eyewitness who saw you with him. And if you're not willing to speak to me, perhaps I should discuss this with your husband."

The queen's mouth tightened more. "He won't believe you."

Three giggling teenage girls entered, each claiming a stall and slamming the door. The queen plumped her breasts in the corset almost to overflowing and pinched her cheeks to a rosy hue. "Meet me at the empty grandstand. I'll answer your questions there."

Ryker was pacing outside. "What took you so long?"

"I ran into the queen. She agreed to a tell all. Girls only."

"Why would she consent to something so incriminating?"

"Told her I have a witness who saw her with Gunnar."

"But you don't have one."

Sara's mouth curved into a smile. "The fact that we're meeting alone on a deserted grandstand tells me it's true. If the courtiers and ladies-in-waiting are still at McDuff's Beans, see what you can glean from them. We'll meet afterward and share stories."

Sara headed to the three-tier grandstand embellished with shields, banners, and colorful pennants bearing coats of arms. She climbed the bleachers to the queen waiting on top, her hands stirring like restless leaves in the wind as she gazed at the jousting arena below.

"I used to watch Gunnar jousting from up here. I'd never seen anybody with such power to control everyone and everything around him. He excited something in me I thought I'd lost."

Sara sat beside her. "Because your husband no longer did?"

"He and I met at a party. I was young and scared, not prepared to be on my own with no job and only a high school education. Six months later he proposed. I didn't love him, but he was kind and would take care of me. I honestly tried to make it work and believed my affection for him would grow in time. But as years passed, all the little things one is supposed to overlook ate away at me until I could barely get through a meal listening to him smacking his lips. His burps and farts became explosions."

Sara nodded. "I understand. Dressing up as a queen on eight Saturdays and Sundays every year was a means of escaping a drab existence. But that wasn't enough, was it?"

Eyes downcast, the queen shook her head.

"Then I repeat, when did you start sleeping with Gunnar?"

"Last year. We got together about five times every week."

"Your husband must have suspected something."

"No, he never did. There was plenty of free time between my queenly duties and Gunnar's jousts. I made up excuses to get away from home midweek and went to his trailer. He always had fresh chrysanthemums on the table and made such unbelievable love to me. I was walking on clouds."

"Your tiptoeing in the sky didn't go unnoticed by one of the ladies-in-waiting. She spread the word among the girls."

The queen shrugged one shoulder, seeming not to have the energy for both. "Didn't matter. All I cared about was his promise to take me on the road at the end of this year's fair. I dreamt of nothing else the ten months between and was ready to give myself wholly to him. The Friday night before opening, I went to his trailer with the knight fighting a dragon on it. My heart was thumping in my throat. I knocked five times before he answered. He looked surprised to see me and asked what I wanted. His words were like a slap on bare skin. Stunned, I reminded him of his promise." The queen lowered her head as if communing with her lap. "You're bound to hear awful rumors about him, but others didn't know Gunnar the way I did. As he gradually shared a painful childhood, I thought my love was strong enough to overcome it."

A possible lead. Sara pressed the record button on her phone. "Do you mind?"

She shook her head. "No, go ahead. Both parents were killed in a car accident when he was eight. He had no family and was put into foster care. He kept hoping the next parents would love him, but they didn't or couldn't. Always changing schools, he learned people were only in his life for a moment, so he didn't believe in attaching himself to anything or anyone. To make things worse, he had really bad skin. Girls shunned him and the boys bullied him." The queen's eyes closed and then slowly opened as if erasing tears. "That Friday night was the last time we spoke. He'd already moved on to someone else."

"That must have made you very angry."

"More hurt than angry. I didn't kill him. I loved him."

Sara recognized the longing in the queen's eyes. She'd walked on those same clouds with Michael and lost her footing too. But now, she had a job to do. "I'm sorry but must ask where you were between midnight and two yesterday morning."

"At home with my ever-faithful husband."

"And he'll vouch for you?"

"Of course."

"Just one more question then. Do you know of anyone who wanted Gunnar dead?"

"Any of the knights. He was like the bullies who tormented him. And maybe Nicu the fortune teller."

Sara drew back. "Why him?"

"Pure jealousy. Gunnar replaced me with Nicu's belly-dancer lover. I've heard rumors of other women too, probably to make up for the girls he couldn't get in school." A disconcerting silence.

"Is there something else?" Sara asked quietly.

"All those things he did. Were they because of what happened to him as a kid, or are some people just born evil?"

Sara sighed. "Sorry, but I've never found the answer to that question. You've been a great help. Can I buy you a cup of coffee?"

"No thanks. I'd rather not be seen talking with you."

As Sara descended the bleachers, the question of evil took her back to when she was seven. Her mother had grown increasingly more disturbed, erupting in frequent bouts of hysteria. One night, she'd cornered Sara at the top of the basement stairs and struck her, shrieking everything wrong in her life was Sara's fault. When she covered her head to deflect the blows, her mother shoved Sara down the stairs and left her bleeding on the concrete floor.

45

Two days later, Aunt Mary, who regularly conducted séances and spoke to the dead, showed up at the house saying a spirit had summoned her. She wore rosary beads and clutched a Bible to her chest. "A malignant force has captured my sister's soul. I've come as the archangel's divine messenger to rescue her from perdition."

From the doorway, Sara could see her mother lying in bed. Aunt Mary sprinkled holy water and blew on her sister's face. Then she shouted, "In the name of the almighty God and Jesus his only begotten son, I cast out you noxious vermin, all unclean spirits, all satanic powers of lust, alcohol, drugs, anger, deceit, and greed. Let go of this weak woman and allow her to return to the Holy Spirit who protects her." She drew the sign of the cross over her sister and spoke, "The sacred Sign of the Cross commands you be gone. Satan, the master of all deceit, enemy of man's salvation, you must leave this body in peace."

The projectile vomiting and head spinning in the *Exorcist* had scared Sara months earlier. Terrified of hearing the devil's voice, she ran to the kitchen and hid scrunched in the corner of a closet behind brooms, buckets, and mops.

Trembling. Listening.

While her aunt kept repeating the incantation, Sara cowered in the dark loneliness of her broom closet and created a virtual safe place for retreating to whenever life closed in on her.

Finally hearing nothing, she crawled out. Aunt Mary had left as quickly as she'd arrived. As the screaming episodes continued for months, Sara didn't know whether an evil spirit possessed her mother or it was all due to the drugs and alcohol.

# Chapter 5

While Sara engaged in the girl's only chat with the queen, Ryker returned to McDuff's Beans. Young courtiers prone to gossip about their elders were his target. He shook his body to loosen up and not appear threatening but more the fatherly, sympathetic type—the man he wished to be.

They were conversing quietly among themselves, sipping coffee, and eating donuts. It took every bit of self-control to refrain from buying two chocolate-covered ones. Sara would undoubtedly smell it on his breath and berate him. "May I join you?" he asked.

One of the courtiers made room for him at the center table.

He wiped his brow. "Whew, I appreciate a spot in the shade. I just moved from New York and haven't acclimated to this heat and humidity yet. Are you all on summer break?"

"We all go to the same school and work the fair together," said one of the boys.

"It's a righteous job," said his buddy next to him, "getting paid to chill with kickass people."

Ryker laughed softly. "I'm jealous. At your age, I had to sell shoes to fat old ladies with smelly feet who insisted they wore a smaller size." He looked around. "Your king and queen seem to have disappeared."

The boy on Ryker's right whispered, "We think things aren't going too great at home."

"How so?"

One of the ladies-in-waiting spoke next, "They usually drive in from town together but not today. He got here twenty minutes before her, and they didn't touch or speak a single word during our visitor greeting. Then she disappeared."

The corners of Ryker's mouth turned downward in a show of sympathy. "A marital spat?"

"Seems like it's been rocky for a couple of weeks. We've heard them arguing."

Ryker had honed his interview techniques over many years with the NYPD and knew how to ease into a discussion. He leaned forward resting his arms on the table to encourage confidentiality. "You're a bright group who keep your eyes and ears open. I bet you know more about the village than I can learn. I've heard unpleasant stories about the knight that was murdered."

Silence. Glances darting at each other, nail chewing, nervous twisting of long hair.

"It's better to be open with me. Don't worry. What you say here, stays here."

A well–endowed young lady fidgeted with a red ribbon on her blouse. "First weekend, he caught me on our way to the grandstand to preside over the joust. He ran his finger down my cheek and said how pretty I am. Would I tie a gold ribbon on his lance for him to be my champion? I was flattered until he invited me to his trailer to celebrate the victory."

One of the boys took her hand. "I convinced her not to go."

"A very wise decision," said Ryker. "I admire a man who steps up when needed."

"He came on to me too," added a girl with wavy blond hair. "I was having lunch in the food court. He sat beside me, laid his hand on my thigh, and began massaging it. I totally flipped out, jumped up, and left my meal on the table."

"He did similar things to all of us and threatened retaliation if anyone told," said another.

Ryker arched back. "Nobody reported him?"

"You didn't dare," said the boy across from him. "I confronted him once. He dragged me into the knights' stable, threw me face down in the stall of the most irritable horse, and got it all worked up. I was scrambling on my hands and knees to keep from being trampled. One struck my leg so hard I thought it had broken."

A girl swept long hair over her shoulder. "After that, we'd all had enough. I finally told my dad. He's the blacksmith, the only man strong enough to take on Gunnar. They had it out behind the stable. My dad whipped him bad and said he'd kill him if he laid a hand on any of us again."

"And did he?"

They all shook their heads no.

"And when did this beating occur?" Ryker asked.

"About two weeks ago," answered the daughter whose beauty was as imposing as her father's brawn.

"There's been nothing since," said the boy who'd confronted Gunnar. "Everyone else around here is nice and fun to work with or we wouldn't keep coming back. This is our third year."

"I'm proud to have made the acquaintance of such fine, brave young people." He rose and laid his card on the table. "I have to get back to work in that heat. From now on if there's ever any kind of trouble, call me."


Sara phoned Ryker. "It's almost time for the final joust. Knights were on the beggar's list which has been a mother lode so far. Walk toward the arena as we're talking."

"Got it."

"Did you question the royal party?"

"Naturally, I have a way of getting people to open up."

"You didn't—?"

"Use any physical leverage? Heavens, no. These kids not only spilled the beans, they cooked them. Our murder victim was a Lothario chasing after every pretty, young skirt until he slipped up around the blacksmith's daughter. She told daddy, and he beat the shit out of him."

"Good work. Add another suspect to our burgeoning list."

"You upped me with that word. I'd have just said *growing*. What about your chat with the queen?"

"Oh, she slept with Gunnar. The key question is whether the king knew."

Ryker laughed with a sudden burst of wind. "She undeniably confessed to adultery?"

"And put on a convincing grieving lover act that may or may not be true. I empathized with her and our sullied victim. Gunnar fell through the cracks as a kid. Some of us don't make it through painful childhoods unimpaired."

"You appear to have done so."

Had she really? A loner with only a beagle for a friend. "Uh, that jury's still out."

"Au contraire, my lady. The verdict's in and you're free."

"Is *au contraire* one your wife's ripostes?"

"Ripostes. You upped me again. But, yes, that phrase ended many of our conversations."

"Back to the queen. She also gave us a lead. Gunnar traded her in for a belly dancer whose fortune teller—"

"Lover became a second cuckold."

"You've got a one track mind."

"Just been in this business too long."

Sara clicked her phone off and waited for Ryker at the arena.

They entered through the rear where knights were saddling their horses and preparing to joust. They donned plumed helmets, leather tunics and pants. Sunlight glistened off chainmail covering their arms and legs. A knight in a dark green tunic approached them leading a horse wearing a combination of protective heavy leather and blackened plates. A green caparison emblazoned with gold heraldry covered the saddle, body, and tail.

Sara and Ryker opened their badges. He said, "We're looking into the murder of your team member, Gunnar the Undefeated. How'd he get such an imposing name?"

"He earned it. No one ever beat him."

"Do all of you have a nom de guerre?" Ryker asked.

"Huh?"

Sara smirked to herself. Him and his acquired vocabulary. "He means a fictitious title."

"I'm Sir Jasce of Saxony. We can make up whatever we want. I chose Saxony because my great grandfather came from there."

"What's your given name?" Ryker asked.

"Tom Moore."

"And the murder victim's?"

"Francis Tufaro became Gunnar the Undefeated?"

Ryker roared. "*Francis?*"

"You didn't dare laugh like that around him. A new member made the mistake of putting on a curly blond wig and skirt and mimicking Gunnar doing a hula dance with Francis the Delectable written across a blouse stuffed with honeydew halves."

"In some New York neighborhoods, pull a stunt like that and you'd be dead in a dark alley by morning," said Ryker.

"He was gone the next day and lucky to get out of here. Gunnar ran the show. You didn't dare cross him."

"When's the last time you saw him?" Sara asked.

"At dinner Friday night. We always meet to agree on who'll be the victor and who the vanquished. He left around ten minutes before me. I went home at eleven."

"Just one more question. Where were you between midnight and two a.m.?"

His leg trembled, his heel drumming the ground. "Asleep in my trailer."

"Alone?"

"Yes."

His heel beat faster. "When I got up to drain the lizard at one fifteen, a light was on in Warwick's trailer. His is the third one down from mine. I can see it from my window." Jasce climbed onto his saddle and took the reins. "You're hunting in the wrong woods. You might learn something at tonight's party in the Roma camp." With that, he spurred his horse and cantered into the arena.

Sara checked her watch and told Ryker, "We don't have much time and need to split up. Talk to those three knights who've been watching us. I'll wait for the one in black who fought the Viking yesterday. We deemed him capable of violence."

Sara's arms hung over the fence. The queen's question about nature versus nurture had staked out a claim in her mind. Had a wanton gene pool destined Gunnar to lechery? Or had an unloving, bullying childhood impelled him to strike back? The answer had never been clear to her. And what of Warwick?

He had already mounted a black horse. It was prancing in place, tossing its head in anticipation. "Before you ask" he said, "I saw him at dinner too. I left around nine and was in bed by ten."

"Can anyone corroborate that?" said Sara.

"No, I was alone."

"Did anyone see you after you left?"

"Doubt it. And we're done here." Warwick pulled the reins so tightly his horse reared onto its hind legs, pawing the air. He raised his visor revealing the scar of Gunnar's blade on his right cheek and announced to the other knights. "I demand to have the south end of the arena with the biggest audience."

"Just put on a good show," said the herald.

The king, queen, and royal court climbed the bleachers and seated themselves on the grandstand to preside over the joust in fine elegance. Sara and Ryker joined hundreds of visitors on a grassy hill overlooking a sand covered arena surrounded by a cedar fence.

He lay back on the lawn with his hands folded under his head. "I never took time to just relax like this. I kinda like it."

"You need to experience nature's beauty more. It's always been my solace." She leaned back to rest on her elbows. "I hate to interrupt your epiphany, but what did you learn from the knights?"

He threw a handful of grass at her. "Kill joy."

She grinned, pulled a fistful, and let it rain on his head. "Sorry, but we *are* at work."

He rolled onto his side facing her. "Okay. They had all seen Gunnar at dinner Friday night and were home in bed by midnight. He wasn't agitated or nervous, just ordering everybody around as usual. And nobody contested him, not even Warwick who was bold enough to fight the Viking. Apparently those two have been going at it for weeks. What did you learn?"

"Nothing new. Watch. The joust is starting."

Sir Jasce circled the arena waving to everyone and waited at the north end. Warwick galloped to the south on a skittish steed. Squires held the reins while the herald announced, "In the name of God and Saint Michael, commence battle."

"I've come for blood," Warwick yelled and dropped his visor.

Both men leaned forward in their saddles with lances lowered and galloped full speed, hooves tearing up the ground. When steel struck steel, the crowd gasped. The knights rode to the opposite ends, turned, and lit out again, their horses angled at forty-five degrees and digging into the dirt as they rounded corners.

This time, Warwick hit Jasce's shield with such great force it shattered his lance. Warwick's squire met him at the other end with a spiked mace to replace it. He seized the handle and dug his heels deep into the horse's flanks. It reared and galloped at full tilt toward the center where he struck a powerful blow that sent Jasce sprawling headlong into the dirt. Warwick stopped at the end of the arena, his horse dancing in place eager to run again. He withdrew a sword from its scabbard, kicked the animal's sweaty flank, and charged in a wild animal fury. Passing Jasce, he leaned forward and slashed his left arm.

As blood gushed from the wound. Jasce clamped his hand over it and screamed, "You'll pay for this."

Warwick trotted in front of a cheering, whistling crowd. He rose in the saddle and thrust his sword in the air, shouting, "I am master of the Knight's Invincible and will defeat all who dare to challenge me."

"He just shot himself to the top of my suspect list," said Ryker. "That was quite the performance. They made it look so real you could have fooled me."

Sara sat up and drew her knees to her chest. "That was no act. The jousts are choreographed and never include drawing blood. This convinces me more than ever that the murder was a crime of passion and a rennie is involved." She pushed herself up. "That creep Foster is simply using it to undermine the election."

"I agree and we can't stop him unless I discover his end game. He's too predatory and money grubbing to settle for being mayor of a city."

Her phone rang. Caller ID, McBride. *What now?* "Before you start complaining, Gunnar's trailer has a knight fighting a dragon painted on it. Strikes me as kind of ironical since he died in a dragon's belly. Anyway, send the CSI team over there." She paused and exhaled slowly. "Now why'd you call?"

"ME needs a family member to identify the body."

"There aren't any. He was an orphan. I'll bring in one of his fellow knights."

She hung up and arched her back, twisting side to side to stretch and relax. "We need a knight to ID the body. Warwick's already left but Jasce is sitting over there wrapping his arm."

When they approached him, she said, "I could use your help."

"I've already told you all I know."

"Someone needs to go in and identify Gunnar's body."

He sneered. "Quit hassling me."

Ryker yanked him up. "The lady asked politely."

Sara's brows drew together at Ryker as they put Jasce in the rear seat. He needed to chill. As they pulled out of the parking lot, she looked over her shoulder at Jasce. "That's a nasty cut."

"Not the first and won't be the last now that Warwick's taken control. I'm glad somebody killed Gunnar, but it wasn't me."

They reached the morgue twenty minutes later. Jasce entered the cold storage room and balked when the ME pulled the sheet partway down. His face paled to ash gray. His lips moved, but no words came out.

"Is that Gunnar the Undefeated?" Ryker asked.

He flinched and spoke in a suffocated whisper, "Yes, it's him."

Sara studied his face and body language as she pointed to cuts on his chest. "What do you make of those?"

"No idea. Can I go now? My arm needs attending."

"All right. We appreciate your help. One of our officers will drive you back."

After Jasce left, the ME said, "I've gone over all orifices and every inch of skin for evidence or needle marks. I scraped under his nails for traces of skin or blood and discovered no evidence of defensive wounds. But you'll find this interesting. I cleaned the area around the genitals and combed pubic hair. A speck of semen suggests recent sexual activity. We can retrieve cells shed by a woman up to twenty-four hours after intercourse."

Ryker laughed so hard he snorted. "Seems our Lothario died a very happy man."

Sara fired a smoldering look. "Dying is not a happy occasion." She asked the ME. "Cause of death?"

"A dagger driven straight to the heart. The chest lacerations are post mortem. I know there are various types of daggers in the village. This may help." He folded the sheet down below Gunnar's wound. "See that slight depression in the skin here? It was created by the blade guard. I've taken photos and printed copies.

Find the dagger that matches it, and you've got your killer."

Sara let out a fluttering sigh. "There could be dozens of them." Something had been bothering her from the first moment she saw the body. Leaning over to examine the wound, she waved her hand to Ryker and the ME in a come-closer gesture. "See those tiny blue marks on the perimeter? The killer tried to destroy something. Maybe remnants of a tattoo?"

"Could be," said the ME. "Oh, and McBride called right before you got here. He wants you both back at the station immediately."

Sara tramped out to the car. "Probably so he can get all over us for not making an arrest."

Ryker opened her door. "Get in and relax. I'll drive."

When they walked into the station, McBride and five duty officers were crowded in a circle around a TV watching Breaking News. "A brutal killer among us threatens the life of every citizen in Reunion Heights. Once again, our amateurish police chief can't keep his own people in line. Detective Sara Lansing was caught on camera guzzling so much Scottish moonshine she fell flat on her face. A kind stranger had to pull her back onto her feet. Instead of investigating the murder, a second detective was later spotted in the employee parking lot with a young woman."

Blood sped through Sara's veins so fast her head throbbed. She pushed through the circle and confronted a pack of indignant faces. "It's all lies. All of you know me better than that."

"But the video," said a man she'd worked with for five years.

"It was freaking water!"

McBride told Sara and Ryker to get into his office. He looked drained with downward folds along his mouth and gray shadows around his eyes and temples. He glared at Ryker. "What were you doing in the parking lot with a young woman?"

"She's a prime witness giving us information. Foster's behind this report. Someone had to take that video for him. Do you want us to go on camera and debunk the stories?"

McBride slumped in his chair. "No, he wants anything to

keep the story alive and create more damning headlines. He's feeding a hungry press." He tapped a pencil on the table as if pondering. "And we need to offer them an appetizer. You heard about the semen on his pants. Find out who left DNA but don't swab in front of visitors. First thing tomorrow morning, your priority is collecting from all the females he had contact with and not just women with brown hair. I want from every damn blond, red, brown, or black."

Sara's body sank. "That could be more dozens."

"And will take days to get results back. So get on it."

Sara sat across from Ryker after their meeting with McBride. Elbows propped on the desk, she perched her chin in her hands. "The fair's closed during the week, and rennies split to do their own thing. We need to make the most of this afternoon and tonight's party. I'm going back to the village. Coming with me?"

"No, I still cannot imagine why a New York mobster wants to be a mayor here. I'll stop in his campaign office on the pretense of making a major donation."

"Okay, but don't forget tonight's our last chance to observe rennies in action."

Sara climbed into her car, crossed her arms over the steering wheel, and laid her forehead on them. What on earth was she doing? Tomorrow she'd spend the morning collecting DNA when solving the case would send her father to prison for a very long time. He could end up dying alone in a cement cell, never knowing she could have saved him. She tipped back against the head rest. But what if the papers were fake and Possum and Grouper duped her into believing a wanton lie? She tried to visualize what they'd shown her. They were printed on letterhead she'd seen in his office and appeared to be in a format she recognized. But rushed at gunpoint, she hadn't examined them thoroughly. Then there was the picture she'd drawn as a nine year old—irrefutable evidence they'd really been in her dad's house and could have accessed his computer and printer. They'd posed the nagging question of how did he working as a financial advisor amass the wealth of his opulent estate.

# Chapter 6

Sara drove back to the main village entrance, a castle wall. Town criers hanging over the parapet shouted, "Milords and Miladies, Lads and Lasses, we bid thee good day. Prithee tarry a few hours in this most beauteous place. For verily 'twill please you most well."

She flashed her badge to a woman attending the turnstile and entered along with visitors dressed in Renaissance clothing as authentic as any worn by rennies. To take a breather and unwind, she watched the last few minutes of her favorite show.

Ded Bob was a skeleton dummy in a tunic and breeches. His purple floppy hat had a white plume hanging to one side. Bony legs dangling down, he sat propped on the left arm of a man wearing a gauze hood over his face, barring any clue to his identity as he worked the dummy's mouth with his free hand.

Ded Bob slowly turned his head as if making eye contact with the entire audience. "Ahhh, I sing in the skeleton key of R-flat.

> Give me a home where the corpses lie prone,
> Where the maggots and cockroaches play.
> Where the stiffs go to rot in their cemetery plot,
> and the skies are all gloomy and gray."

He scanned the crowd. "Everybody having a good time?"

Loud foot stomping on the bleachers responded. "Good to hear 'cuz

> *I'm getting buried in the morning.*
> *Ding, dong, the bells are going to toll.*
> *Bring on the casket.*
> *Put something in my basket.*
> *But get me to my grave on time."*

The audience went totally crazy, cheering and whistling. The ventriloquist passed his tip basket and exited the stage with the skeleton dummy under one arm.

Sara caught up to him. "I love your act. You're such a creative artist not afraid to push boundaries to entertain an audience."

He removed the hood and pulled a long, blonde ponytail from under a peasant shirt and shook it out. "Thank you. Ded Bob and I try to please."

She presented her ID. "I hate to bother you but want to ask a few questions about the knight found dead yesterday morning."

"I never met the guy personally but certainly knew who he was. Everyone did. To answer the obvious, I saw him shortly after eleven Friday night heading toward the Roma camp."

Sara's breath caught. A verifiable clue when least expected. "You're sure of the time and that it was Gunnar?"

"Ded Bob and I were sitting under my awning rehearsing a new song for the next day. I noted the hour since it seemed late. And it was definitely him. His trailer's right down from us."

"Did you see him return?"

"No."

She walked with him. "I know you're a regular on the circuit and may have worked with the knights before. Have you noticed any kind of confrontations with other rennies?"

He shifted Ded Bob to the other arm. "Sure, in Louisiana just a few weeks ago, the Viking challenged Gunnar to meet in the arena at night. I didn't go but word spread quickly that the Viking held the knight down with his knee on his throat."

"What were they fighting about?"

"No idea. Ded Bob and I stay as far from them as possible."

"How about Gunnar and Warwick the Black?"

"I've only heard rumors of bad blood between them."

"The Scots and Roma camp? Any provocations with Gunnar?"

"None that I'm aware of." He quickened the pace. "If you don't mind, I have a gorgeous lady waiting to fix my lunch."

"Of course. Thank you for your time."

Gunnar and the Viking. That put him at the top of the suspect list, but she didn't relish going to Thor's Treasures. His wild red hair flowing from beneath a winged helmet and an amulet shaped like the jaws of Fenris ruffled even her. She took Wizard's Way to his shop and just observed from a distance. He used a swivel knife to carve a dragon that covered the entire back of a leather vest. His index finger sat in a saddle at the top while the thumb and third finger controlled the blade. Each slight turn cut a scale along the tail that wound around the front. A blade that slices leather with such precision could demolish human flesh.

His daughter approached Sara. "Can I help you?"

"That's a beautiful vest he's working on."

"A customer commissioned it for her husband's birthday and needs it by Tuesday."

Sara picked a business card from the counter that read Stieg Agnarsson Creator of Fine Viking Wear. "That sounds like a true Norwegian name."

His knife paused a moment. He scowled at her. "I'm a direct descendant of the Vikings."

"Then the bus with oarsmen and dragon prow is yours?"

"I'm Karina," interjected the girl, casting a nervous glance at her father. "We have lived and traveled in it since I was seven. My father's taken me all over America to learn by experiencing the real world, not just reading about it in books."

"Sounds like many grand adventures. You've seen far more of the country than most adults three times your age."

Sara liked this unusual girl. Studying her face and build, she guessed maybe eighteen. She showed her ID. "I'm talking to people who might have known the knight who died."

"I heard what happened but never met him, said Karina.

"What about your father?"

Stieg slammed the knife down. His voice dwarfed the space between them. "Don't come here and badger my daughter."

"I'm merely trying to learn all I can about the victim."

"Didn't know the man. Now get out of here. We're busy."

Either the ventriloquist or Viking was lying. She laid odds on the latter but would curb her suspicion for now. "I also have to ask where you were between twelve and two Saturday morning."

"Home with my wife." He put his arm around Karina's waist firm enough that she winced slightly. "And my daughter."

With the girl present, Sara felt things wouldn't go too awry. "I watched you leap over this counter yesterday to grab, shall we say, a rather *healthy* woman. You proclaimed her the fairest lady mine eyes have yet to look upon. Warwick the Black goaded you into what appeared to be the animosity of a long-standing feud."

"Nothing more than our spontaneous entertainment for those escaping their dreary lives."

Sara was searching for how to respond when a teenage boy came to the counter in a spiked helmet, his arms and neck covered with mystical tattoos. He removed an empty sheath from a leather belt and laid it on the counter. "I need a new knife to fit in here."

"This conversation's over," Stieg told Sara and turned to show off his display to a young Viking wanna be.

Perhaps his daughter would answer questions if beyond her father's ear. Sara asked Karina, "Would you mind showing me the way to your mother's booth?"

"Sure, my dad calls her Freya, the goddess of love and beauty."

"I'd like to meet her, but first let's get something. I'm starved."

Sara led her to the food court offering an array of edibles and libations. Picnic tables sat interspersed among large leafy trees. Sara said, "What would you like? My treat."

"A cherry malt."

"That's all? You can have anything you want."

"It's what my dad always gives me when I'm sick or down in the dumps."

"And are you down in the dumps today?"

Karina looked away and was so quiet one could hear a blade of grass in the wind. Sara said, "When I get the blues, my comfort food is mac 'n cheese. It's not all that healthy, so I ration it." She ordered the malt and a bowl of fruit for herself and then parked on a bench with Karina under a live oak. Something about the girl aroused emotions Sara had denied for too many years. She wanted to connect with her. "Being on the move all the time must make it hard keeping friends."

"It is, but I run into really cool people like Naira, the flower-cart girl. We met here two years ago and became best friends. We use FaceTime and Instagram to stay in touch."

"I saw her earlier. Quite stunning with such long black hair and dark eyes."

"Her name means big eyes. Naira's a Seminole and told me how the government forced more than three thousand Indians out of Florida in the eighteen fifties." Karina sucked the thick malt so hard her cheeks caved in. She held her forehead. "Brain freeze."

Sara laughed. "Been there, done that. What'd she say about the Seminoles?"

"Around three hundred hid out in the Everglades and escaped being relocated since nobody could find them. Her tribe calls itself the Unconquered People. Some still live in the swamp, but her parents moved up here to northern Florida."

"Fascinating. A beautiful girl like you must have a boyfriend."

She blushed. "My dad won't allow me to."

Sara turned Karina's chin toward her. "But I think you do."

She blushed redder. "Maybe."

"What's his name?"

"Pan." Karina tapped the straw against the bottom of the cup trying to dislodge a cherry piece. "We met eighteen months ago at a Texas fair, but my father doesn't know. We talk secretly. I give Pan our schedule and he urges his uncle to book the same fairs."

"Seems you really care about him."

"We're going to run away together when he finishes school."

"Sounds like a plan." Sara gathered the next words and lined them up before broaching the subject of whether her father had lied. "I have a feeling all your family wasn't home Friday night."

Karina's face blanched at the words. She gave an abrupt shake of her head.

"I won't say anything to your parents but need to know where everyone was."

"My dad set an eight o'clock curfew, but they're never around to enforce it. He left about eight thirty and my mom fifteen minutes later. They stay out late every night."

"But not together. Where do they go?"

"They never tell each other or me. But I knew they wouldn't get back for hours."

Sara took both of Karina's hands in hers. "This may be difficult to answer, but you need to be honest with me. I've heard stories about the knight who died. Was there ever a time Gunnar said or did anything that made you uneasy?"

Karina folded in on herself and murmured only loud enough for Sara's ears, "At a fair last spring, he kept telling me how alluring I am and that I'm so mature for my age."

Sara sensed something communicated but not said. "Nothing more than that?"

Karina sat quietly tapping the straw.

"It's okay. What you tell me will remain our secret."

"At the Louisiana fair right before this one, he surprised me in the dark as I was going home. He pinned my arms behind my back and . . . and pushed himself hard against me."

"Oh, sweetheart. What did you do?"

She straightened her back and thrust her chin forward. "I'm a Viking's daughter. I kneed him where it hurts. When he grabbed himself, I made a break for it."

She was one tough kid. A humorous pleat formed at the corner of Sara's mouth. "That was incredibly brave. Your dad seems very protective. Did you tell him?"

"No way. I'm scared of what he'd do. Pan doesn't know either. Only my friend Naira."

"Not your mother?"

"No, and you must swear to never tell her. She'd say it was my fault. I can't talk to her about anything. I don't exist in her world."

"I'm sure that's not true."

"Yes, it is."

"Then it's her loss and nothing about you. I know how it feels to live in the shadows without love. I used to hide from my mother in a safe place. I still escape there in my head."

"Really?"

"When I'm sad or the world overwhelms me. You need to find your own safe place."

"Pan lives in a castle turret. I feel safe there."

Sara had rarely let people get close to her, yet here she was sharing secrets with someone she barely knew. Having lost her appetite, she tossed the remains of her fruit in the trash. As they walked, Sara wished her father had stayed to buy comfort treats like a cherry malt, but he left when she was ten.

Her mother's drinking and fighting had driven him to scream, "If I don't get out of here, I'll go crazy."

Sara had followed him to the bedroom, dimly lit from a single bulb in the ceiling. The foul smell of alcohol, smoke, and discarded cigarette butts made her queasy. Drab wallpaper with stars that had lost their shine peeled away from dust-covered baseboards. Her father opened a worn brown suitcase on the unmade bed and began whipping clothes from the dresser and tossing them inside.

He shut it and cinched the strap. She clung to him. "Please take me too. I promise to try harder and harder to always come out on top. I'll be a winner for you."

He held her for the longest time, caressing her hair. "I love you sweetheart, but it's not possible. Courts always award custody to the mother."

"Even drunken ones that hurt you?"

"It's wrong but that's how the law works."

He kissed her goodbye, turned, and walked out the front door taking nothing with him but a suitcase full of clothes. The most important person in her world had left, casting her adrift with no life preserver. Every night for the next six months, she stood at the window waiting for him to return and rescue her. The pain of his departure dulled with time but hadn't diminished. And now faced with a decision about his life, she'd do anything to prove worthy of his love. No matter what the cost.

"Here's my mother's shop," Karina said, drawing Sara back to the present.

The red sign read Asgard Jewels. Stieg's goddess of love and beauty was tall and slender with large, round amber eyes. Sunlight filtering through her long hair gave it a gossamer quality like a spider's web.

An assortment of earrings, necklaces, and bracelets lay on the counter and hung on rotating racks. As Sara and another customer browsed the collection, Freya asked if they'd like to use the mirror. The other woman held several pairs of gold earrings up to her face and turned her head side to side. Sara chose a pair of silver ones. "Gorgeous. Did you create these?"

"I make everything I sell."

"But I help." Karina handed Sara a matching necklace. "I made this one last week."

Her mother put Karina's back and chose another. "This goes better with them." As she reached high on a rack, an avalanche of colorful bracelets slid toward her elbow, two of them composed of turquoise beads resembling those found in the swing.

"Everything's lovely," Sara said, "but I can't shop on the job, perhaps later in the week." She showed her ID. "I'm talking to people about the knight who died early yesterday morning. Did you know the man in this photo?"

"I'd heard of him but didn't know him."

Sara fished through a bowl of green, ruby, gold, and turquoise beads. "You have quite an impressive collection."

"I use a variety and also sell them to rennies and visitors."

Sara replaced a handful of turquoise ones. "I'm asking where everybody was between midnight and two Saturday morning."

Freya's muscles hardened from her shoulders up through her neck. "At home with my husband and daughter all evening."

That didn't line up with Karina's curfew story. Sara's gut said Freya was lying right to her face, but she pinned accusations under her tongue. "There appears to be tension between your husband and a knight called Warwick the Black."

"Nothing more than two stupid grown men trying to best each other." She pushed past Sara. "Excuse me. My customer's waiting."

Sara walked outside with Karina. "Why'd your mother say you were all home together?"

"I don't know, but you should go now before my dad comes."

A scary father and an estranged mother, no wonder Karina planned to run off with Pan. But with no official school records, employment would be daunting. She left and called Ryker. "What did you find out?"

"There's a luncheon tomorrow for major backers. Invitation only, but I'll get in."

"Instead of helping me? We're down to seven days."

"Then I hope you came up with something."

She gnashed her teeth in an effort to restrain her tongue from lashing out at him. "Okay, here it is. A reliable source said at the Louisiana fair a few weeks ago, the Viking challenged Gunnar in the arena at night and held him down with a knee on his throat. Now get this. At the same fair, Gunnar came on to the Viking's daughter."

"Talk about a motive!"

"Ya think? The same source saw Gunnar heading to the Roma camp around eleven. The Viking and his wife both lied about where they were Friday night. And she has a large bowl of beads that might match the ones found in the swing."

"Way to go, Miss Detective. I'm done here and will meet you at tonight's show and tell."

Suspects were piling up, but time was growing shorter. And then there was her father issue. Sara strode down Bacchus Lane so lost in her thoughts about the case that a sudden movement startled her. A bare-chested boy with shaggy legs, horns, hooves, and the tail of a goat sprang off a boulder and danced around her playing a sprightly tune on a flute. No older than seventeen or eighteen, he had wispy, brow-skimming bangs over blue eyes rimmed in green. Downright handsome.

"Good morrow, sweet lass. Verily, thou art as comely as a spring morn."

"And who might ye be?"

"The Greek god Pan, protector of shepherds, goatherds, and their flocks."

Ahhh, Pan, Karina's secret boyfriend.

He lightly tapped his head. "Perchance thou wouldst enjoy a pair of these beauteous horns or another uncommon adornment." He escorted her to Mythological Jewelry that sold unicorns, fairy wings, hair armor, satyr horns, and elfin ears. "My mother created them. My uncle owns the shop."

"Do you all travel together?"

"No longer." His voice cracked. "My mother died of cancer nineteen months ago."

"Oh, I'm so sorry. I'm sure you really miss her and your uncle does too."

"We still have each other. Most of the time I share a crowded space in his trailer, but here I live in a totally awesome castle turret over the Mail Works and can see the entire village."

A polar shift from a voice like shattered glass to exuberance over his lodging? She didn't quite know what to make of him. Sara showed her badge. "I'm looking into the murder of the knight and could use the vantage point of your turret. May I go up there?"

"Glad to." Pan led her across a drawbridge into the showroom. "During the week, the owner stays busy making chainmail bikinis, jockstraps, hoods, and vests to go with his daggers and swords."

"Impressive."

They climbed a spiral staircase to a turret with tall windows on two sides. "Watch out for bats," he said. "There's no glass and they love castles."

A smile tugged at her cheeks. "You're joking."

"No. Had one last night, but it didn't bother me. Maybe didn't like how I smell." His only possessions appeared to be a sleeping bag and air mattress, guitar, backpack, and odd pieces of paper stuffed between cracks in the stone wall.

Sara moved to the only picture. "Is this your mother?"

His body grew rigid. "I already told you she's dead."

His mother a forbidden topic, Sara changed the subject and stood at one of the windows. "There are so many trees it's hard to get my bearings."

He pointed to the jousting arena, petting zoo, elephant ride, and Roma camp all located on the perimeter to bring in animals.

"Where's the dragon swing? I can't see it through the forest."

"Over there on the other side of the lake?"

"Did you hear or see anything Friday night?"

"No, I'm usually here playing my guitar or doing homework for the online classes my uncle pays for."

"What are you studying?"

"To be a veterinarian. I love animals. Moving all across the US, I've seen elk and prairie dogs in Colorado and whales off the coast of California."

What a perfect fit for Karina, two nomadic kids living true life adventures. This boy touched her the way Karina had. She wanted to connect and there was time to share a story before the party. "I'm into animals too. I saw this awesome water-holding frog in Australia. Droughts can last years. In a rainy season, it gains fifty percent of its body weight in water and burrows deep in the mud. Then it sheds its skin in one piece making a cocoon, wraps itself inside, and hibernates until rains return. Guess the first thing on its mind when the frog crawls out."

"Food?"

She giggled quietly. "Nope. Sex."

Pan's eyes widened. "Really?"

"It rushes to find a mate so their young can fill their bodies with water, burrow, and wait for the next rains." She jiggled one of his horns. "I have to go and you should get back to work."

Sara descended the spiral staircase and exited through the Mail Works showroom. As she crossed the drawbridge, Grouper was sitting on a stone block at the bottom. "Such a handsome young man living high up in the castle and that pretty lass."

The muscles in her jaw hardened. "Go near either of them and you're dead."

# Chapter 7

Sara found Ryker in the Roma camp wandering among shops for henna tattoos, belly dancing costumes, and books on incantations and toad lore. He'd stopped at one selling small cloth bags of magic love potions.

She sneaked up behind him. "Got a hot date tonight?"

He jumped like a scared rabbit and turned, red faced. "I . . . uh no . . . but sometime, maybe. I like women and miss having one in my life. I've tried but no luck. I'm just a rusty old clunker with spongy brakes, no shocks, and threadbare upholstery. My battery doesn't start and I leak oil. I need replacement parts."

She tucked a smile inside. "I know a good body shop that can help with weight loss and giving up cigarettes."

"I tried that once but my warranty has run out."

"Moving down here bought you an extended one."

"But I'm only here temporarily and doubt New York accepts warranties from out of state."

"You'll eventually succumb to our charms. Look at this great place. It's my favorite camp."

"I've heard bad stories about the Roma people."

"Your blind ignorance is showing again. Nomadic people get wrongfully blamed for all sorts of junk. The fair gives them a just chance to earn a living selling goods made by their skilled artisans, dancers, musicians, food, and fortune telling. I traveled a lot when racing and it was a good life, much more satisfying than sitting in a stuffy cubical."

Sara wandered toward an old woman cooking in a cauldron over a wood fire, her face darkened by wind and smoke. "I love the authenticity," she said. "These aren't characters playing a role."

Sara introduced herself to the woman. "Your dish looks and smells like a tasty stew."

She continued stirring. "We make it here with beef or rabbit, but hedgehog baked in clay is our favorite. Wrapped in grasses it is a cure for poisoning."

"Must be hard finding it here. What is your name, please."

"Nadya."

Sara smiled. "I'm very happy to meet you."

Above the bleating of goats rose a mellow flute followed by the wail of a fiddle. Soon tambourines introduced seven musicians playing soulful tunes on violins, flute, and dulcimer. Compared to the Roma women's flowing skirts and bright scarves, the men dressed rather plainly in baggy pants tied at the ankle and leather sandals. But rings adorned every finger, and long pieces of colorful fabric wrapped around their heads hung to their shoulders.

"Their lifestyle brings back my free spirited days," said Sara.

"You miss them?" Ryker asked.

"Yes, in a way. Their wagons are called vardos." Running her fingertips along brightly painted panels depicting the worship of nature and spirits, she imagined traveling with a troupe through the Romanian forests.

"I'm hungry," said Ryker. "Onward to a food table." He nodded toward the fairy. "She's alone. I'll take my plate and sit with her. It makes me feel like I'm with my daughter."

"I understand your objective, but we're here to observe our suspects. Stay focused on the job."

Lazzero showed up and nuzzled her. "Evening, beautiful."

*Give it a break.*

Sara headed for the shade of a hickory tree and sat on a hay bale using the trunk as a backrest. Lazzero infringing on her spot didn't buoy her mood. She inched away but stayed amiable enough to glean his insight. "You're an astute observer. What do you think is going on with the Viking? I watched him vault over his counter for a kiss from a woman strolling with Warwick."

He shrugged. "I've heard rumors. Maybe just to provoke him or perhaps not getting enough at home?" Lazzero lifted a thread of Sara's hair and curled it behind her ear. "Are you getting enough at home from someone new?"

She moved two more inches. "No, you soured me on the idea."

"So you'll continue to shut everybody out of your life. How's that been working for you?"

"Better than the alternative."

"I don't buy it. We all need to love and be loved. Look at the Viking's daughter and her flower–selling friend. They know what it's all about and aren't averse to a little romance with those young squires who attend the knights."

Karina was headed toward the squires with a bowl of Roma stew and two cabbage rolls, but her father intercepted her. After a short verbal exchange, she turned instead and joined two young women who ran a feather shop next to her mother's.

"As you can plainly see," said Lazzero, "daddy doesn't allow her the luxury of being with young men. And yet, you deny yourself such pleasure."

He lightly kissed Sara's ear causing an uneasy ripple through her. She was about to shake him off when a reprieve arrived with a contingent of knights no longer clothed in Renaissance garb. They pushed two tables end-to-end and began feasting on wild boar sausage and bratwurst. They pounded their steins calling for beer from big bosomed women in low cut dresses who supplied them with fresh brew and ample kisses.

Stieg Agnarsson, the Viking, jumped onto their table, tilting sideways and hopping on one foot to maintain balance. His beer sloshed on Warwick's stein and plate.

The knight swung both legs over the bench and rose to his feet. "You barbarous pagan."

"You impotent adversary, shoddy horseman, and coward."

Two squires grabbed the knight's arms to restrain him. He announced, "We'll finish when you're sober. There's no satisfaction in defeating a drunk."

The Viking slid off the table onto the bench and lapsed into silence, staring at Freya as she emerged from the forest shadows. He swung an arm toward her. "Behold Hel, who hath ripped a hole in my heart."

She strode up to him. "You're despicable. Possessed by gods you can't control, you've lost your way." She threw a drink in his face and stalked off, having disgraced him in front of everyone.

*Whoa.* Sara hadn't seen that coming.

An ominous silence filled the air as everyone waited for the Viking's response. The musicians quickly enlivened the party by playing a passionate song. Six dancers in jeweled skirts hanging below their navels crossed soft arms and graceful fingers over their heads and framing their bodies as their hips moved in fluid circles. Fringed bras decorated with coins and colorful glass beads glimmered in the fire light.

One stood out from the others in a purple bodice that laced up the front and both sides. Three rows of coins on a triangular scarf jangled with every sway of her hips. A sheer skirt parted exposing the full length of her thighs. Clicking finger cymbals, she slowly lowered herself to her knees and arched backward, her black hair spilling onto the ground. Arms stretched outward, she rolled her body from belly to breasts and back again in slow sensuous waves.

A silky, turquoise veil revealed only dark eyes as she rose and moved slowly through the crowd, teasing men by trailing the end along their shoulders. When they tried to catch it and pull her back, she wriggled just out of reach. She chose the Viking and ran her fingers up through his beard and was about to kiss him.

Out of nowhere, the queen charged, arms flailing, slapping the dancer's face and body. "You scheming slut, worthless whore!"

The belly dancer grabbed the queen's hair and whipped her head around as if trying to rip it off. Both women shrieked, kicked, and punched in a fiery rage.

Sara scooted off the bale to interrupt a cat fight before claws were drawn. The king got to them first, clutched his hysterical wife, and shook her. But the queen kept lashing out and wouldn't shut up. He finally took her by both arms and pulled her out of sight still writhing and shouting.

Stunned, Sara thought the queen had reconciled herself to Gunnar's betrayal. Watching how easily the belly dancer's sensual flirtations enticed men must have set her off. This was the woman who'd stolen the queen's lover even though she appeared to have one of her own.

A dark–haired man wearing gold earrings and a red silk scarf took her in his protective arms, holding her so close a fly couldn't squeeze between them. Soothing fingers twined through her hair as he kissed her lips and neck.

"Who's that?" said Sara.

"Nicu, her fortune-lover."

The very man the queen presumed would seek revenge. As Nicu lifted the dancer and carried her toward the vardos, Sara shook her head in disbelief. "He's taking her after she just teased other men and tried to seduce the Viking?"

"A year ago, he caught her with a Scot and almost killed him. I was surprised to see them together again, but they appear to have added a freedom clause to their relationship contract."

"A handy arrangement. What else do you know about him?"

"Not much. We have nothing in common."

"You mean other than bedding belly dancers?"

His mouth tightened in a stubborn line, "I told you it was only once and meant nothing. Now I presume you'll place him high on your suspect list."

"Get it through your head I cannot discuss a case."

He slid his arms around her waist and gently drew her close. "But you can confide in me."

"Also get it through your head that *we* are not gonna happen."

Ignoring him, Sara sent a text to Ryker. "What d'you think?"

"Same old, same old. Fighting over power, sex, jealousy."

Sara nodded toward the wagons. "He took her behind them. Let's go see."

They came upon an old man grooming a vanner draft horse bred for power to pull Roma caravans. Its feathery hairs starting at the knee covered the entire hoofs. Sara sifted her fingers through a white tail that touched the ground. "He's a magnificent animal. You brush him with much love."

The man's wrinkled mouth had no clear outline. His eyes were a dull gray, the spark having long since burned out. "I'm grateful to the Roma camp. They gave me a home when my wife died five years ago and left me alone. We had no children."

She wanted to console him but couldn't find more poignant words than, "I'm sorry for your loss. I'm detective Sara Lansing and this is detective Ryker Harris. Your name please?"

"Yoska."

Ryker kept shifting his weight, folding and unfolding his arms impatiently. "I have a couple of questions. A man and woman came back here quite upset."

Yoska paused as if trying to remember. "Yes, her face was wet with tears."

"What did they say or do?"

Aging spots mottled the thin tissue on his arms as he traded the brush for a curry comb. "He shook her and kept wanting to know if she was sleeping with that knight again."

*Again?* Sara tried to appear casual by rubbing her hand over the animal's smooth flank. "You're sure he said again?"

"Yes."

"And how did she answer?"

"She walked away from him crying that it was over a year ago. Then he went after her."

"Where'd they go?" Ryker asked.

Yoska pointed at two horse trailers and trucks rigged to pull the vardos. "Past those."

"Just one more question," said Sara. "Did you see someone come into camp shortly after eleven on Friday?"

"A man."

Her ears perked up. "Who?"

"My old eyes don't work so good in the dark, but he argued with another one."

"Who and about what?" Sara asked.

"I . . . I don't know more."

"You've been very helpful." She gave him her card. "If there's anything else, call me."

Ryker laughed as they strolled back through the camp. "So the cuckold knew all along. He just shot up higher on the suspect list which now includes a probable second cuckold. The man who just carried off that seductive belly dancer needs questioning."

"Go for it and when done with him meet me at the crime scene. I have my own theory."

# Chapter 8

For time alone to think, Sara left the cook fires of the Roma camp and avoided well-traveled paths. Beads of water glistening on the grass blades made them shimmer. Dewdrops clung to her pant legs hitching a ride. Overhead in the clear night sky, scattered stars sparkled like silver sequins.

Inhaling the lingering aromas of kettle corn, turkey legs, and roasted nuts, she heard a soft swish of air. "What the . . . ?"

The dragon swing was moving with Lazzero standing inside. "Good e'en, sweet lass. "Wouldst thou fly to yonder sky with me?"

"Dammit. You startled me."

"Flying dragons banish the cares of the day and calm the soul. Come aboard."

"Only if you promise to behave yourself." When the swing glided toward her, she extended her hand. Lazzero leaned over the wing and helped her into the belly. It felt good to unwind a few moments and let the chilled, night air caress her face. The moon darted in and out of tree tops as the swing soared higher. "What're you doing out here so late?" she asked.

"Just patiently waiting. A trained detective would surely visit the crime scene. I knew you'd come to figure out what happened."

"Ryker and I are working on it. You cannot be involved."

"But I want to be *involved* with you and have a proposition."

"Hah, your propositions aren't exactly breaking news."

"I'm proffering an adventurous trip to someone who should

be traveling instead of decaying here. For two years, I've wanted to add an ornate hawk eagle to my show. It will boost me above all other US falconers with its gorgeous plumage and long spiky crest it can erect in a crazy hairdo. A falconer in northern Argentina is retiring and has one for sale. I've already arranged to go down and take a look." Lazzero sat beside her and ran a finger along the back of her hand. "You'd make the journey infinitely more pleasant."

"Can't be done. No time off. And I wouldn't go anyway."

"Your mind and body will atrophy staying in one place. You're meant to fly."

"You broke my wing. I can no longer soar."

"I will lift you up again."

Ryker arrived just in time to keep the dialogue from turning ugly. Sara grabbed one of the wings ready to disembark. "Lazzero was just telling me about this special raptor he intends to buy in Argentina. He's about to leave now."

The falconer hopped out and slowed the swing as it passed by. He helped Sara down and held onto her hand as he quizzed Ryker. "What's a New Yorker doing in Florida?"

In a snarky tone. "Enjoying your warm southern hospitality."

Sara wriggled free. "We're lucky to have him. Now if you don't mind, we need to work."

Lazzero sauntered off and called back over his shoulder. "I'll phone tomorrow. Commit to at least considering joining me in Argentina, all expenses paid."

Ryker gave her a dubious look. "Free trip to South America? Something's fishy. Where does a guy like him working Renaissance fairs get that kind of money?"

"It doesn't matter. I'm not going. He and I are done."

Ryker squinted, peering closely at her face. I've been looking into people's eyes long enough to know when someone's lying to herself. I see a woman courageous enough to kayak down raging rivers and bushwhack through jungles but is terrified of love."

"I don't want to talk about it. Back to our case."

He lit a cigarette. "If you insist. I checked. Friday night had a full moon. Our killer could have seen Gunnar from a distance."

"Or didn't have to if she was already here."

"She?"

"We've assumed it required a man's strength. What if it was a woman? After watching this evening's cat fight, I've come up with a new theory and want to test it. Climb inside and lie on your back in the belly the same way we found our victim."

He choked on a laugh. "A bloody body was just in there."

"Superstitious?"

"Who me? Afraid?" A cigarette dangling from the corner of his mouth, Ryker stepped in.

"Now lie down."

Once he was settled and gave a quirky smile, she climbed in and carefully placed her knees on either side, straddling him. His breath escaped in a cloud of smoke.

"Take it easy," said Sara. "You're acting like a nervous tart on her first job instead of Gunnar the Undefeated, a known Lothario."

His brow wrinkled like a walnut shell. "Don't compare me to that lascivious creature."

She threw her hands in the air. "Okay, you're Prince Charming if that's what it takes. Now imagine you're dazed and recovering from the most mind blowing orgasm of your entire life. Basically, brain dead."

She mimicked the stabbing scene from *Psycho*. "Would I have the strength to drive a weapon deep enough into your chest and shoulder to cause severe bleeding?"

"Oh, darlin', I do like your MO." He took a long draw from the cigarette and exhaled slowly. "Was it good for you too?"

She smirked. "Just answer."

"You surely would."

"My point exactly. Now stay there." Sara dismounted, stood outside the swing, and hovered over him with her hand raised as if to strike. "What if this stupefying orgasm put you to sleep, and I'm a vengeful lover thrusting a blade over and over?"

"But what happened to that steamy lady I just had sex with?"

"She may be an accessory to murder, merely a witness to the act, or have already left."

Ryker sat up and climbed out, brushing himself off. "I felt disgracefully vulnerable lying there with you hanging over me."

An awkward silence tempered their walk to the car. Ryker gave a small, wretched smile. "If it was me in that swing, I would have fought back, and there'd be defensive wounds. But the ME said there weren't any."

"He may have passed out after sex. Have you never done so?"

"No comment."

"Oh, come on."

"Let it go."

"Sorry." From the parking lot, Sara called McBride, "What did CSI find in Gunnar's trailer?"

"Someone had dumped every drawer and shelf onto the floor looking for who knows what? Robbery wasn't the motive. They left a sword with a jeweled hilt and a wallet full of twenties and a credit card. Wasn't drugs either. Four bindles taped to the underside of the toilet lid? Any decent junkie would have found them."

"We've added two more suspects, but it's all conjecture. I'll get on the DNA tomorrow."

"And I'll discover how Foster fits into all this," Ryker added.

When she hung up, he walked a couple of yards away and lit another cigarette with his back to her, smoke swirling about him.

"Something's bothering you," she said.

He paced slowly and spoke in a muted voice. "All day long, I've been thinking about what you said. I plead guilty to manhandling Jasce. When it comes to defending women, I lose control at times and am struggling to change. Bear with me."

This bear of a man had a tender spot in his heart. "If you ever want to talk," said, Sara, "I'm here."

"Thanks. See you at the station tomorrow."

As Sara drove off, Ryker leaned against his car and imagined his mother standing beside him. An only child, he worshipped her. She was his entire world, and his father didn't deserve to enter it. Every night, he'd stop at a bar, come home late, and demand dinner be hot and on the table the moment he walked in, no matter what the hour. On Ryker's fifth birthday, dinner was ten minutes late. His father's jaw tightened. He took the empty dinner plate and hurled it across the room, narrowly missing her head.

"For our son's birthday," she said in a meek voice, "I made something special that took a little bit longer. You'd be pleased."

"I'll be pleased if you do things the way I ask!" Then he slapped her so hard she fell to the floor. Ryker grabbed the rolling pin and charged him screaming, "Get out of here. I hate you."

The next years, his dad hit her so often she was embarrassed to be seen outdoors. She covered her body and face to hide bruises and wore sunglasses over blackened eyes. Ryker pleaded with her to leave him, but she made the same excuses heard over and over in domestic cases: money, fear of being alone, an overwhelming sense of unworthiness.

As his mind replayed that fatal, winter night, anger slowly rose thru Ryker's body and settled into his shoulders that arched back and locked themselves. He was eleven and sitting in the living room watching TV when his dad flew into a drunken rage over his steak being a little dry even though he was three hours late. He grabbed the fireplace poker, swung it around, and struck Ryker's mother. She fell against the brick hearth and lay motionless, blood trickling from the side of her head. Ryker held her sobbing until his nose was so stuffed up he couldn't breathe. "It's my fault for not protecting you," he wailed again and again.

His father was gone when Ryker stopped crying. He called

his grandmother who brought the police. When they caught his father six months later, Ryker was summoned to testify against his own dad. The DA charged him with voluntary manslaughter, but he got off on a technicality beyond the comprehension of an eleven year old. From then on, Ryker swore to defend women and make sure the law didn't let monsters like his dad slip through its fingers.

Sara left Ryker and took a long route home on a winding, country road that passed by her father's place. She'd done so many times before and never stopped after he shut her out of his life. But she needed answers now. Rounding the sharp curve behind her, a driver's high beams blinded the rearview mirror. She flashed lights as a signal to pass, but the car pulled alongside and forced her off the road into a shallow ditch. She threw the door open and jumped out ready to knock somebody's head off.

Grouper walked jauntily toward her. "Off to see daddy?"

Sara planted both feet squarely in front of him. "I've had it with you creeps and am arresting you for extortion."

"Oh, I don't think so," Possum mused. "That would send dear daddy to prison for a very long time." He circled her. "You'll do no more little replays of the murder or question other suspects." His breath smelled like rotten eggs as he spoke in her ear, "It would be such a tragedy if the boy in goat legs and the Viking's daughter met an unfortunate accident."

Sara whipped her gun from behind and pressed the muzzle at his belly. She ground the words out between clenched teeth, "Go near either one of them, and I'll blast a hole in your gut."

Grouper guffawed. "You'd never get away with it."

"Nobody will miss you except that swine you work for."

"If we don't report in by nine thirty, he'll ping our phones and come after us."

"But he'll never find you stuffed in a remote, forty-foot well."

A cocky grin. Possum said, "He has all your dad's files stored on his computer. If you don't slow down and let this investigation run out, justice will be served."

"Who's justice, yours or mine? Get the hell away from me."

She drove her all wheel Outback out of the ditch and another mile to her dad's locked gate. A long driveway stamped like natural stone ended in a roundabout with a marble fountain in the center. Indigenous flowers and trees added to the entrance of a modern concrete house accented with floor-to-ceiling glass on three sides, creating a synergy between indoor and outdoor spaces. A forested area with walking paths led to a lake.

*I'm here, dad, a maelstrom of loving, hating, doubting, needing you. The physical barrier is easier to surmount than the emotional chasm between us. Seeing news of the election, you don't have a clue of your role in it.*

Sara draped her arms over the steering wheel, torn between her job and a man for whom she never felt worthy of his love. She came to him eight years ago bearing racing medals to show she was his winner. He seemed proud at first but then made excuses for not getting together. To prove she could come out on top, she chose the ultimate challenge, Everest, but failed by stopping three hundred feet short of the summit. They hadn't spoken the six years since. *Why am I putting myself through all this agony? Because you're still my dad and I love you.*

Sara drove slowly forward watching his house disappear in the rearview mirror. Her mind too muddled to think any longer, she went on home. As she pulled onto the driveway, her headlights shined on the neighbor's fence. Ralphie's ball sat wedged between the pickets beside a folded paper taped to the cross bar. Were they going on vacation and needed her to take care of him as she'd done before? She opened the letter and read in bold red, all caps.

"Beagle fur would make a nice handbag."

Sara crushed the note and tossed the ball into their yard. She went straight to bed, punched her pillow into shape, and lay on her stomach with both arms around it. When that didn't work, she flip flopped from side to side like a fish out of water. Thinking about Ralphie made sleep impossible.

# Chapter 9

Monday morning, Sara's phone alarm rang at 7:00 a.m. Her hand shot out from under the blanket and tapped it off. She did not want to go to work and spend the day testing reluctant women for DNA. And then there was Ralphie. The note was a threat and she needed to counter it. Having oatmeal and black coffee, she devised a plan to save her furry friend. She headed to her neighbors and rang their bell. A lady in her late sixties answered in her bathrobe, a wiggling, jumping beagle at her feet.

"Sorry to bother you," said Sara. "I just wanted to alert you. We've been receiving calls of dogs disappearing from their yards. We're on it and will find the culprits by the weekend at the latest. But until then please don't leave Ralphie alone outside. Stay with him at all times until you hear differently from me."

"Thank you for warning us. Ralphie watches for you to leave every morning and come home each night."

"I love him. He's a very special dog."

They were good people and would keep her best friend safe. Now off to work. Ryker met her in the parking lot. "You're late and in trouble big time."

"The thought of having to collect DNA kept me awake most of the night. What needed to be said next lodged in the back of her throat. "You do realize this means you getting Celine's."

"No, no. I can't do that. She's innocent."

"Doesn't matter. He demands samples from every female

who had any contact with Gunnar. Do you know where she lives?"

"I can find her but am still stressed about doing this."

"You've said talking to her is like being with Dulce. Here's an opportunity to practice a difficult conversation you may encounter with her."

He opened the station door and followed her in. "I'm honestly not trying to subvert your investigation, but there's far more at risk here than an election. And the chief's gonna lose if I don't dig up enough dirt to take Foster down. While you're collecting DNA, I'm going after him."

"That doesn't get you off the hook. I'm leaving Celine's DNA to a father figure. Have it in by early afternoon. We need to ship to the lab ASAP. You know it takes days, and my time's running out."

She entered McBride's office anticipating a tirade. He stood looking out the window. His shoulders rose and fell with labored breathing. "The slanted news coverage shows Foster will stop at nothing to undermine us." He turned toward her with folds along his mouth like the parentheses for a typed sad face. "I've lived here since I was three, married, and raised my family. You have to solve this." With an angry sweep of his arm, he wiped all the papers off his desk. "Find out who was in that swing with him. I need credible DNA results. It takes priority over all else."

"If you want it done fast, get me some help."

He sank onto the chair, drummed his fingers. "Understood. I called Kathleen DeVries forty minutes ago."

"Good. She's always ready to help."

Ten minutes later, the volunteer housewife arrived. In her thirties, she had short, naturally curly hair and silver fingernails.

"Thanks for coming," said Sara. "I've assembled forty buccal swab kits. Let's get this show on the road."

They drove to the village deserted during the week when the fair was closed. Shop fronts were shuttered. Barren stages played to silent audiences. The only sound was the crackle of empty candy wrappers under Sara's feet and the occasional banner flapping. She inhaled hot, humid air instead of the sweet smell of funnel cakes. "Finding the women could be tough," she told Kathleen. "Rennies take Monday off, and many go into town for grocery shopping, getting their hair done, movies."

"Where do we start?"

"With the Roma camp." Sara gave her a small evidence bag and the single brown hair found on Gunnar's body. "As I swab each cheek, do a visual check for a hair matching this one."

Empty tents dotted the camp. Smoldering embers from the morning fire. The mournful tune of a dulcimer. Sara saw the old woman from last night sitting alone by a vardo. "I've got to check something," Sara told Kathleen. "Gather the belly dancers together and explain why we're here."

Nadya was sewing silver beads on a bra. "That's lovely. Who's it for?"

"Adara."

"Which one is she?"

"The most beautiful. Her name means *beautiful*."

"But they all are."

As if insulted, Nadya took the beads and went inside without a word.

*What's that all about?* Kathleen had assembled the dancers. None of their attire matched the turquoise beads. Surely, they owned multiple outfits. Determined to locate the one in question, she knocked on the door of Nadya's wagon.

No response.

She rapped harder.

The dark haired fortune teller who claimed the belly dancer the night before marched toward her. "What's going on?"

Sara showed her ID. "I'd like to search this wagon."

"Not without a warrant. It's a private residence."

"Then I need to see the person in charge."

"I'm the one in charge—Nicu he who foretells the future. And I guarantee no good will come of you invading our privacy."

*Arrogant toad.* "I deal with facts not crystal ball gazers."

"I don't need a ball, tarot cards, or tea leaves to see your aura," he said circling Sara.

She brushed him aside. "There's no scientific proof of auras."

"Then call it vibes if you must. But I sense great turmoil within you, restlessness, regret." He stared at Sara as if he owned her. "You envy our freedom and want to be off seeking adventure instead of being held captive by walls and ceilings."

His words struck a barren place inside. She paused, her heart racing down a dark, lonely street. Sara harnessed her emotions and replied, "I'll be back with a warrant."

She spun around and strode to the dancers. "Good morning, ladies. As Mrs. DeVries explained, we're here regarding the death of the knight Gunnar the Undefeated. We believe he came in contact with someone Friday evening. I'd like to get a DNA sample from each of you simply to clear your name."

"Do we have to?" one asked.

"Strictly voluntary at this point."

Kathleen gave her a consent form and Sara explained, "You have the right to speak to a lawyer before signing."

She shrugged. "I don't have one. Give me the pen. I'll do it."

Sara explained, "I'll rotate the swab along the inside of each cheek and place it directly into a collection tube. Mrs. DeVries will write your name and date of birth, seal it, and place it in a single envelope. All to ensure that no results are mishandled. Everybody got it?"

They all nodded and patiently waited a turn. The Roma queen was the last to step forward. "Your name please," said Sara.

"Adara."

The one for whom Nadya was sewing beads. As Adara opened her mouth, Sara noticed Nicu watching from a porch.

He hopped off, marched toward them, and grabbed Adara's arm. "Hold it. You're not collecting hers without a warrant."

"I'll look guilty if I don't." She jerked free. "I'm innocent and going to give it."

With an exasperated look, he pivoted on the heel of his boot and stormed off.

"Go ahead." Adara opened her mouth, but continuous bodily movement made collection difficult.

"Thank all of you," said Sara.

As they left, Kathleen said "This is so exciting. I've never been here when the fair's closed. Where to now?"

"The Scottish camp."

Sara hadn't discerned any liaisons between the knights and Scottish lasses, but that didn't preclude Gunnar defiling one of them. The contentious climate between the two camps was hard wired for vengeance.

A deflated, twenty-foot Loch Ness Monster lay on the ground at the entrance. No skirl of bagpipes. Balgair strutted toward them, bare chested, his hair damp as if just showered. The well-defined pectoral and bicep muscles seemed to spark Kathleen's interest. "Welcome, Detective. You're here again."

"We believe Gunnar had contact with a woman Friday night. I'm collecting DNA from any he might have known."

"Our bonnie lasses aren't akin to those braggarts."

"Then there should be no reluctance in giving samples."

Arms akimbo, he assumed the bold stance seen at the Scottish party Saturday night. "Is this really necessary?"

"It's the best means of clearing them."

"A moment please." He left and returned with two full cups. "Prithee enjoy a sip of our fine bevvy whilst I find our lassies."

A tiny pleat in Sara's cheek hinted at a smile. "Is it mere water or hundred-seventy proof moonshine?"

A twinkle in his eye acknowledged he knew she was onto him.

After Balgair left, a rosy blush crawled over Kathleen's face. "Why would anyone give herself to a knight with him around? He could have anybody he wanted."

Sara grinned. "Want me to fix you up?"

"I wouldn't know what to do with a man like that."

Balgair returned with ten comely maidens who readily made themselves available to sample while he chaperoned. Sara thanked him for his cooperation.

"Is that like his harem?" Kathleen asked.

"No idea. That was easy enough, but the next one won't be. I've clashed with the Viking and don't want him around when I go for his wife's DNA. I'll duck out of sight while you just saunter past Thor's Treasures to see if he's working."

When Sara was tense the final minutes before a race, she used to stretch her quads. Waiting for Kathleen, she stood on her right leg and grabbed the other. She kept her torso straight, drew the left leg back, and held it for thirty seconds. She'd done both sides twice by the time her accomplice returned.

"He's there and didn't seem aware of me."

"Good. Now we need to find his wife and daughter at home."

In the rennie camping area, they came upon Jasce sitting on his trailer step ten feet straight across from Gunnar's. Did the knights camp together like settlers circling their wagons?

Farther down, Kathleen came to an abrupt halt at the sight of sixteen oarsmen painted on a Greyhound bus. "Look at that."

"It's show time," Sara said and knocked.

The two bus doors opened outward. Freya stood at the top of three stairs, holding a robe closed in front. "You again."

"May we come in."

"I've answered all your questions. I'm busy now."

Sara climbed onto the first step before Freya could shut the doors. "Police business. It won't take long."

Freya shrugged but her eyes betrayed something was amiss. "Come in but wait over there." In bare feet, she padded to the rear and pulled a curtain behind her.

Sara entered. "I've never been in a converted bus like this."

A kitchen counter, sink, fridge, stove, and microwave lined

the center aisle. A storage closet separated it from the small bathroom. On the other side were two easy chairs, a couch, dinner table for four, and a TV.

She looked around. "I wonder where their daughter sleeps."

"We've got a small trailer." Kathleen jiggled the table slightly. "Ours folds down into a bed for my ten year old."

The goddess of love and beauty tumbled from her Olympic throne by returning to the room in wrinkled pants, a sloppy shirt, and cigarette. She inhaled deeply and blew smoke upward fanning out along the low ceiling. "Now what's so important?"

Sara waved smoke away from her face as she explained the reason for a DNA sample.

Freya sat on the couch and crossed a leg over the opposite knee, bouncing her foot. "I was nowhere near Gunnar that night."

"Then this will only confirm your absence."

She took another revolting puff and exhaled. "My husband already vouched for our being together here all that night."

"And your daughter too?"

"We never allow her out after dark." Freya ground the butt to a nub in an ashtray. "So, I see no reason for agreeing to your test."

"I can get a warrant."

She raised one shoulder in a gesture of indifference. "I'm not giving it."

"I'll be back."

Outside and beyond Freya's earshot, Kathleen asked, "Do you believe her?"

"No, she's so full of it and has someone hiding behind the rear curtain. I'm quite sure it wasn't her daughter. Unfortunately, we need her sample too. I have an idea where she is but will go alone. We've tested everyone we can for now. Here are the keys to the car. Take the envelopes and I'll meet you there in a few."

Sara walked to Pan's turret, perturbed at being forced to ask a child for a test to prove she didn't have sex with the man who tried to molest her. The Mail Works was closed. Sara entered from a rear door and stood a moment at the base of the circular staircase to compose herself before climbing to the top.

She stopped outside the curtain to Pan's room. "It's Detective Lansing. Is Karina with you?"

He pulled the curtain back. "Come in. I'm showing her online pictures of mountain gorillas in Uganda. My dream is to go there and see them in the wild someday."

"I had that dream too," said Sara, "and never thought I'd make it there, but I did and you will too. The adults are used to humans and pretty much ignore you. But the little ones venture close and stare as if to say, *you don't look like my mother.*"

Pan's laugh eased the situation and lowered Sara's heart rate. "I'd like to talk to Karina alone, just girl chatter."

She and Karina went downstairs to an empty showroom. Sara paused searching for the correct words. "Sometimes I hate my job like right now. My boss ordered me to get a DNA sample from every female Gunnar contacted."

Karina shuddered. "But he didn't do anything."

"I know. This is the worst part. You don't have to comply, but it can confirm you weren't with him Saturday morning. The test doesn't hurt and takes only a minute, just like in movies." As Sara gently swabbed both cheeks, she asked, "Any idea why your mom wouldn't give one?"

"Uh, uh," Karina uttered with her mouth wide open.

"You can close now." Sara placed the swab in a collection tube and labeled it.

"You mustn't ever tell Pan or my parents about Gunnar."

"I won't. If your dad knew, it would make him a most tenable suspect." She wrapped her arms around Karina and held her for a moment. "Better get back up so Pan won't worry."

Relieved that was over, Sara went to the parking lot where Kathleen waited, continually twisting her watch band and almost hyperventilating.

"You all right?" Sara asked.

She paced. "I just couldn't hold it any longer and went to the Royal Flush. I swear I was only gone a couple of minutes." Kathleen chewed on her lower lip. "Did you get what you wanted?"

"Yes, and I couldn't have finished so quickly alone. You seem awfully hot and tired. Go home now to your family."

When Sara returned to the station, McBride confronted her the instant she walked in. "What took you so long?"

"People aren't exactly eager to donate their DNA. Did Ryker show up with a sample for a girl called Celine?"

"If so, he didn't give it to me."

Not surprising. She knew he'd lose his nerve. She picked up some more swab kits and told McBride, "I still need to test the day workers living in town."

"Then get on it. These tests have to ship out this afternoon."

Absolutely no idea where any of them lived, Sara called the fair's personnel office for phone numbers and addresses. The king and queen both had strong motives. She'd go after her first. They lived in a modest house with the neglected yard of two seemingly unhappy, disinterested people. She rang the bell.

The queen answered. Seeing Sara, her brows shot up. "What are you doing here?"

When Sara began explaining the test, the queen hushed her and stepped outside, pulling the door closed behind her. "I beg you, not in front of my husband."

"The party scene proved he knew about you and Gunnar."

"But not that I was in his trailer a week ago."

"What? You told me—"

"I had to lie. I'd made my own key last year and went to his trailer last week to look for that Romani woman's clothes." Anxiety flicked across the queen's face. "I was only there a few minutes and heard someone talking outside, so I split."

"I still need to get a DNA sample from every woman who had

even the slightest contact with Gunnar."

"I'll give one as long as my husband isn't brought into this. He's watching TV with headphones and doesn't  know you're here."

"That means from all the ladies-in-waiting. Choose a suitable place and call them, including the blacksmith's daughter."

"Please remain out of sight while I slip inside for my phone."

An hour later, the ladies-in-waiting had been rounded up at a picnic table in a nearby park. They seemed nervous since Gunnar had made advances to each one. Sara explained the sample would only indicate if they'd been with him Friday night. Any other time was irrelevant.

She swabbed everyone with no reluctance and went directly to the station where McBride was pacing in the hot parking lot. He was going to have a heart attack if he didn't calm down. "Couldn't you wait until I came inside?"

"We have new clues. The brown hair found on the victim isn't human, and the killer was right handed."

"Terrific. That narrows it down to only ninety percent of the population and sundry animals." She closed the car trunk. "I've got all we need and am getting out of the sun."

In a conference room, she laid the envelopes out for shipping by FedEx First Overnight. Something didn't add up. She counted them, checked the numbers against her list, counted again. She was short four tests, one from the Scots and three from the Roma camp. *What the...?* Seems Kathleen's hyperventilating and stammering wasn't due to heat and fatigue. Discovering missing envelopes had spooked her. The goons must have followed her and stolen enough to send Sara the message they were onto her every move. To find the women and retest now was an onerous task that would only add fuel to Foster's rebuke of McBride as incapable of handling his own people. Foster had declared war and would take no prisoners. Sara had to choose which side to fight on.

# Chapter 10

Monday morning, Ryker lit a cigarette and smoked it all the way to the nub to ease his tension before knocking on the door of a VW bus. Its iridescent fairy wings painted on the sides shimmered in the sun.

Celine's eyes opened wide. "Detective, why are you here?"

"May I come in?"

She stepped aside. "Of course."

The interior had a small kitchen, bath, table and bench that turned into a double bed or couch. "Cute place you've got."

"Thank you, but why—?"

Searching for the right words, he raked both hands through the sides and back of his hair. "To ask you something I'd rather not. I'm working on the case of the slain knight. Forensics shows he was with someone shortly before death. Our police chief demands we collect DNA samples from every woman Gunnar had contact with."

She wilted. "I would never hurt anyone."

"I know. I know. And I'm sorry but must do my job."

She twisted a lock of hair. "Would you ask such a question of your own daughter?"

"In the same situation, I'd have to."

"Then I guess it's okay."

Ryker swabbed gently and apologized again. He left shrouded in sadness. There could be a Gunnar in Dulce's life, and he couldn't protect her. She still refused to answer a phone call, text, or email.

To quash thoughts of missing his daughter, he got into his car, breathed deeply, and tried to clear his head. But time alone wasn't his friend. It awakened memories of what estranged her. He could only blame himself for being too absent in their lives, working a job that destroyed many marriages. His wife had to raise Dulce with little help from him. For twenty-one lonely years, they both lived in fear that the next time they saw him, he'd be lying on a mortuary slab. They endured out of love that he didn't deserve.

His wife had pancreatic cancer. Even under the best possible care, she survived six months in unbearable pain. The day she died, his team had finally arrested a serial rapist who murdered girls the same age as Dulce. Ryker was so focused on grilling that piece of human garbage for the location of a girl thought to still be alive that he didn't hear his daughter's call. When a deputy alerted him that his wife had just passed away, he lost it. Two officers had to calm him enough to drive home.

Racing into the house, he found Dulce sitting at her mother's bed, her eyes swollen and red. "I'm here, sweetheart," he said and put his arms around her to share their grief.

She shrugged him off. "Quit pretending you care. Where were you when Mom needed someone to wipe her brow and cool a fever, to read to her at night, to hold her while she slept?"

His eyes filmed over. "I loved her with every part of my being as I do you."

"I hate you for putting work ahead of us and will never forgive you for not being at her side when she took her final breaths. Don't ever try to speak to me again." Dulce refused to sit with him at the funeral or stand next to him at the graveside. She disappeared the following day without a word.

Needing to pull himself together now, Ryker kept repeating his mantra aloud. "Guilt's a toxic emotion. Let it go, let it go." By the time he arrived at the county seat, he'd composed himself well enough to come off as confident and businesslike. He stood at the information desk, lightly tapping his fingers on the counter. With a genial smile, he asked the woman, "How are you this perfect day?"

"Stuck here until five."

Ryker leaned forward just enough to connect without being overbearing. "Then I wish the most beautiful evening for a lady as lovely as you."

A pink hue flooded her cheeks. "What do you need?"

"Information about a company in this county?"

"Go to this website." She wrote it on a card and slid it over to him. "It should give you most of what you need."

"How kind of you. Can you also get information relating to the specific licensing of a company?"

She added another site.

"My lady, you're a bewitching jewel. Perhaps you can help me with one more thing. The Renaissance village leases the property from Reunion Heights. I'm rushed now but would be most appreciative if you could find when that lease expires. Here's my card."

She blushed. "I'll do my best."

One down. On to the next. In all of Ryker's NYPD investigation of Foster, they had never come face-to-face during an arrest or in court. He drove to the campaign office and strutted through the door as an anonymous benefactor.

A receptionist greeted him. "Welcome to our operation. We've put together a team capable of making this city greater under the new leadership of Corbin Foster. Unlike his incompetent opponent, he's a master builder and will create state wide recognition of Reunion Height's prosperity and forward looking goals."

"That's why I'm here." Ryker extended his hand. "Lee Wright from central Texas. I follow the money and am ready to move on to the next big project. Folks say this Corbin Foster fellow has what it takes to get the job done. I just sold a large scale development with a multi-million-dollar return on my money. I want to see if he's got the savvy to make an even greater profit in his economic climate. I'll begin by personally making a sizeable contribution to ensure his election."

Her entire face lit up. "He'll be quite pleased but isn't available until tomorrow morning. He's hosting a luncheon this afternoon at the Azure Moon Hotel. It's by invitation only."

Using his most–winning smile, he whispered in a lilting tone, "Don't suppose you could wangle one for me."

"I'm really sorry but this is for his biggest benefactors."

Ryker raised and lowered his shoulders with an exaggerated sigh. "Guess I'll move on." He opened the door, stepped outside, and walked slowly, expecting her to come running after him like a used car salesman trying to close the deal.

"Wait," she yelled, catching up to him. "I'm quite sure he'll be interested in meeting a man of your stature. I've written a note for Susanne at our check-in table. My number's at the bottom if she needs to verify."

He bowed with a broad wave of his arm, having no clue where the Azure Moon Hotel was.


Sara was packaging the swabs when he arrived. "Here's Celine's."

"Didn't think you'd do it."

Head lowered and rubbing the back of his neck, he murmured, "Wasn't easy for me."

"I'm sure it was quite difficult but good work. What else did you accomplish while I spent the entire morning sticking swabs in reluctant women's mouths?"

"From a county clerk, I got two web sites to search Foster's business." A cocky swagger and he rolled back on his heels. "You may find this implausible, but I can turn on the old Ryker charm and elicit information from even the tightest lips. At his campaign headquarters, I introduced myself as Lee Wright from Texas with loads of money to contribute if the cause is right. He's hosting a luncheon today downtown at the Azure Blue Hotel by invitation only. I finagled one."

"You have twenty-one days before the election to get enough on Foster to discredit his campaign while I have only seven more days to solve this murder before the fair closes. But you go right ahead and enjoy your meal while I work my butt off looking for daggers matching the guard imprint."

"I'll do more than discredit him. I'll put his a*ss* behind bars in an orange jumpsuit."

"Love that image."

She left Ryker hovering over google maps to locate the hotel and drove to the village to search booths selling potential weapons. McDougal's Armory, Earthen Metalsmith, and Eternal Blades didn't make or sell daggers matching the guard.

Sara had a special interest in the Mail Works. She found the owner, a man in his mid-forties with dark brown hair and matching goatee, using two plyers to connect steel rings in rows.

"What are you making?"

He pinched three together. "A knight's chainmail gauntlet."

"Looks like it would take an incredible amount of patience."

He set the plyers down. "Is there something you need?"

She showed her ID and surveyed the display Pan had shown her on the first visit. "You have quite a collection of daggers."

"They're popular with visitors."

She picked up one resembling the photo of the guard imprint. "I heard you used a blade to thwart sexual advances to a young fairy by the knight found murdered Saturday morning."

"I didn't cut him, only warned to never touch her again." He straightened his shoulders and pushed his chest out. "Somebody has to stand up for the young ones here."

"Like the boy you allow to sleep in your turret?"

"The satyr? He's a good kid hauling a heavy load of sadness."

"I sense it too." Sara chose a second dagger. "These two have guards matching an impression left on the victim's body. May I take them to forensics?"

"They're yours. I've got nothing to hide."

He'd come across as sincere and honest. She doubted any blood trace would show up. But her next stop at the Tempered Forge strained her credulity. The blacksmith had already beaten Gunnar and threatened to kill him if he ever came near any of the ladies-in-waiting again. She found him using long handled tongs to pull a piece of steel from the fire. Then holding it on the anvil, he pounded with a heavy hammer.

She yelled over the clanking, "The blades you sold the knights and zookeeper, were any of them daggers?"

He turned the metal and struck it again. "All of them."

"All three? You're sure?"

He dipped the steel in water to cool. "I already told you."

"I understand but forensics says the murder weapon was a dagger. My boss insists we check every one in the village and bring in those matching a particular guard imprint."

He shot her a glance as hot as his forge. "Listen, lady. I don't have time for this. You're not taking anything out of here."

"Afraid I have to if I find a match." She compared the photo to every guard in his inventory and came up empty. "Were the ones you sold the same as these?"

"I don't remember. I create different styles. Now get out. I'm in the middle of a battle axe on commission."

*You need to dip yourself in water to cool off.* And she needed coffee. McDuff's Beans remained open during the week. She went there and ordered a black cup. Sipping from the cooler edge, she surveyed the area and recognized the two mud wrestlers at a table on her left, three of the singing nuns on her right, and the tree man on stilts covered by leaves, all of them seemingly innocuous. Ready to leave, she picked up a plastic cup and burger wrapper left on a table and walked to the trash bin.

Standing beside it, Possum opened the swing lid for her. "We warned you to stop working so fervently on this case."

"It's my job."

"Slow down, keep your mouth shut, or it's *bang, bang* dead."

Her brows drew to a deep V as she got right in his face. "Get out of my sight or pay the consequences."

Muscles knotted in the back of Sara's neck. She twisted her head left and right to relax them before tackling her next owner—the keeper of the petting zoo. When she opened the gate, a creaking hinge must have set off a food bell because animals swarmed on all sides, grunting, squealing, braying, and bleating. Pretending to defend herself, Sara managed to pull a brown hair from one of the goats to compare back at the lab with that found on the body.

The man in charge shambled up to her. Mud and hay coated the cuffs of his pants. He reeked of goat dung wafting about him. His large rumpled frame looked as though his skin hung too loosely on his body.

She presented her badge. "I'm Detective Lansing looking into the knight's death Saturday morning."

"Heard he got cut up really awful. He was like them yukky maggots I found on a dead cat."

"How so?"

"Ask anybody. They'll tell you." He swatted a goat trying to eat Sara's shoelaces.

"I'd like to hear it from you."

Another swing at the goat. And a miss. Eyes to the ground, he kept rolling his head back and forth. "He was always bullying me and calling me bird brain and doofus 'cuz I take care of animals." He frantically waved his arms in every direction. "Look at all them pigs, rabbits, chickens, sheep, and six goats that don't care about nothing. They chew on anything looks like a plant. And so curious, them goats'll do anything to get outside the fence."

"And what's that got to do with the knight?"

"Four nights ago, that pig was so drunk he come stumbling in here, open all my gates, 'n chase every animal out. Stomping and screaming, shooing 'em all over the village."

Did Gunnar prey on everyone? "How'd you get them back?"

"Good people with flashlights. But ya can't herd goats like sheep. They jump every which way. Took hours to find 'em all. They had to wrestle 'em down and carry 'em back, clothes all covered with dirt and hair."

"That must have made you very angry."

"I . . . I hated him but would never kill nobody."

"We know the murder weapon was a dagger. You bought one from the blacksmith."

His body pitching from side to side, he avoided eye contact. "For protection."

"From Gunnar?"

"Him and everybody else. Nobody likes me 'cuz I'm different. I gotta have something to defend myself but ain't never used it."

"We're collecting all that might match the guard impression in this picture. I'd like to see yours if you'll get it for me."

He galumphed toward the shed with the stealth of a pregnant hippo, returned minutes later, and plunked the blade clumsily into her hand.

"Good selection. Such a very handsome one."

His head bobbed. "Uh-huh, first one I ever owned. When I was growing up, my mum said knives was too dangerous, and I couldn't have none."

"I'll put yours in a bag with your name and promise to bring it back. I'm sorry but am asking everyone this question. Where were you Friday night and very early Saturday morning?"

His eyes shifted from her. "Right here in this yard. I can't never leave them animals alone."

Sara felt something moist and sticky on her ankle. She peered over her shoulder at a grotesque creature made entirely of spare parts—a pig body thickly covered with bristly hairs, donkey-like ears, a naked tail tapering to a point, big claws on its front feet, and a long nose. A stringy tongue flicked out of its tubular mouth at her leg again.

"What is that?"

"An aardvark."

She smiled. *Ah, yes, the all-time, favorite Renaissance pet.*

Sara left him wrestling two goats to keep them from making a bolt for the open gate. She sympathized with this scruffy character more comfortable with four legged animals than those on two. He was such easy prey for the cavalier knight, but she didn't quite know what to make of him. A little dim, a lot paranoid, but capable of murder?

On her way to interrogate the knights, Sara stopped at Fay's Fruit Cups where the pulp had been removed from an orange and replaced with sorbet. She dipped the tiny wooden spoon in as she strolled toward the jousting arena. Four knights were engaged in mock battles wearing sweats rather than armor or chainmail. The only vestiges of the weekend attire were sheaths and scabbards attached to their belts.

She stayed a safe distance eating sorbet and watching them thrust, parry, block and retreat in a display of grand bravura. Sara sashayed up to them and flashed her badge. "I'm Detective Lansing investigating Gunnar's death."

"You won't catch any of us wailing over his dead body," said a knight with long, dark hair and matching stubble.

"I understand, but forensics identified the murder weapon as a dagger with a guard matching this photo." She opened the app on her phone. "I need to compare it to your blades."

They all took a look and proclaimed, "Not any of ours."

"Then you'll have no problem showing me."

One of the knights cupped both hands over the pommel of his sword and leaned on it in a broad stance. "And why would I?"

"To clear your name and not force me to get a warrant."

He looked over his shoulder and laughed at the other two. "Detective lady wants to see our blades."

One swaggered toward her, pumping his hips forward. "Have something I'd rather show you."

She calmly set the sorbet down, pulled out a pair of cuffs, and reached for his arm. "Are you certain that's what you'd like to do?"

"All right, all right. Come on guys, help me."

She scooped out another bite of sorbet as they emptied their sheaves. "Thanks, I appreciate your most *cordial* cooperation, but none match."

Next, Sara needed to find the two knights who had purchased the blacksmith's daggers. She knew where Jasce lived and went to the off-site camping area. She intended to squeeze the truth from him and rapped on the door of a trailer with a gold lion on a green shield. "It's Detective Lansing. I need to talk to you again about the dagger you bought from the blacksmith."

"Why?"

"To see if its guard matches a mark on Gunnar's body."

"Mine's plain, nothing special about it."

She wedged her foot between the door and jamb. "I also need the name of your alibi for Friday night."

"I . . . I can't," came a muffled reply.

"Would you rather continue this conversation down at the station where you could be charged for withholding information?"

"He was with me the entire night," said a voice she instantly recognized as Balgair's, head of the Scottish clan.

# Chapter 11

*W*hoa. She never would have tagged them as a couple. Kathleen would be quite disappointed. Balgair invited her to enter. "Would you like some coffee?"

"Uh-huh, sure, thanks," she said stepping inside.

Both men were in robes sharing a late lunch and newspaper like an old married couple. Sara hoped her presence didn't inhibit them. Balgair got a mug from the cupboard and filled it. He sat beside Jasce and motioned her to join them. "Sugar or milk?"

"No thanks, just black."

She sat across from them and tented her hands. "Sorry to intrude. I'm just following up on every lead. Forensics confirmed a dagger was used in Gunnar's death. According to the blacksmith, Jasce purchased one last week. The timing raises questions."

Balgair laid his arm along the seat back of his partner. "We've tried to be discrete, but Gunnar lived ten feet across from us. At two in the morning about ten days ago, he came home wasted and tried breaking down our door thinking it was his. I made the mistake of shoving him off the step and dragging him to his trailer."

"We hoped he was too drunk to remember," said Jasce. "But the next day, he blackmailed us threatening to tell everyone what fucking faggots we are."

"Would that disclosure have been alarming in today's world? Attitudes are changing."

"Not as much as you'd think," said Balgair. "A knight and head of the Scottish clan? Our images and reputations would have been ruined. We've managed to keep it a secret for five years."

"Five years, and a secret? How'd you ever pull that off?"

"Jasce sends me the Knights schedule and I coordinate ours as best I can."

Like Karina and Pan. "Were you intending to kill him?"

"No, never," said Balgair. "We'd use it only to defend ourselves if he came at us drunk again."

"Jasce, do you still claim to have seen nothing Friday night?"

"Just a light in Warwick's trailer at one fifteen like I told you."

Sara finished her coffee and wiped a small spill from the table. "I'm not accusing you, but I still need to see if the guard on your dagger matches an impression left on the body."

Balgair rose from the bench. "I'll get it."

She rotated the empty mug between her hands, hoping for a mismatch, but the guard he brought was identical. Sara labeled the blade and put it in an evidence bag. "Sorry, but I have to take this to the forensics lab."

"Anyone can see it's clean," said Balgair.

"They have a way of finding things others miss. Do you own a similar one?"

"No, only a sword."

"And what about the men in your camp?"

"Nothing resembling this one."

"I'll return it when forensics has finished." Sara got up and paused at the door. "And don't worry. I see no reason to mention your relationship to anyone. It's none of their business."

She had no problem with their situation but was skeptical of them providing alibis for each other. They had means, opportunity, and motive. Not relishing more brain damage from Warwick who also bought a dagger, Sara called Ryker. "After leaving me to search for daggers by myself, you'd better have come up with something."

"I found Foster's real estate license. Florida has no reciprocity with New York. He had to jump through hoops getting one here. I also checked his name in the Florida Public Records and couldn't find any charges against him."

"He hasn't been here long enough plus he needed to keep his nose clean to run for mayor."

Ryker chortled. "I guarantee you things will get very swampy if he's elected. Now I'm off to attend a luncheon."

"Watch your back. I doubt Foster's there alone. From what you've said, he could have brought henchmen from New York."

She watched her own back on the path to Warwick's trailer, the third one down from Jasce's. The door was ajar. She gingerly stepped onto the first stair and peered inside. Warwick was scrubbing his helmet with a Brillo pad.

It seemed better to step right in and apologize later than to ask permission. "Hello, it's Detective Lansing. Sorry to bother you. That's an impressive helmet. What are you doing?"

"Preventing it from rusting." He sneered at her. "And what are you doing here?"

"A dagger was used in Gunnar's murder. I'm collecting any that match a guard impression on his body. You and Jasce recently purchased one. She removed a blade from the sheath on the table and compared it to the photo.

"Get your hands off my personal property."

"Can't. It's a perfect match. Forensics will need to examine it."

"I had nothing to do with his death. I was home in bed by ten that night."

"I haven't accused you of anything. However, I know Gunnar was responsible for that scar on your face."

He touched it. "Could happen to anyone in the final joust."

"But the story is he struck when you were down. That would infuriate anybody."

Warwick hurled the Brillo pad across the room. "Quit pushing me. I was bitter but not enough to kill that tyrant."

"Yet you benefited from his death by rising in power over the Knights Invincible."

"Somebody has to control those artless gudgeons. You should be looking at that Viking instead of me. He's an arrogant ass who thinks he's a Norse god we should all bow down to."

His temples were throbbing. The veins bulged. Time to make a quick exit. She stuck her head out the door and looked up and down the row of trailers as she was prone to do now with Possum and Grouper always right on her tail. Neither of them in sight, she stepped outside, relieved that it had gone quicker than expected with Warwick.

Nicu the fortune teller was near the top of her suspect list. Jealousy was a powerful motive, and his lover flagrantly flirted with other men. Sara walked the village perimeter to the Roma camp and spotted him coming out of a turquoise vardo trimmed in light orange filigree over the door porch railing.

"Still longing for our life of freedom, can't bear to stay away?" he asked.

She sauntered to him. "Did you not *foretell* the true nature of my visit? I'm looking into the knight's murder."

"Means nothing to me." He sat down, cigarette in hand, feet resting on the top of four orange, filigree stairs.

"Gunnar was seen entering your camp around eleven Friday night and was overheard quarreling with a man. My gut says that other man was you."

He inhaled smoke and blew it in the air around her. "Wasn't me. I was in bed by ten thirty with my bewitching lover." He yelled inside. "Detective's asking about Friday night."

Adara stepped onto the porch in a simple peasant blouse and skirt, her hair flowing below her shoulders. "What's going on? Did I miss something?"

"I told her how we were in bed by ten thirty." He tipped his head back and peered up at her as she rubbed his shoulders. "Isn't that right, my beloved temptress?"

"Yes, at ten thirty and I'll attest to our not getting much sleep." Smiling, she spoke in his ear loud enough for Sara to hear. "I hope you haven't revealed any of our carnal pleasures."

Sara let out an exasperated sigh. "I didn't come for chit chat about your sex life. The murder weapon was a particular type of dagger. Nicu, I need to see the one you're wearing."

"Not getting it without a warrant. And you haven't shown up with one yet."

Sara folded her arms over her chest and curled her hands so tight the nails dug into her palms. "I'll get it one way or another and the *another* won't turn out well for you."

Nicu flicked his cigarette butt at her and withdrew the dagger from its sheath. "This what you want?"

"Precisely. I'll return it when forensics is done. Anyone else in camp have a similar one?"

"Not a soul. Now get out of here." He pushed off the porch and stormed past her, leaving his belly dancing lover on her own.

Sara noticed bruises on her arm. "What happened there?"

Adara glanced at the marks. "Oh those, I was trying to calm a nervous horse."

"Not from when Nicu grabbed you at the Saturday party?"

She tilted her head to one side like a dog trying to understand. "Why do you keep coming here and bothering us?"

"I'm questioning everybody about their relationship with the knight. What was yours?"

"Hmm, same as others. He made himself exquisitely visible in the village."

"When was the last time you saw this *exquisite* specimen?"

"One day last week. Don't remember which." With a seductive smile, she swayed holding onto an orange post supporting the roof. "We spoke a few times about fairs we've worked and how hot it is here in Florida." Her eyes swept over

Sara's face and hair as if assessing a rival for men's attention. No contest. She'd win.

"Do you own a belly dancer's bra with turquoise beads?"

"I have many bras but only wear gold and silver."

Sara gave her card. "If you think of anything."

Adara glanced at it, shrugged. "I have nothing else to say."

Another dead end. Now the most daunting—Stieg Agnarsson. She strolled back through an empty village where on weekends a Renaissance world sprang into life with thousands of visitors and rennies dressed in colorful costumes, music filling the air, and audiences clapping and howling. Wonderful shows like Ukulele Wielding Nuns, Sisters of Perpetual Inebriation, and Cirque du Sewer. Sara missed the gaiety of days not clouded by a murder.

She arrived at a sea of tents and trailers and located the bus painted like a Viking ship. "Anybody home?"

"Who wants to know?" said a rough male voice.

"Detective Lansing. We've spoken before. May I come in?"

"If you must."

Sara climbed the three stairs and edged past Stieg's ethereal goddess in the doorway.

"You have no right to intrude in our private lives," said Freya.

"Private? Him calling you Hel who ripped a hole in his heart and you tossing a drink in his face was a public spectacle, one your daughter should never have to witness."

"Do you have children?" Freya said.

"That question's not pertinent to this investigation."

"Well, do you?"

"No."

"Then don't patronize us."

Stieg was carving more scales on the leather vest. Glaring at her, he slammed the knife on the table. "When are you going to quit hassling us with these murder accusations?"

"I haven't charged anyone yet."

"Yet you're here again?"

"A dagger murdered Gunnar. I noticed you had some on your shop counter. I'm collecting any with a specific guard. I need to see all of yours."

He placed his index finger in the knife's saddle. "That is also not pertinent to the investigation."

"My boss insists. I need all of yours."

"Daggers are for sniveling, lily livered curs. I use swords."

Sara had run down a six-foot-three, tattooed, biker, but the unrelenting, malevolent temperament of this man unsettled her. She wasn't letting him off the hook. "I heard you've tangled with Gunnar numerous times."

"That man was a goatish molester of women who regarded himself lord of the realm."

"A position you covet."

His jaw clenched. "What are you insinuating?"

"Nothing, just seeking the truth. Do you still maintain being here with your wife and daughter that entire night?"

He called to Freya who had retreated to the bedroom, "She's accusing us of lying about Friday night."

She stepped from behind the curtain, her mouth in a straight, expressionless line. "I made myself perfectly clear this morning."

Sara had no doubts about a third party in the bus earlier. She wanted to call them out as liars but wouldn't compromise Karina's trust. "And I'm making myself perfectly clear. Give me access to the daggers in your booth or I'll get a warrant."

"Just take her there," Stieg grumbled.

As they walked, Sara deplored Freya's failure as a mother but would use her vanity to get information. "Karina's quite attractive. She takes after you."

"No, she's a rather plain child."

"Does she have a boyfriend?"

"She's much too young."

"At eighteen?"

"Her father won't allow it. He's fiercely protective."

*Enough to kill?* "I didn't see her in the bus earlier."

"I don't know where she goes, don't ask, and don't care."

Sara could barely tolerate Freya another moment but needed to dig deeper. "What do you do when you have free time?"

Freya merely picked up the pace with no hint of her late exploits. At Thor's Treasures, she opened the padlock and raised the boarded front. "We've got nothing to hide. Go inside and look all you want. Then get out of my sight forever."

Sara surveyed the weapons on the display counter. Nothing.

"Why are you going back there?" Freya asked when she went behind a screen to the rear of the booth and discovered a trove of blades among a stockpile of metal and leather goods. Extracting them one by one, she found a match and bagged it.

"I'll return this as soon as forensics has finished."

Apprehension that flooded every tiny wrinkle at the corners of Freya's eyes and mouth added a bounce to Sara's step. The goddess of love and beauty was aging just like everybody else.

Sara left Freya closing the shop and went in search of Karina who'd witnessed the public disgrace of her parents. Pan's turret was her safe place. Sara entered through the rear door of the Mail Works. She took two steps at a time up the winding staircase and stopped outside the curtain. "Hi, it's Detective Lansing."

"Come in," said Pan.

She drew the curtain aside hoping not to interrupt a romantic tryst and found them on the mattress playing cards. "What game?"

"Rummy five hundred." He moved over to give her a space and then pondered a moment before making a fatal discard that gave Karina the complete pile. "She usually wins."

*Not always. She didn't win the luck of the draw when it came to parents.* "You're a good sport, Pan. But I can't keep calling you that. What's your real name?"

"I just go by Pan."

"Your last name?"

"Don't use one like Eminem and Ice-T."

"Why not your mother's?"

He glowered at her. "Because she left me."

Suddenly the room was thick with tension. Her heart ached for him. She wanted to hold him and make him feel loved but feared getting too close. Instead, she simply referenced the picture on the wall. "She's wearing a lovely blue necklace."

His mood abruptly changed. An aura of sadness engulfed him.

Sara said, "I know how hard it is when someone you love is no longer present in your life. I've been there too, and it takes years to ease the pain."

She turned to Karina who had her own issues. "I just spoke to both of your parents. They're sticking to the story all three of you were together Friday night."

"That's not true. They stay out late every night. I don't know where they go or what they do and don't care as long as they leave me alone."

"Why's that?"

She gave a little shrug.

"It's okay. What time did you leave Friday night?"

"We left here early and went to the Enchanted Forest where we found a beautiful spot to sit by the lake and watch the sunset. Pan played his guitar for me."

He gazed at Karina. "I was composing a song in my head about us being together as the sunset glowed in distant clouds, turning them flaming orange with purple on the frayed edges."

Such a sweet, sensitive boy. Sara smiled at the two innocents trying to find normalcy in an irrational world. Karina was looking at Pan the way Sara used to at Michael but never at Lazzero. No wonder he strayed that night.

"That sounds very romantic. Karina, what time did you reach

the bus?"

"A little after eleven and nobody was home. I dozed off and never heard my mom come in. The next morning, my dad was passed out on the hood with his legs around the dragon prow. He lay there facing the Valhalla of his beloved gods."

Sara turned to Pan, "On your way back here, you could have passed the swing. Did you see or hear anything?"

"No, I took a shortcut past Dunk the Duke to get home quicker and write the song down before I forgot."

"I'm sure it's beautiful. I'd love to hear it sometime but can't now. Go ahead and finish your game. I have to work."

Sara descended the staircase, wondering if they'd have the courage to strike out alone as she'd done at sixteen. She'd had no other choice that night. Her mother's new boyfriend had brought Ingmar Bergman's *Seventh Seal* to the house. He explained the symbolism to Sara, a rapt audience of one, while her mother sat in the corner drinking. After he left, her mother smacked her in the face, accusing Sara of sleeping with him. She raced to the bathroom and tried frantically to lock the door, but the latch wasn't long enough to fit the hole on the striker plate. Sitting with her hands and feet hard against the floor, she pushed back on the door to hold it. Forty minutes later, the house grew silent. Sara tiptoed past her mother passed out in the living room, packed clothes in two bags, and left never to return again. But nightmares of not being able to lock a door still haunted her.

On her own and broke, she found an abandoned log cabin in the mountains and got a job waiting tables. With nature as her only friend, she communed with babbling brooks and wind whistling through trees. Then ten years of a solitary life changed forever.

Hiking a steep path in the Rockies, she heard, "On your left," from behind and stepped aside to let a mountain biker pass. His well toned, calf muscles flexed with each stroke of the pedal as he maneuvered over rocks and roots.

He stopped at the turn in a switchback and waited for her. "I watched you from below and have never seen a woman climb so fast and aggressively before."

"I've been doing it most of my life." His curly, blond hair and bronzed shoulders in a tank top distracted her into silence.

"Hello?" he said smiling, "do you also ride?"

"Huh? Oh, I've gone to Moab, Utah for fat-tire weekend and done the Slickrock Trail."

He dismounted and leaned the bike against a tree. "Good to know. Ever kayaked?"

"On class four rivers such as Gore Canyon and the Narrows on the Cache la Poudre."

His gaze wandered the length of her and aroused unfamiliar sensations she didn't know how to interpret. She continued up the dirt trail, hoping he'd follow. He pulled his bike from the tree and walked it beside her. "I'm Michael."

"Sara." She focused on the ground to avoid tripping over rocks and making a fool of herself.

"Do you live near here?"

"About forty-minutes away."

"Maybe we could meet at a trailhead for a hike and end up at a lake for a picnic."

A warm flush spreading through her, she'd entered a new emotional territory with no GPS to guide her. Now six years after their marriage ended, Michael still resided in her thoughts.

# Chapter 12

Ryker called the hotel for the time of mayoral candidate Corbin Foster's luncheon. He had long enough to go home and change into a proper business suit. Then he put Azure Blue Hotel in his GPS and headed out, thinking about Sara. She wasn't pleased with his plan and rightly so. He should be working the fairgrounds with her but didn't know how to connect with those rennies. They were her domain. This type of detective work was more his style and could help her and the chief if he dug up some dirt on Foster.

Ryker arrived thirty minutes early in time to scout the hotel. Laughter came from the bar four doors down from Meeting Room five. He wandered up to three business suits with starched white shirts and solid colored ties and took a stool at the end.

"You fellas here for Corbin Foster's luncheon?"

The closest man asked, "Who wants to know?"

Ryker reached out to shake his hand. "Lee Wright all the way from Texas to meet the next mayor of Reunion Heights. Heard he's got a talent for turning things into big profits."

The man stirred his martini. "Heard it where?"

"From friends well connected in the business world."

The man looked him over. "You're not wearing the name tag to get in. This luncheon is by invitation only."

Ryker removed his from a pocket. "And I've got mine."

The three rose from their stools. "Then you need to check in with the receptionist and get a name tag like everybody else."

Ryker poured a cup of complimentary coffee and strolled over to a stylish woman in her early thirties. "Here's my invitation to the luncheon. Guess I need a name tag from you."

She scrolled three long pages. "You're not on here."

A list of Foster's donors and their companies. He wanted it. "I explained to Heidi at the campaign headquarters I'm just in from Texas and interested in backing the best man running for mayor. I heard he was a shoo in against some senile police chief. When she told me he wasn't available today, I put on my Texas drawl and said, 'Ma'am, I ain't no corn fed boy. Ah'm a self-made meeyenair.'"

"Do Texans really talk like that?"

"Just for fun like do y'all know wheech way's to the restrums?"

She giggled.

Shifting his weight, he spilled coffee on the sleeve of her white blouse. "Oh, oh, so sorry. Clumsy me. I didn't mean to. I'll get a wet rag from the bar to wipe it off."

She held up both hands. "No, that's all right. I know it was an accident. I'll go to the restroom and wash it off if you'll take care of the desk for me."

"My pleasure. It's the least I can do."

She pushed out of her chair. "I'll be right back."

"Take all the time you need."

He immediately got behind her desk and used his camera app to shoot the list of names and companies.

The phone still in his hand, he heard her speaking to someone around the corner. He quickly put it to his ear and pretended to be conversing with an associate. "It should be an interesting meeting. I'll call soon as I'm done."

A stain still on her sleeve. "Soap and water didn't do it, but my cleaners can get it out."

Ryker pulled a ten from his billfold. "You must let me pay."

"Thank you. I appreciate that." She penned his name on a tag with *Foster for Mayor* printed on top and gave it to him. "I hope you'll become a member of our team. We don't have any Texans."

Ryker clipped it to his lapel and entered Meeting Room five. How could someone seemingly as gracious as she be taken in by this charlatan? He scanned the area for a fast head count. Twenty tables seating six each, mostly men. He pulled a chair back from the table closest to the exit and sat down.

"Mind if I join you?" he said before anyone could balk.

His table mates ignored him and continued their discussion. All appeared to be involved in construction of some kind. Finally, one turned to him. "And what is your field?"

*Think quick, think.* "I'm of the opinion that solar power is our only answer," he said, slowly articulating each word as he searched their faces. A low chuckle escaped him. "It's hardly as if there's no surplus here in sunny Florida."

The man directly across from him had doubts about Ryker written all over him and opened his mouth but stopped when the host tested the mike. "Can everyone hear me?"

"Yes," came shouts from every corner.

"Then let me begin by introducing the man who will become the next mayor of Reunion Heights with your generous help." He opened his arm toward the side to usher Foster in.

The entire room stood, cheering and clapping as he entered and took the mike. He stood beaming and soaking in the adoration of his benefactor audience. Ryker rose and could barely stomach participation in the idolatry of this fraudulent New York drug lord.

Foster opened both arms upward as if invoking the gods and then lowered them signaling his minions to sit down. Ryker held his tongue as he watched a first rate hustler who believed there's a sucker born every minute, and they'd come to idolize him.

Foster ranted, "Police chief McBride is so unqualified he can't manage his two amateurish detectives who in three days turned up nothing regarding the murder of an innocent knight in our famed Renaissance village. As your mayor, he'd plummet

Reunion Heights into crime and such darkness where no one's safe on the streets." Foster stopped center stage and paused, holding everyone firmly in his grasp. "So I ask you, how could such an incompetent man possibly take charge of our beloved city. We must stop him."

Donors rose again, clapping and cheering for the chosen one.

"Thank you. Please be seated. I know I can count on all of you to help me win this election. Under my leadership as its mayor, the city will flourish and become greater than ever in its history." He strode back and forth promising his personal backers they'd reap profits beyond their wildest dreams.

Ryker understood politics is a beauty pageant, and Foster was charismatic. Coiffed hair and perfect, white teeth. With the energy of an overcaffeinated hamster, he presented himself as a highly successful businessman. McBride came across as a hometown boy. Voters would know and trust him for his twenty years of dedicated service, but that might not be enough. It all came down to solving the crime and unmasking Foster.

Ryker ducked outside the rear door and called Sara. "I showed up at the luncheon with Lee wright's personal invitation."

"The one your irrefutable charm snared at his headquarters?"

Pleased with himself, he said, "Yes, and there's a lot of money in that room fawning over Foster. I accidentally spilled coffee on the receptionist's blouse. When she left to clean it, I photographed four pages of donor's names and their businesses."

"And what will you do with those?"

"Not sure yet, but there's something nefarious going on. Like Foster saying help him get elected and you'll get . . ."

"What?"

"To be determined." He paused. "Oh, almost forgot. My charm coaxed a lady into checking the village lease. It's for ten years."

"Told you it was long."

"But what you didn't say is the lease expires six months after the election. If Foster wins, he'll have time to install sycophants willing to push through not renewing it."

"But for what purpose?"

"Don't know but finding out who's backing Foster will expose his agenda. There's a reason he chose to come here of all places."

Sara went in early Tuesday morning and slid low in her chair behind the computer to remain out of McBride's sight. Her suspect list was multiplying like Florida's Burmese pythons, but she had no definitive answer for him. She quietly worked on the weekend and Monday reports, omitting all references to Possum and Grouper. Hearing McBride's door open, she lifted her head to peer over the top of the monitor. *Damn here he comes.* She'd waylay him by going on the offense. "Where's my warrant to search the Roma vardo?"

"Judge wouldn't sign it. You don't have probable cause."

"And when do we get the tox report?"

"Tomorrow."

Arms crossed and his brows knit closely together, he peered down at her. "And when do I get an arrest?"

"I have viable suspects but am running into a head wind until we get DNA results and a forensics report on the daggers."

"And Ryker?"

"Fixated on Foster, he went to his donor luncheon yesterday and suspects something nefarious but has no evidence."

"Send him in when he arrives."

After McBride closed his office door, Ryker whispered behind her, "I'm here." He dropped a bag of day-old, fried funnel cakes and apple cider donuts on her desk. "Have one."

"The thought of ingesting cold oil makes my stomach churn."

"Fair's not open yet. They're left from last night." He bit into a fried donut and talked with pieces of it tucked in his cheek."

"Quit sabotaging yourself." Like a naughty cat, she pushed his bag off the counter into a waste basket. "McBride's all strung out over this election. You'd better have something."

"Foster's donor list is a coterie of the very wealthy. While you lollygagged around the village, I was bent over a computer all day researching their names and companies but only finished the first page." Keeping his back straight, Ryker bent his knees enough to lower himself close to the floor. His hand was about to reach inside when Sara grabbed the basket, pulled it under her desk, and held it captive between her feet.

*"Hump,* I pity any kid having you as a mother."

*Like you're a parenting expert? Stop, cool down, take another direction.* "Why are you so obsessed with Foster?"

For once, Ryker appeared stuck for words. Then through a rumbling, phlegmy cough, he said, "My somewhat heavy-handed interrogation of a murderous rapist tarnished my reputation. To restore it, I need to nail Foster down here in Florida when everyone in New York failed."

"Where's your path to redemption?"

"I keep asking why Florida?" Ryker picked up a folder and rolled his chair back to hers. "Look at their businesses. Demolition, construction industries, major retailers. Two of them are based in New York. Don't you find that a bit odd for a local election? I also recognized the name of a New York thug for hire." He lowered his head and looked at her with basset-hound eyes. "I need to spend most of the day on the second page and could use some help."

She rubbed her temples and slowly drew her fingers down her face. "Might as well. Without any test results, there's not much going on here."

He played up the poor-puppy look again. "A petite favor, *si vous plaît.* First check the village perimeter gates to see if a hired killer could have entered at night."

"Only if you promise to search for your daughter."

"You're like a pit bull yanking on my pant leg."

She bared her teeth. "And I don't let go easily. Now promise."

"You win." Ryker pushed off her desk and rolled back to his.

Sara gathered the reports, slunk into the chief's office, and handed them to him. "Ryker's busy following up on his visit to the luncheon. I can't do anything right now and want time to look into something that's been percolating in my mind."

"You got it."

Those blue marks on the body's chest area had perplexed her from day one. What did they mean? Obviously significant enough to create a post mortem shit storm. But who and why? She had to inspect the body again. Sara drove to the morgue and entered the storage area, a cold room of tile, stainless steel, and porcelain. The silence in the empty space was a bit unnerving. "Hello?"

The coroner entered from the back, eating a sandwich. "Sorry, didn't have time for breakfast. What do you need?"

"I'd like to see the body brought in Saturday morning."

"Ah, the man murdered in a dragon swing. Most interesting." He opened the door to a refrigeration unit housing stainless shelves and trays. He pulled Gunnar out on a gurney, "Someone's here to visit you."

*OMG. He's talking to the dead.* Surrounded by nothing but corpses, she'd go nuts too. "You only need to uncover the chest."

He folded the sheet down to the waist. Sara leaned over the wound. "I'm still curious about these tiny blue lines. Could they be the remains of a tattoo the killer tried to eradicate?"

"I've seen stranger things."

She stood back up. "But why? What possible significance can it have?"

He covered the body. "Sorry. Facts are all I can give. Motives are not my bailiwick."

"But they're mine. Sorry to interrupt your brunch."

Sara exited trying to configure the tattoo in her deliberations. Needing expert advice, she drove to the village to consult the owner of Ink Legends. The shop was closed, and no one was about. She went to McDuff's Beans, one of the few eateries open for rennies, and found two morning denizens, their eyelids half mast, jowls sagging, zoned out. Nobody home there.

She figured the man in charge of the pachyderm ride couldn't escape the daily chore of caring for a five-ton animal. He'd be around and might have a clue where the tattoo artist hung out. Taking a short cut, Sara skirted an anthill to ward off a likely Brazilian disaster. She and Michael had stopped to watch a family of capybaras standing on a river bank as if comatose—a caiman smorgasbord. They didn't notice ants crawling up their legs until the first cranky insects stung and released a chemical signaling dozens of others to attack.

*Dammit, Michael, quit following me everywhere.*

# Chapter 13

An elephant flapping its big ears as she entered the compound forced Sara's thoughts back to the case. A whippet-thin man in his mid-forties exited a barn with a pitchfork full of hay. "Don't worry. He's just cooling himself." Jeans hung on his bony pelvis like clothes on a wire hanger. Long brown hair was pulled back in a ponytail. The aroma of hay and oil wafted around him.

"What's his name?" she said.

"Bo Jangles. And I'm Alex but everybody calls me Scratch on account of this scar." He lifted his shirt to bare a long gash down the full left side of his back.

She cringed. "How'd that happen?"

"Bo ran under a low branch with me riding him. Elephant's a dangerous animal. You gotta be careful working with five tons." Scratch pulled an apple from a bag on the ground, sliced it in half with a pocket knife, and handed it to her. "Wanna feed him?"

Sara held the apple in her palm. Using two opposable tips at the end of his trunk, Bo gently picked it up and put it in his mouth.

"That same trunk can rip trees outta the ground," said Scratch.

"I've seen it happen." Sara opened her ID. "I'm looking into the knight's death Saturday morning."

"Only spoke to the guy a few times."

"Know why anybody wanted him dead?"

"Couldn't say. But I saw him with many different women."

"Which ones?"

"They all look the same in those dresses that push everything over the top. Heard he got cut up pretty bad in the dragon swing. Weird place to die."

"It's certainly a first for me. Have any idea why he'd be there so late at night?"

"Probably drank too much and passed out." He gave Bo a light slap on the rear. "Working with something this big and dangerous, you gotta keep your wits about you at all times."

"How long have you two been together?"

"Seven years."

"Hah, That's longer than many marriages. I must ask where you were between midnight and two Saturday morning?"

"Right here where I always am. You don't pack an elephant's bags and catch the next bus outta town."

"You've got the biggest trailer I've ever seen. It must be quite an operation moving him from fair to fair." As she promised Ryker, Sara walked behind it to an eight-foot wooden gate on the village perimeter. Two cars were parked inside. "Why's it open?"

"A hay delivery arrives every other day. At night, I chain and padlock it."

To appear indifferent, she went back to Bo and ran her hand over thick ridges covered with short bristles of hair. "The skin's so dry you must go through a gallon of Oil of Olay every day."

He didn't seem to find that as humorous as she did. He'd been studying her as if she were a bug pinned to a museum wall. "Why are you here?"

"I'm looking for the owner of Ink Legends."

"How would I know? I've got nothing to do with him."

"I'm just asking around the village, and it's pretty empty."

"Try the petting zoo. He's stuck here with animals too."

Sara took the perimeter path accompanied by mockingbirds singing bits and pieces stolen from other birds. Their songs always caught her ear. The zoo keeper was raking fresh dung into a foul–smelling pile. He had to be aware of her presence but kept his eyes to the ground.

"Good morning. I'm searching for the tattoo shop's owner. "Know where he might be?"

"Rudd hangs out at the Smiling Gator."

Rudd? At last, a real name. "I don't know where that is."

Still with no visual contact, he mumbled, "Twelve miles out on Rangeley Road. Front part is a good restaurant. In back's the bar where he goes."

"How would I recognize him?"

"Tattoos?"

What a dumb question. And she thought *he* was the slow one.

"I'm also reverifying where everyone was between midnight and two."

His head rolled side to side. "Will I get in trouble?"

"Not if you tell me the truth now."

He tamped the pile. "Some nights I just gotta get away from animals. I stayed at the Smiling Gator till closing at two."

"Can anyone confirm that?"

"The waitress and bartender."

"What about Gunnar, the knight? Did he go there?"

He leaned on the rake with both arms. "Nah, never seen him. He's more a drug man."

An unforeseen freaking lead. "How do you know this?"

"Wednesday, I come home tipsy, stagger past his trailer, and hear him arguing about the coke he bought not being pure."

"Who was he talking to?"

"I don't know nothing about voices and was too drunk. My feet go one way and my brain the other. I crash into his trailer. A really bad mistake. Gunnar comes flying out the door and grabs me by the throat. Says there will be *severe consequences* if I tell anybody what I heard."

"Then Thursday, he let all your animals loose. And on Friday, he was dead."

"I didn't do nothing. Honest, I didn't." His hands kept rubbing over each other. "I was scared to admit being gone that night."

"I understand. And just so you know, visitors love coming to your petting zoo. You do a wonderful job."

He looked away blushing.

Sara left him talking to pigs and drove twelve miles from town to the Smiling Gator. Ten people queued up outside a place she'd never heard of. Eating out never made sense to her when it was cheaper and healthier to eat at home. She displayed her ID to those in line, cut to the front, and got through the door. Every seat was taken. They obviously hadn't come for the ambiance of cracked vinyl booths, dusty pictures on the wall, or six customers crowded around old wooden tables meant for four. But the waitress seemed to know every customer and their usual order from a menu written on a wall chalkboard.

"Excuse me," she said to a waitress, "There's a bar?"

Chewing gum, she gestured with her thumb toward the hall past the kitchen. Cigarette smoke invaded Sara's lungs and burned her eyes the second she stepped inside the back room. She hated Florida law that banned smoking 100% in restaurants but still allowed it in bars as long as food sales were no greater than 10%. A clever businessman was running two separate establishments under one roof. Enveloped in smoke, she covered her nose and wound her way between tables of boisterous men.

"Is there someone named Rudd here?" she asked a bartender with thinning, gray hair and a heavily pock-marked face.

He jerked his head toward three pool tables. Sara squeezed through a crowd of players to a man who had to be Rudd. His body looked like an autobiography etched in ink, a fascinating read if she had time to decipher it.

"Are you Rudd?" she asked.

"Who wants to know?"

She flipped out her ID. "I'm investigating the knight's murder

Saturday morning."

Bent over at the waist, he held the front of the cue between his thumb and first finger, took two warm up strokes back and forth, and then sank a ball in the corner pocket. He circled the table for the next shot. "Heard some guy got sliced up bad but don't really know any of them. Rather come here most of the time."

"I need your help in identifying some marks on the body that look like tattoo remnants. Would you be willing to accompany me to the morgue?"

He stood the cue on end. "Right now?"

"I'd greatly appreciate it. Time is critical."

Rudd handed the stick to his partner "Always good to rack up a few points with the cops for future offenses."

He followed her to the morgue in his pickup and looked a bit uneasy when entering. "Ain't never been in a place like this before."

"It won't take long," she reassured him as the coroner pulled Gunnar out minus his earlier dialogue with a corpse. "Tell me what you see," Sara told Rudd.

He examined the blue marks emanating from the chest and shoulder. "They could be remains of a tattoo. Looks like somebody tried to destroy it." He stepped back and studied Gunnar's face. "Hey, I know this guy. I did a tattoo for him three years ago, and the asshole skipped without paying. Whoever murdered him did the world a favor."

"Do you remember the image?"

"No, done too many since then." He pulled out his phone. "I'll take a picture and check it against my design books."

"Please, and ASAP. Here's my card. Call if you find it."

"I'll do my best to hurry but have many books to go through."

As Sara returned to the station, questions for which she had no answers rumbled in her gut such as what to do with this tattoo thing. On arrival, she went directly to the breakroom and toasted a bagel to appease her stomach before answering to McBride. No such luck. He spotted her trying to sneak to her computer and gave the two-finger signal to get in his office.

He closed the door behind her and sat at his desk. "The tox screen came back. Seems our knight had cocaine hydrochloride in his system. Maybe his death had nothing to do with power or sex but simply a drug deal gone bad."

Sara took the chair across from him and tore a piece off the bagel in her lap. "Could be. The keeper at the petting zoo overheard him arguing with someone in his trailer about the coke he bought not being pure. That's another possible lead, but I'm working on the brutal destruction of the tattoo. The killer obliterated it for a reason. I tracked down Rudd, owner of Ink Legends, and took him to the morgue. He remembers doing one on Gunnar and vouched what a sleaze he was. He took a picture of those blue marks and will call if he can identify them."

"What good will that do?"

"Who knows? But they've been bugging me from day one. It's better than just sitting on my hands waiting for test results."

She stuck the bagel piece in her mouth and walked out to her desk to begin a day report, her heel tapping on the floor, waiting to hear from Rudd. Ninety minutes passed. Impatient, she was about to drive back to Ink Legends when he phoned. "I found the tattoo in an artist book. Wanna meet at McDuff's?"

"You bet I do."

"How long till you'll get there?"

"Depending on traffic, fifteen to twenty minutes unless I turn on the siren and speed. Which I won't."

"See you then."

As Sara drove, the obvious question *what good will that do?* bounced around in her head. It was only a shred of hope. Her phone rang. Incoming call on the dashboard read Lazzero. Groan. Was he never giving up? "I can't talk now. On my way to Ink Legends in the village."

"Meet me at the Kokeb Grill for lunch. It has your kind of grub, hummus and veggies."

"Can't. Gotta go. This is too important."

She made it to McDuff's before Rudd and waited anxiously for him. He walked in a few minutes later, his art meticulously placed to create a living video as his muscles contracted and released. He touched the photos icon on his phone. "Take a look at the knight."

"It's too small to see the details. I need to go to your place and take pictures to enlarge on my computer and print out."

"Whatever suits you."

They reached it ten minutes later. Rudd held the door for her. "Huh," he said. "Thought I closed this."

"You normally leave your shop unlocked?"

"During the week, nobody's around but rennies. We trust each other. Nothing I have is of value to anyone other than tattoo artists. And I'm the only game in town."

A chair and table similar to ones found in a dentist's office or doctor's exam room took up most of the center. Sara picked up a handheld, gun shaped instrument. "What's this?"

"A tattoo machine with a foot pedal that controls the speed, sort of like a sewing machine. It can pierce the skin and deposit ink fifty to three thousand times a minute."

"Sounds too painful."

"That tattoo you want is right over there." A book was open to a picture of flying dragons. He flipped through several pages. "I saw it right here."

She turned back to the page. "Looks like one was ripped out."

"Can't be." He ran a finger down the jagged seam. "It's gone. I swear I didn't tell a soul about this."

"I believe you. Somebody didn't want me to find it."

"Who, why?"

"I have no idea. At least you got a phone shot." She gave him her email address. "Please send so I can enlarge it."

The theft gave greater credence to her theory that the tattoo was significant to the killer, but she didn't know what to do with it. Needing to turn her thoughts elsewhere, she reluctantly agreed to have lunch with Lazzero at Kokeb Grill.

He was already seated when Sara came in. First thing out of his mouth was, "You look like your goldfish just died."

"I'm in no mood for this and shouldn't have even showed up. There are far more urgent issues to deal with than listening to you." She pushed back from the table and started to rise.

He stopped her. "Wait. You need to at least eat something. I'll order the hummus plate."

She did feel a bit light headed. The bagel wasn't making it. "All right go ahead and add sugarless iced tea."

"Got it. This case must be really wearing you down."

"In ways you'll never know." The iced tea arrived with a straw. "What's with these people? These straws aren't biodegradable and will turn into micro plastics floating in an ocean mass."

"Don't use it then."

"They already tore the top off, not allowing me to refuse it." She folded the wrapper accordion style.

"The case?"

"You know I can't discuss it with anyone."

"I'm not just anyone."

She threw the paper accordion at him. "Why are we here?"

"To talk about us."

"There is no *us*."

He took her hand. "But could be if you come to Argentina with me for a couple of weeks."

"I'm not wandering down another dead end with you."

He leaned toward her. "Look me in the eyes, and you'll see that I've changed."

"You know the old saying about a leopard's spots."

He pulled back. "I'm not asking for a lifelong commitment,

just a brief trip for a free spirit who thrives on flowing with the wind. I'm offering to pay your way and will throw in an extension to Iguazu Falls, the largest waterfall in the world surrounded by a tropical jungle. Just your kind of thing."

"I'm well aware of them."

"Then why decline my offer?"

"The same reason I don't walk barefoot on volcanic rock."

"Huh?"

"To protect myself." She wriggled off the bench. "Gotta go."

"But you didn't eat."

"No appetite."

"And no answer?"

Not when she didn't trust his agenda. He'd snooped and read her text at the party, knew she was heading to Ink Legends, and kept trying to involve himself in the investigation. Had he done Gunnar in for humiliating him with a dead pigeon tossed on stage? That didn't seem likely. A more disturbing thought crept into her head. Had her rebuff of his advances caused him to become a mole for Foster?

# Chapter 14

None of the daggers contained blood residue or showed any link to the murder. Returning them was an unwelcome task, especially to Nicu. If he weren't so annoying, Sara would sympathize him for being with a woman whose blatant sensuality had no bounds. Sara went to the Roma camp and found no one except Yoska. The veins in his hands were like tracery in a leaf as he carefully brushed the long, flowing mane of a brown and white vanner pinto. There was a peace about him she yearned to find in herself.

He crossed strands of brown hair over each other. "That's lovely. Why do you braid it?"

"To keep it from tangling and getting dirty. And to make my horses beautiful."

She lifted the forelock and feigned stroking it as she compared the single hair found on Gunnar. The match wasn't conclusive. She returned the sample to its evidence bag and slipped it into her pocket. "I'm here to return a dagger to Nicu. Where can I find him?"

He shook his head and continued working.

"May I leave it with you?"

He simply motioned toward the ground. Sara knelt and laid the dagger two feet from the vanner's hooves. "Thank you."

Warwick and Jasce were next. At the arena, the village beggar was cleaning the grassy hill overlooking the sand covered field. She climbed up to him. "Where is everyone?"

He stabbed a paper cup and stuffed it a large bag hung over his shoulder. "Some women in town invited the knights to a party. They left two hours ago and will drag themselves in early morning, waking everyone in the campground."

She walked alongside him. "Have you seen or heard anything unusual since we last talked?"

"Just some folks sneaking around at night."

"Who?"

"It's too dangerous for me to be naming anybody. You need to go away."

Sara was about to ask *dangerous how* when giggling and shouting suddenly rang through the air. "What's that?"

"Young squires in the arena showing off for girls. All of them in a whole lotta trouble and gonna get hurt riding the knights' horses and playing with lances like they're jousting."

Sara did not need this now. Was nobody in charge? She gave him the daggers. "Please make sure Warwick and Jasce get these."

The slightly skunky smell of weed told Sara all she needed to know. They were so busted. She slid down the grassy hill and hurdled over the fence. The teens split like popcorn bursting, but she caught Naira and Karina who were too high to run.

"What were you thinking?" she said.

Karina folded and dropped to the ground. "Doesn't matter. It's all over. All the king's horses and all the king's men couldn't put Humpty together again."

Sara lifted her. "Get up. You'll be fine. You were flying high and had a bumpy landing. How'd you two get into this mess?"

"One of the squires brought a stash, and we all wanted to try it," said Naira.

"Which squire?" The girls exchanged furtive glances. "Who?"

Naira rapidly shook her head *No* as Karina muttered, "A male friend of hers."

"And where'd he buy it?"

"I . . . I don't . . . don't know anything," said Naira.

"If I find out that either of you isn't being totally upfront with me, you'll be charged for withholding evidence." A lemon-lipped smile between them suggested they were hiding something.

"I'm waiting."

Naira gulped. "My friend wrinkled his nose and said the guy had mud and hay on his pant legs and smelled bad. Please don't let on I told you. Can I go now? I'm not supposed to be here during the week. My mom thinks I'm in town shopping."

"All right, but make yourself available for more questioning."

Karina's body sagged. Sara pulled her back up and steadied her. "This will not sit well with your father."

"I must be strong and face up to him." Her cheeks puckered as if to keep from crying. "But I can't do it alone. Come with me."

This must be the kind of torture parents go through, but Sara would have braved it for kids like Karina and Pan. After an hour of strolling around the village to bring Karina back down to earth, she took her home. The dragon prow projecting from the bus daunted trespassers better than any security system. Sara took a long quavering breath before knocking. The door opened and a blast of cold air swept across her face as Stieg's presence consumed the entire space—his formidable eyes glaring at her. "What do you want now?"

"I brought your daughter home."

He yelled at Karina as she climbed the stairs, "Where've you been, and why's this woman here?"

"She and some friends were at the jousting arena," Sara said following her in.

"What *friends*?"

"Six squires and five other girls who work here."

Karina's voice faltered and then rose an octave as if her throat had stretched too tight. "We'd all smoked some weed and were a little high."

"Weed? That puking Warwick needs to keep his curs in line.

This is his fault."

"No, it's mine. I'm old enough to make my own decisions."

Her father's menacing stare bored right through her as he emphasized each word. "Not as long as you still live under my roof. You're grounded until the fair closes Sunday."

Sucking in air so fast it made a whistling sound, Karina flung herself at him.

Sara caught her arm. "Easy."

Stieg pushed them both away and was out the door, three stairs in a single stride. Sara laid his dagger on the table and told Karina to sit. "I can put you in a safe place until this blows over with your dad."

Her chin quivered. "You don't have to. He's never hurt me or my mom physically."

"But he seems so—"

"Warlike, barbaric, like a volcano about to erupt?"

"That pretty much describes him." Sara sat across from her and rested both arms on the table. She leaned forward and held Karina's hands. "I'm afraid for you."

"He can't help it."

Sara pulled back, her face contorted in disbelief at the girl's defense of him. "Why?"

"His grandfather Geir raised him after both parents died in a car accident when he was only four. He brainwashed my dad into believing he had to live and die as a Viking. To him, courage and honor are more important than life."

"How do you know all this?"

"From my mother. She fell in love with a strong, handsome man who vowed to always protect her. And he has both of us. I've heard the story so many times I can repeat word for word how he and Geir lived in an old stone house in Grindavik, Iceland where Vikings settled and their language is still spoken. Geir discovered they were direct descendants and filled my father's head with stories of the Norsemen and their gods. When it was time for Geir to die, he wanted a Viking burial at sea. In the middle of the night, he made an eleven-year-boy carry firewood down to their small fishing boat and build a platform. Geir made him swear to maintain their Viking heritage and explore the world with courage and strength. Then he set sail with the tide on a moonless night, leaving my dad standing alone on the shore. Moments later, orange and red flames shot into the black sky, setting it aglow. And Geir was gone."

"Oh, my God."

Tears formed on Karina's lashes like morning dew on slender blades of grass. She wiped them with a napkin. "My father kept his word. We've traveled all over the country in this crazy bus made to look like Geir's Gokstad ship. He's shown me things such as this amazing orchid growing in the desert. It was clinging to a rock wall to catch every precious drop of water seeping between layers of rock. I remember him holding one on his fingertip, dabbing it on my mom's cheek, and saying, 'Life's full of such fragile beauty. It's a Greek Siren enticing us with such sweet music that I'm helplessly seduced by it.'"

"That's terribly romantic."

"Yes, he used to always say things like that to her."

"Used to?"

"Not so much now. But he taught me to celebrate life and gave me courage. We stopped for a picnic near a waterfall in Wyoming. With a horrendous roar, water shot off rocks far above our heads in great, white sheets. 'We have to go out there,' my dad yelled pointing to some boulders in the middle of the river, just above a second set of falls.

"He turned to me. 'Ready? We can't experience the falls just standing here. We have to feel it.' He hopped onto a large, slippery rock and held a hand out to me.

"I stood glued to the shore. 'C'mon, Karina. You can do it. I'll catch you.'

"I took a huge gulp of air and jumped. He caught me in his

arms. We made four more leaps onto a rock barely large enough for one. He stood behind me holding me firmly by the shoulders as we stared at the falls high above our heads. Mist sprayed in our faces as we watched the water shoot over the top, drop in silence, and then explode in a mountain of white.

"'Y–e–o–w,' he shouted over the loud roar. 'It's the lightning of Thor's hammer crackling through our bodies.' I threw my arms out, dropped my head back with my eyes closed and mouth open to catch the spray. 'Y–e–o–w.' My voice echoed off the rock walls of the canyon. I yelled again and again and couldn't imagine anything better in this world than standing there with him."

Karina plucked at her fingers. "But he changed, became angry, as if Viking gods have taken possession of him."

"Your dad's not Thor. Maybe he's afraid of losing you both."

"But if I don't stand up for myself and what I want, I may never find me." A minor tremor rippled through her. "Please don't tell Pan. He's totally against alcohol or drugs and gets really moody at times. I don't want him to be disappointed in me. When he's done with school, I'll go with him no matter where or when. I don't care what my dad says. I hate who he's become."

"No, you don't. You're unhappy with him right now but are still that little girl standing in the middle of a river, mist spraying in her face, and yelling 'Y–e–o–w'. Find her again and remember how she felt."

"That girl's gone. My mother used to wear brightly colored blouses with huge sleeves that ruffled in the wind like wings. To me she was a beautiful butterfly flitting from flower to flower but always just out of my reach. Now I can't even stand to look at her or my father."

Sara said, "My dad left when I was ten, leaving a hole in my chest where my heart belonged. It grew deeper and darker until nothing could fill it. Don't let your present feelings lead you to say or do something you can't take back. Otherwise, that emptiness will eat you from the inside out." Sara squeezed Karina's hand.

"You need to take care of yourself now. We'll talk again later."

Sara left remembering Naira's comment that the dealer had mud and hay on his pant legs and smelled bad. The zookeeper had motive, means, and opportunity. Had he conned her by playing the innocent victim with his oafish mannerisms, frightened look on his face, and unsettling current in his voice? Sara had believed his alibi that the waitress could attest to his presence at the Smiling Gator and didn't bother to verify it.

She went to her car and sat there. If only for a few moments, she needed serenity from the lies and threats consuming every second of her thoughts. She turned on the classical station to *The Hoedown* from Aaron Copeland's *Rodeo* and luxuriated in the lively, upbeat music. When it ended, she could no longer ignore the facts, no matter how implausible. She'd drive back to the Smiling Gator and rectify being duped.

She parked in the only vacant spot and went directly to the back room. The same bartender was wiping glasses and setting them on a shelf. Sara asked, "Does an unkempt man smelling like dung come here frequently?"

"Oh, yeah, about four times a week."

"How about last Friday?"

He rinsed two margarita glasses. "Can't remember. He always sits at Charlene's table. He has the hots for her but doesn't stand a chance. She's miles out of his league." He signaled a waitress with blond hair piled high on her head and a pencil stuck behind her right ear. "Come here a minute. Lady has a question about the guy from the fair who always sits at your table."

Charlene set a tray of empty glasses on the bar and ordered six margaritas. "What ya wanna know?"

"Was he in here last Friday night?"

"Yes, ma'am."

"How can you be certain it was that night?"

She chomped on some gum with her mouth open. "'Cuz he gave me a free ticket for the fair the next day. He's so proud of working there and wants to show off his animals."

"And what time did he leave?"

"Same as always. After closing at two."

"You're sure of the time?"

"Positive. He offered to give me a ride home. I thanked him but already had plans to meet up with the fair's blacksmith."

"Meaning you might have accepted the ride otherwise?"

The waitress raised one corner of her mouth. "Nah, not really. He's nice enough but not for me. Ya know, kinda slow and simple."

The bartender put a sixth margarita on a round serving tray. "Charlene, here are the drinks for customers at table eight."

She picked up the tray and held it over her head on one hand. "Told you all I know."

"Answer two more questions," Sara said. "What time did the blacksmith arrive for your date?"

"About two fifteen."

"And what about a man covered in tattoos?"

"Ya mean Rudd? Comes here a lot but not on that night."

"How can you be sure?"

"Believe me, Honey, Rudd comes in here? Everybody notices."

One of her thirsty customers yelled, "Hey, Babe, what are ya waiting on?"

She winked at Sara. "Gotta take care of my payin' ones."

Sara used the restroom before walking to her car and clicking the key fob to chirp twice. Opening the driver's door, she noticed the front tire had been slashed and was flat. She checked the back. That too? She stomped around to the passenger side. Both slashed and flatter than armadillo roadkill. For a finishing touch, a large dent on the rear bumper.

It had to be Possum and Grouper who were likely watching her reaction "Weren't two tires enough?" She spun around. "Come on out, show yourselves."

Resounding silence.

The door still open, she sat sideways on the driver's seat with her feet on the ground. *Now what?* She didn't want to call Ryker or McBride and try to explain why someone would select her personal car out of an entire lot to puncture all four tires and damage her bumper. Plus Foster's thugs were clearly watching with the usual threat if she told anyone of their meeting. No other recourse, she leaned backward over the console to open the glove compartment, dig out the card, and call AAA for a tow truck. ETA fifty minutes.

When the driver finally arrived, he introduced himself and hunkered down to inspect the tires. "Looks like somebody cut them deep. Any idea who?"

She gave a dismissive wave. "Probably some drunk kids who thought it would be *totally* cool or *righteous.*"

He pushed back onto his feet. "Most drivers need to replace a single flat. Good thing you told us about all four." He backed the tow truck in front of her car and lowered a flatbed. Once her car was loaded, she gave him the auto shop address and got in the cab.

On their way back into town, he asked, "Did you report this to the police?"

"Think they'll do anything about it? Corbin Foster running for mayor claims the whole police department is incompetent."

"Lived here all my life and never had any problems with them. But they need to catch whoever murdered that guy at the fair. My wife and neighbors are pretty scared having a killer on the loose."

"I understand and am sure the police are doing everything possible to find him."

# Chapter 15

At the auto shop, Sara waited for the store owner to check his inventory in a computer. "Looks like I don't have the tires you want, but they're in stock at the warehouse and can be here by tomorrow afternoon. Will that work for you?"

Sara's insides lifted and sank. "Guess it has to. How long to get the bumper fixed?"

"My body man's working on another car but might be able to get to yours later tonight."

She was in the lobby googling for a taxi number when Ryker called. "I'm done researching all the benefactors. Can we meet at the station in twenty minutes?"

"Uh." She paced in front of the check-in counter. *Need a story, got to have a story.* "I'm without a car right now."

"Why?"

"Tell you later. I could use a lift. Pease come to Roger's Auto Shop on Mapleton."

Watching for him through the window, Sara came up with a reasonably true explanation for why she needed a ride. When he arrived, she picked up the police and personal belongings gathered from her car and went outside.

Ryker loaded her gear. "Christ, you look like something the cat dragged in."

She sneered. "And good afternoon to you too."

He opened the passenger door and bowed before her with a

flourish, raising his left arm high in the air and then lowering it. She couldn't help chuckling.

"So what's with your car?"

"I went to a bar twelve miles out of town called the Smiling Gator to confirm a suspect's alibi. The place is really popular. The parking lot was crowded, and you know what that's like. Idiots not paying attention as they back out of their spot. Someone rammed into my rear bumper and gave it a sizable dent. The repair man can't get to it until morning."

After a long pause, Ryker looked over at her. "Sure it wasn't you who bumped into someone?"

Sara's body shook as if he'd tasered her. "What an asinine comment. Why would you say that?"

"You'd just left a bar. I saw you downing a stein of beer in the Scottish camp."

"It was freaking water.  I was no more drunk than you were behaving inappropriately with Celine. I don't ever drink. Period."

He held his right arm up as if to shield himself and whispered, "Because you're a recovering alcoholic?"

"What?"

"Well, your mom was, and some kids go right down that same path their parents did."

"Want to know why I don't? I saw too much. After my dad left, holidays at our house were Bacchanalian orgies with bounteous clusters of grapes and cases of skid row wine." Sara gazed out the window. "My mother's best friend always sat in a stuffed red chair by the kitchen door. The more she drank, the more she broke out in these purple blotches on her face and arms. She looked like a human tie dye. I can still smell urine dribbling down the cushion and soaking into the carpet. One time, I squeezed past her for a glass of water, but she grabbed my arm and wouldn't let go. She said I had to write on her headstone, 'the cats crept into the crypt, crapped, and crept out again.' She kept repeating it."

"You still remember the words."

"It was a catchy little phrase imprinted into my young brain"

"Where was your mother all this time?"

"Lying naked on some long–haired stranger placing grapes into his mouth one by one."

Ryker stopped and stared straight ahead, tapping his thumb on the steering wheel. "I'm almost afraid to ask if she's still alive."

"Nope, died eight years ago. All that childhood stuff's too long ago to be relevant. If you go this way, we can access the outer gate of the pachyderm ride. As you requested, I checked the perimeter entrance and saw two cars parked inside."

He glanced at her as if awaiting a deeper emotional response. When she offered none, he made an abrupt right turn. "I don't like that place already. Our governor signed the Elephant Protection Act prohibiting the use of elephants in any form of entertainment."

"And you know all of this because—?"

"Heard about it constantly from my wife. She volunteered for the Animal Legal Defense Fund."

"I'm more impressed every time you speak of her."

"She was a better woman than I am a man."

"Don't denigrate yourself. You fought for your beliefs."

Ryker turned away, looking out his side window. "Tried to."

Sara gave him a little elbow bump. "Hey, my friend, cheer up. Things are starting to come together. Tox report showed cocaine in Gunner's body. This hapless chap who runs the petting zoo overheard him arguing with someone about coke he bought not being pure."

"You believe him?"

"Think so. It was his alibi I confirmed at the Smiling Gator."

When they arrived at the elephant compound, Ryker left the engine on. "Stay here, this one's mine."

Sara opened her mouth to confront his sexism but decided he needed this. Ryker ran low to the ground, took pictures of the plates, sped back, and hopped into the driver's seat. "Got 'em. Let's get outta here."

She yawned. "Good skulking, my speedy road runner. Didn't think you had it in you."

"And you have nothing left in you, Miss saggy endurance racer, I'm taking you home. We can check these tomorrow."

When he pulled into her driveway, Sara felt obliged to invite him in as a thank you. She used the key pad to open the garage door and entered through the laundry room where she set her keys and badge on the washing machine.

Ryker stood in the middle of the kitchen surveying the room. "No magnets on the fridge, no dishes in the sink. Nothing sitting out other than a coffee maker and toaster." He slid his hand across the counter top. "Spotless. The place doesn't look lived in."

"I call it my no clutter zone. Make yourself at home. I'll bring coffee out when it's ready. Sorry I don't have any fried donuts or fritters. How about veggies or fruit?"

"Pass on the rabbit food." Ryker called from the living room, "Where are all the racing photos and travel souvenirs? I expected shelves of medals and plaques, carved elephants and giraffes from Africa, or Aboriginal paintings from Australia."

Sara brought out two tall mugs and set them on the table. "I'm a minimalist. Racing and traveling force you to pare down to bare essentials. My mantra is less is more."

"You don't have less. You have nothing. No pictures of siblings, parents, grandparents, friends, cats, dogs, even you as a little girl." He chuckled. "Now that's one I'd like to see."

"Had none of the above."

"So you're a soul drifting alone in the world. Who'll come to your funeral?"

She leaned back against the cushion. "Don't think I'll be aware of those in attendance."

Ryker carried his coffee into the hallway and opened a closet door. He winked at her. "I've got my own personal search warrant for photos of your ex. You were married seven years and did some pretty damn exciting stuff. What happened to him?"

"I haven't told anyone the full story, so why should I now."

He gave a naughty grin. "Tit for tat. Show me your secrets, and I'll show you mine."

Sara smiled for the first time that evening. This paunchy New Yorker was growing on her.

He returned to the couch and stretched out with his feet on the coffee table and hands clasped behind his head. "I'd rather be here than in an empty hotel room."

"That's where you're living?"

"I wasn't sure how long I'd be here."

"Okay, you ready? Michael and I wanted a new challenge—to summit Everest, the roof of the world."

His brows arched and his mouth dropped open. "I thought you were bat–shit crazy before. Now I'm sure of it."

"We flew from Kathmandu to the Lukla, airport, one of the most dangerous in the world."

Ryker turned sideways with his arm across the couch back and leaned toward her as if to catch every word. "Then you headed straight for the top?"

She laughed out loud. "My New York friend, it takes eight days of acclimatizing just to hike thirty–seven miles to the base camp at 17,600 feet. From there, it's four to five weeks preparing your body to survive in thin air at 29,032 feet. People die of altitude sickness."

"I'm beginning to question your decision making, and that's not a good trait in a partner."

"Long story short, you have to wait for a weather window of four to six days when the winds are favorable for summitting. Everybody going up at once causes a major traffic jam. Michael raced ahead of the crowd in the Death Zone where the air's so thin your brain and lungs are starved for oxygen. Your body slowly begins to die." Sara got up for more coffee. "Bored yet?"

"My flabber is gasted but not the least bit bored. Continue."

"I was totally done in and thought I was hallucinating when I caught up to him propped against a rock, close to death at 28,700 feet. He'd used too much oxygen and emptied the cylinder. A famous climber Ed Viesturs said, 'Getting to the top is optional; getting down is mandatory.' I couldn't bear to leave my husband and would share my oxygen while Pemba our Sherpa guide went down for more. I took three deep breaths before removing my mask and placing it over Michael's face. Dead eyes stared back at me. Feeling lightheaded, I put the mask back on and breathed deeply to ward off hypoxia. Then I exchanged oxygen between us every sixty seconds. Between pulmonary or cerebral edema and hypothermia, the chances of either of us getting out alive were diminishing rapidly. I became drowsy but stayed awake long enough to place my mask on Michael before nodding off. I don't remember anything until someone yelled, 'Wake up,' and clamped a mask down on my face. Pemba had brought oxygen and two more Sherpas. They loaded Michael and me on stretchers and carried us down through the Death Zone to base camp."

"Why isn't he here with you now?"

"After I risked my life to save his butt, he left me three months later. I haven't seen him since."

"Then why's he still roaming around in your head?"

"We had shared what could have been our last breaths. You can't just forget moments like that."

"But you could breathe life into new moments with Lazzero."

"Yeah, right, let me know when you decide to begin breathing with your daughter."

Ryker's chin dented. "It's been too long a day for us both."

Sara walked him to the door. "Thanks for everything."

After showering, Sara pulled a box from beneath the bed and withdrew her favorite selfie of sitting with Michael in their tent at 19,000 feet. They were so cold and so in love. She put the simple wooden frame on her nightstand and whispered, "Goodnight."

At 3:00 a.m., the sky cracked and boomed, jarring her from a restless sleep. She shot straight up. The hairs on her arm stood on end as electricity charged the air. After her father left, she'd learned to sleep like antelope whose ears remain active to warn of danger. Always listening, not for green-eyed monsters under the bed but the sound of her mother's footsteps on the stairs. Sleep no longer an option, she fell back and burrowed under a pillow to drown out the sound.

# Chapter 16

Dawn struggled with heavy, black-tinged clouds veiling the sun. The air was thick and damp as Sara waited for Ryker to come for her. With only five days left, she felt like a dog chasing its tail.

He arrived with gray circles under his eyes and hair unkempt, clearly having not slept either. "I hated the lightning last night," he said. "It reminded me of holding my daughter during storms and promising everything would be all right. Daddy's here, but I wasn't often enough to ease her fears."

"I'm sure she knew daddy loved her. This job takes a heavy toll on us all."

"It knocked me flat on my face, and I can't seem to steady my feet. You showed me your secrets last night. I'll show you mine on our way to work."

Ryker had finished the story of his wife's death and daughter's estrangement when they reached the station. He straightened his hair in the rear view mirror and thrust his chin forward in an air of confidence.

As soon as they walked in, McBride ordered them to his office and slammed the door. He paced the room like a caged lion. "It's Wednesday already and you've brought me nothing."

Ryker let out an explosive breath. "Maybe not quite zero." He opened his photo app and brought up the license plates. "Sara and I saw these parked inside the elephant enclosure last night. It might lead to something." He gave the numbers to Andre in I.T.

"Please run them ASAP."

Sara stood behind the monitor. Her stomach tightened when Grouper's and Possum's faces popped up on the screen.

"The vehicles are registered in New Jersey to Hugo Young and Levi Ward," said IT.

"Any violations or other information?" Ryker asked.

Andre shook his head. "Sorry, nothing."

Sara wanted to scream *They're Foster's henchmen* but couldn't risk her acquaintance.

"It was worth a try," said Ryker, "but that outer gate allowing ready access still compels us to pay the elephant trainer a visit."

McBride called after them, "Bring me facts not suppositions."

As they got into his car, thunder rumbled in the distance and ominous clouds darkened the entire sky. Sara fastened her belt. "Last night, you hounded me about Michael. Now it's my turn. You promised to look for your daughter. Don't you love her?"

"More than my own life, but I just told you how she doesn't want me in hers."

"Of course she does. I can speak as a daughter. We love and need our fathers no matter what has passed between us."

He twisted a gold wedding ring on his finger. "I don't deserve to have another woman in my bed again or my daughter speaking to me. I wear this to remind me of how badly I failed."

"You'll find someone. I'll help you create an online dating profile once you lose that weight and quit smoking."

He laughed. "I'd have better odds winning the Nobel Peace Prize." He pulled out of the station lot. "Tit for tat again. You say daughters need their dads. So where's yours?"

Pressure at the back of her throat warned her not to go there. She wasn't ready.

"Sara? You interfere in my life and relationships telling me what *I have to do* but refuse to answer a simple question like where's your dad?"

She swallowed hard to shrink the lump lodged in her throat.

"He owns a financial management company. We haven't spoken in quite some time."

"Weeks, months?"

"Years."

"You hypocrite!"

He pulled into a parking space and slammed on the brakes. "We're not working one more minute on this case until you walk into his office and make up."

"I can't."

"Can't or won't? I'm serious. Give me the address. We're going to see your father."

Sara bit the insides of her cheeks to keep tears from trickling down the sides of her hair. "I said I can't. And that's final. Now head in the direction of the village so we can get back to work."

Ryker's shoulders puffed up like a vulture ruffling its feathers. "Not a chance." He googled nearby financial management offices. Four came up but only one with the name Lansing. A Cheshire-cat grin spread across his face as he turned back onto the street.

She saw words floating about in her brain, but they eluded her before she could pull them together in a coherent way to speak to her father now. She was a police officer. He'd committed a crime punishable by years in prison and had abandoned her twice. But could she forsake him?

Ryker broke into her thoughts. "What's going on with you and your dad?"

"It's complicated."

"Don't give me that cliché. Everything in life is. Details."

"He views life as made up of two kinds of people, winners and losers. I was expected to always come out on top, no matter what the cost."

"And you didn't on Everest. I don't know which one of us is the greater failure as a father. Your forgiving him offers me hope."

They arrived at the twelve story office building. Her body felt like rusted hinges unable to move. Ryker held the car door open for her. "I'm going to stand here all day, not accomplishing a thing, if you don't exit this vehicle right now."

She stepped out grudgingly.

They entered in a revolving door and checked the business directory. Ryker ran a finger down a long list of names to Nathaniel Lansing Financial Management Suite 700. He ushered Sara into an elevator and pressed the UP arrow. Dreading her first encounter with her dad to occur in a public space, she held her breath every time it stopped to let someone on. Seventh floor, the door opened.

"Wait out here," she told Ryker. "I need to do this alone."

A detective no longer racing or climbing, her life was radically different from when she last walked into his office six years ago. But nothing had changed here other than Barbara, the fifty-year-old receptionist. She was heavier and her hair had grayed. "May I see Nathaniel Lansing?" said Sara.

"I'm sorry, he isn't here. Can I help you?"

"Um, no. I need to see him personally."

"I'm afraid that's not possible. Mr. Lansing started working from home almost six years ago." Barbara wrapped a curl around her finger. "Wait a second, you're Sara. I wouldn't have recognized you if it weren't for all those pictures on his desk."

*What pictures on his desk? Taken when? Was he in them too?*

"He admired your courage and decision on Everest and never quit bragging about you not letting mental or physical hardships stop you from coming out on top in those adventure races."

Sara's emotions climbed in and out of the darkest places so many times in the minutes it took Barbara to utter these few words that everything below her throat went limp. It all made sense now. He'd detached himself from her not out of disappointment but love to shield her from his legal problems.

Waiting in the hall, Ryker pressed the elevator button.

"How'd it go?"

"He wasn't there. He works from home now." She scowled at the disapproval written on his face. "Drop it. I'll take care of my problems when we're done. This case has been creeping forward with the speed of a sloth crossing a road. It has to take priority."

"You're making the same mistake I did, letting work be more important than your relationship."

"It has to right now."

Exiting the building, Sara spotted Grouper watching her from across the street. *Get out of my life!* she screamed in her head, but her cry was drowned out by thunder rumbling and trees moaning in the wind. Lightening turned the bottoms of torn clouds a pale gray, and the sky opened in a torrent.

"Run for it," said Ryker.

They covered their heads with their arms and raced to the car. Sara jumped in and shook water out of her hair. "I did as you asked. Now get back on track. One of the boys caught with weed said the guy who supplied it had mud and hay on his pant legs and smelled bad. I don't think the zookeeper's got it together enough to pull off a murder. He also has an alibi."

"That leaves the elephant trainer. My money's on him and his outside access. We're going back there."

"You did notice it's currently raining heavily, right?"

"Couldn't be more perfect timing. He's staying dry somewhere and wouldn't expect us to show up." Ryker's mouth jerked into a ragged grin. "Adventure racer afraid of a little moisture?"

"Not on your life. But let me take the wheel. You're not used to driving in Florida downpours."

They switched seats. Sara turned on the wipers but could see only penny size drops pelting the windshield. They passed two cars stalled in flooded low spots on the highway. Riding higher than some, they skimmed across the asphalt on a shallow sea. When they reached the village, Sara dropped Ryker near the pachyderm compound. "Wait here and I'll park in the visitor lot. Don't act on anything until I get return."

He saluted. "Yes, ma'am."

All the way around to the visitor lot, Sara groused to herself for allowing him to cajole her into pursuing an arguable lead during a storm. She checked his trunk, no umbrella. Didn't it rain in New York? She'd have to hoof it in long pants and a short shirt.

Lighting crackled and trees waved in the wind, swirling and tossing their branches A limb snapped and struck Sara's upper arm. Blood oozed down to her elbow and wrist. She wiped it on her pants leg and kept running through the deserted village, slipping and sliding in mud. Covered in it and bent over, hands on her knees, she saw Ryker fifty yards ahead nosing around Scratch's barn. *Don't do it.*

In front of the building, Bo Jangles swayed back and forth, straining at the shackle on his rear leg. A blast of thunder tore through the clouds and flicked a jagged tongue of lightning to the ground. The elephant bellowed and curled his trunk.

"Get out of there," Sara yelled, but the storm swallowed her words and spewed them out in muted whispers.

Drenched with wet hair plastered on her face, pulse roaring in her throat, she ran closer when Ryker started walking toward the forest as if he'd spotted someone. "Wait for backup!"

Lightning skittered across the clouds like a rock skimming on water. Bo trumpeted and lurched forward tugging and tugging against the chain on his rear leg.

Suddenly Scratch emerged from the barn with a bolt cutter and snipped through the chain. In a violent twist, five powerful tons of disturbed beast wrenched free and charged toward a small wood, trumpeting louder, ears flapping. Thunder splintered the air into a thousand pieces, startling him. He veered headlong onto Ryker's path.

Lightning slashed a scar across the sky and the forest wailed.

"Ryker!"

# Chapter 17

Sara's breathing and heart rate soared with a sudden burst of energy. She raced toward the forest, ignoring the pain in her arm. As Bo's hulking body bore down on Ryker, she hurled herself at him shoving him from the elephant's path. Sara hit the ground inches from Bo's rear leg. As he lifted his massive foot, she stared at the soft underside of five tons about to crush her.

Memories flashed. Her father holding her, Michael yelling *on your left,* the whir of hummingbird wings.

When Bo's foot came down, she felt the earth move and rolled out of the way. A rush of wind brushed her as he plowed past into the forest, ripping limbs from trees like a child pulling twigs from a sapling.

Wind and rain stung her face. She scrambled shakily to her feet. "You okay?"

Soaked to the skin, covered with mud, Rykerseemed disoriented, running his hands all over himself. "No broken or missing parts." He looked up at her in a dazed expression. "You saved my life."

"T'was nothing. Just rescuing a gallant fighter in distress. Call McBride to get animal control here. I'm going after that creep."

Mud sucked at her feet as Sara scrambled to the barn. She gripped her pistol with both hands and slunk along the wooden front until able to peer around the open door. "Police," she announced and slipped inside, aiming in every direction until certain all was clear. The rapid clicking of an engine sounded at the rear exit. She dashed through the door, gun raised. "Halt, police!"

Spinning tires shot mud and gravel at her as the truck peeled out. She fired at the wheels and then called for an APB. "Red Ram thirty-five hundred leaving Renaissance village. White male, mid-forties, brown pony tail, thinnish, long gash down full left side of back. Wanted for attempted murder."

Ryker lumbered into the barn. "I heard shots."

"Fired but missed the damn truck in this lousy visibility." She holstered her pistol. "Why on earth did you proceed on your own without calling for backup? You could've been killed."

"Another of my failings is I tend to close my eyes, lower my head, and charge. I was waiting for you but heard talking inside the barn and wanted to catch him red handed. The door was slightly ajar, so I peered through the crack."

Sara clamped her mouth shut to keep from reprimanding him more. He didn't need her frustration and anger. "What'd you see?"

"Small coke baggies and a man leaning over the table sniffing through a straw, probably checking if it was pure or cut with some white crap. Suddenly, thunder rattled the walls and freaked the buyer. He threw the door open so hurriedly he didn't see me pressed against the side of the barn. When he sped toward the woods, I had to go after him. Follow the coke."

At a table with cut off straws, razor blades, and small mirrors, Ryker pinched a white powdery residue and held it to his nose. "Cocaine, it must be stockpiled somewhere."

"That his associates won't want to lose. The word's probably out already."

"And I'm gonna find his cache if I have to tear this place apart. I want enough to put those vermin away forever."

While Ryker overturned fruit bins, Sara assessed McBride of the situation and asked for two squad cars to load the evidence.

Nearest one was ten minutes away. The sky moaned as wind and rain emptied more trees of greenery. Waiting under the eaves, she got a text from the garage saying they'd finished her car.

Police arrived at the rear gate. She went out and assigned four officers to help Ryker gather evidence. They dumped trash barrels, cut into hay bales, combed through all possible storage areas, and removed cleaning supplies from shelves. Then they inspected every inch of the elephant trailer.

Ryker gave them instructions. "When you're done, please take detective Lansing to a garage for her car on your way to the station. This was my first elephant encounter. I need time to absorb what happened and get myself together."

"We can meet later to discuss our findings," he told Sara.

"Got it. I need to go home too."

Ryker strolled until hidden in trees and then ran to his car. He needed to get there and back while a police presence deterred anyone from entering the scene. The tentacles of Foster's drug ring had infected New Jersey. It was no coincidence those two cars were parked in a drug dealer's lot. The license plates had sounded an alarm howling in his head, but he'd kept quiet rather than create false hopes. He returned and parked out of sight for a stake out replete with bottled water and packaged snacks routinely stored in his trunk. Only one car remained. He'd wait for its owner to reveal himself.

Wind scattered the last moist clouds across the sky and then died down. Slivers of sunlight glistened on leaves still wet from the rain. Ryker munched on potato chips, string cheese, and a candy bar. He sat bolt upright when a figure emerged from the Enchanted Forest and stealthily made his way to the car. Ryker sniggered. Too bad the parents did nothing about that nose. He turned the key in his ignition. *Levi Ward, where will you lead me?*

Working in New York for his entire career, Ryker considered

himself a pro at stake outs and tailing someone. He followed Levi half an hour across unfamiliar parts of town into an industrial district with a labyrinth of streets and buildings. A GPS was his only hope of getting out. Levi parked beside the other Jersey car in front of what appeared to be an abandoned two story building. Ryker stopped at a safe distance, turned the engine off, and reached for a bag of caramel corn. The aroma of some cooking was his catnip. He plopped some in his mouth.

*So what are you thugs up to?*

Twenty minutes later, Ryker pulled forward over the steering wheel for a closer look. The man himself, Corbin Foster, stepped from an Audi RS7. Out came Ryker's camera for proof of collusion with two dubious characters associated with a known drug dealer. One, two, three quick snapshots before Foster disappeared in the building. Sara was still stuck with her belief in the rennie-crime-of-passion verdict. After two decades of pursuing Foster in New York, Ryker knew the scum wouldn't hesitate to order a hit on a knight to get what he wants. But there was no verifiable proof. Nothing happening in the old building, he jotted down the address and left for the station.

When he walked into the office, Sara said, "Feeling better?"

"I took a long nap and need coffee to recharge my brain."

She slumped in her chair. "McBride's waiting for us and we've got nothing tangible. No DNA results yet, a futile weapon search, and suspects popping up like whack-a-moles." She pushed to her feet. "Guess we'd better report to him before he has a heart attack."

They stood at the chief's door. Sara gave Ryker a little body check. "You first."

He stepped aside and bowed with his ostentatious flourish. "Oh, no, ma'am, ladies first."

"Enough already." She entered, shoulders rolled inward and

head lowered.

"It's about time you two got in here."

Ryker said, "We searched every inch of the elephant trainer's barn and trailer and uncovered a large cache of drugs. The guy's a shrewd dealer using the cover of a child friendly, animal lover. The elephant gave an excuse for always being on site to make covert deals, needing a separate entrance, and using a storage area large enough to squirrel away drugs among bales of hay and bins of fruits and vegetables."

"And you talk about the ideal means of transportation," Sara added. "No highway patrol would do a thorough search of a trailer with a five-ton elephant inside."

An officer stuck his head in, interrupting them. "Excuse me but the APB picked up a man in a Red Ram thirty-five hundred."

McBride slammed his fist on the desk. "Finally, some kind of progress. Read him his Miranda and put him in the interrogation room. We've got him on drugs. Let's nail him on murder too."

All three stood outside a small barren room with nothing on the walls, only three chairs, and a table. They watched Scratch through a one way mirror. He sat slouched low in the seat, one leg crossed over the other knee, foot bouncing.

"Let him simmer a few minutes," said McBride.

"Far as I'm concerned, he can sit there for hours until reaching a boiling point," Ryker added. "That son of a bitch tried to kill me."

When the foot bouncing accelerated and sweat dripped from Scratch's face, they decided he was sufficiently uncomfortable. "I'll remain out here to observe," said McBride.

Ryker winked at Sara. "Good cop, bad cop?"

She strutted past him. "Whatever floats your boat."

They entered the interrogation room. When she took a seat across from Scratch, he asked, "What the fuck am I doing here?"

Ryker swung a wooden chair around with the back facing the table, straddled it, and folded his arms across the top. "That's no way to talk to a woman. We just want to ask a few questions."

Scratch flicked a piece of hay off his sleeve. "I got nothing to say until I make my one phone call."

"A search in your barn turned up a large quantity of drugs."

He picked more hay from folds in the cloth. "Must have been planted by somebody." He raised his upper lip in a sneer. "Could have been you. And where's my elephant?"

Sara riveted her eyes on him. "Elephant's fine. Animal control tranquilized him so he won't hurt himself or others."

"I gotta go feed him"

"You're not going anywhere," said Ryker. "We have a witness who says he bought cannabis from you and another who overheard you arguing with Gunnar about impure coke two nights before he was killed."

"Can't pin either of those on me."

Sara pictured Scratch slicing the apple for her to feed Bo. He'd held the pocket knife in his left hand. Forensics concluded Gunnar's murderer was right handed. The bolt cutter. She hadn't made the connection in the thunder, lightning, and a bellowing elephant." Sara stood up. "I'm dehydrated after being on the go all day and need a soda. How about either of you?"

Ryker shook his head.

Scratch ran his hand down his throat. "I'm so dry I can hardly speak. This is police abuse."

"I'll get us something."

Taking her time to let him sweat more, she moseyed down the hall to the break room vending machine, inserted two one-dollar bills, and listened to each can drop. Her detective work was correct but would not please McBride.

He was waiting by the interrogation room. "What's going on? We're not here to provide refreshments to the likes of him."

"Pay close attention."

She walked back inside and held both cans up. "Which do you want, Pepsi or Doctor Pepper?"

"Pepsi."

Sara tossed the can to Scratch and watched him snatch it in the air with the left hand he'd used for the bolt cutter. She signaled Ryker into the hallway.

"What's so urgent that you had to interrupt an interview?" McBride asked.

"The insufferable excuse for a human being didn't kill Gunnar but tried to Ryker. Remember forensics proved the murderer was right handed. I saw him use the bolt cutters with his left."

"The sky was dark and it was pouring rain," said Ryker.

"That's why I tossed the can to confirm it."

McBride began his interminable pacing. On the second pass by Sara, he said, "Fantastic, great job on proving *who didn't* do it! I need to arrest *who did* to protect my city and its community." To the end of the hall and back, he stopped in front of Ryker. "Get two deputies from the front desk to haul that stinking piece of rubbish to a cell."

When all five entered, Scratch stiffened. "Now what the fuck is going on?"

"We're holding you on possession and distribution of illegal drugs plus the attempted murder of a police officer," said McBride.

"I didn't try to kill no cop."

"We've got the elephant chain and bolt cutters in the evidence room with your prints on them. Deputies, book him and escort him to a cell."

Holding Scratch by each arm, they escorted him out the door with him yelling, "You can't do this. I'm calling my lawyer."

"You be sure to do that," said Sara.

In the empty room, all hope seemed to fade from McBride's face. "This isn't getting any closer to solving a murder and saving the city. It's Wednesday night. You've got until Sunday night when the village turns into a ghost town."

Ryker wasn't ready to divulge his findings without proof and disappoint McBride again. He simply said, "I'm trying to gather political ammunition to bring Foster down."

McBride shook his head. "It's a waste of time. Anything you come up with would need to go to court. That could take months. The election's in less than three weeks."

Sara bit the insides of her lips to keep from voicing her frustration and upset the chief even more. She quietly uttered, "That gives me four days. Once we get the DNA, I should be able to make better headway. Right now, I need a good night's sleep."

After learning about her dad and almost being trampled by a raging elephant, Sara just needed to get home and have time alone. She made a bowl of oatmeal, sat on the couch with her legs folded under, and tried tying loose ends of the case together. Motives centered around sex and power, the two elements Lazzero claimed men fought over. But what about women whose emotions were equally strong? It was as if she'd laid out a 1,000–piece puzzle with an irregular border and couldn't even put the outside together. She leaned against the couch back in thinking mode. What if the motive didn't originate here? Rennies working fairs all over the country were bound to encounter each other. Her eyes popped open. That was it, one of the missing outside pieces. She used her laptop to search the Knights Invincible web site and clicked *Contact us.* No response. Oh, that's right, site manager's dead.

She phoned McBride. "When forensics searched the victim's trailer, did they find any kind of documentation about which fairs the Knights Invincible worked and when?"

"If so, they didn't think it important enough to even mention or bring in."

*Huh,* she'd conduct her own search in the morning. Too busy and tired each night, she hadn't remembered to bring in the mail yesterday. The Tuesday flyers had the weekly grocery ads for sales beginning on Wednesday, and she always checked for deals.

Sara padded down the driveway to the mailbox, pulled the steel latch, and reached inside for the folded papers. Something slid out and hit the ground at her feet. She shined her phone's flashlight and jumped straight back from a dagger lying on the sidewalk. She spun around and looked for cars or pedestrians that didn't belong there. No one.

Mail tucked under her left arm, she used a newspaper to lift the dagger, carry it inside, and set it on the kitchen counter under an overhead light. The guard didn't match. Who gave it to her and why? Could be anyone she'd hassled in the last few days. She mulled over their names and faces while flipping through the paper. Nothing of interest on sale at the first store. She opened a second flyer and found a white piece of printer paper inserted in the middle. Someone had cut out different letters and pasted them together in a colorful collage. "Talk to anyone and blood will flow."

The threatening note paired with a dagger erased any doubts Sara had about the sender. Foster's goons were constantly in her face. They knew she'd collected daggers, and Grouper had seen her coming out of her father's building. Their message was short but explicit. Sending it in a letter collage prevented tracing it back to them. But maybe they weren't so smart after all. She got the fingerprint kit out of her trunk and dusted black powder on both sides of the blade and handle. Nothing. She dusted the letter's entire page, front and back. Zero prints. Their calling cards had been wiped clean. Taking them into the station would only raise questions she couldn't risk answering. Sara pictured Foster as a turkey vulture circling overhead waiting to rip her father, McBride, and Reunion Heights citizens into fresh carrion. She slid the knife and paper under her mattress. First solve the murder and then get revenge on Possum and Grouper.

Her phone rang. She checked the caller ID. McBride. "Hello."

"We finally got the DNA."

She held the phone closer to her ear. "And?"

"DNA from a woman you swabbed named Adara Rowell matched the DNA found on the victim. She had sex with him shortly before death."

Sara fell back down and threw her arms out, not knowing whether to laugh or scream.

# Chapter 18

Thursday morning, Sara tried to work the DNA news into her equation. She and Ryker had concluded a woman on top of a man lost in the throes of an orgasm could thrust a direct, fatal stab to his heart. But then why would Adara willingly give up her DNA? Nothing made sense. The more likely suspect was Nicu or another betrayed lover seeking vengeance.

When she arrived at the station, McBride was in a meeting with his supervisor, and Ryker was busy at the computer. She poured two cups of coffee, rolled over to him, and lightly banged into his chair like an amusement park bumper car just for some much needed levity. Then in an earnest tone, she said, "Did you send Scratch a Get Wellephant card?"

He snickered and bit into a fried apple donut.

"Seriously? What about the weight loss program?"

"I can't concentrate on an empty stomach. Know what you get when you cross an elephant with a parrot? An animal that tells you everything it remembers."

"Hah, get me one of those."

"Glad to see you can still find the humor in things. There have been times when I felt incapable of every doing so again."

"This will cheer you. DNA came back. Seems our Roma queen was out for a good time on that Friday, yet Nicu claims to have been home with her all night. She hasn't denied his alibi. I think she's afraid to speak up. I saw bruises on her arms."

A dreamy smile formed on Ryker's lips. "Ah, Adara, the embodiment of pure sensuality. She's the main attraction. All other dancers are simply backup."

"Your lust is showing."

"Not lust. I just believe a thing of beauty is a joy forever."

Sara wrinkled her brow. "You're quoting Keats now?"

"What can I say? My wife was a *sagacious* woman and used to read him to me."

"Love your word choice. But beauty or not, she's a seductive tease. And that skyrockets Nicu to the top of our suspect list. He had motive, means, and opportunity plus a matching dagger."

A piece of donut bulging in his cheek, Ryker said, "And how do we prove it?"

"Not sure, but we're derelict in our duties if we don't pursue this further. I'll get a warrant to search their wagon."

"You already tried."

She gloated. "But this time we have DNA for probable cause." She called McBride to get a warrant for Adara's vardo.

While waiting for the judge, she told Ryker, "I've got another theory. What if the motive didn't start here? Rennies travel all over the country. They're bound to run into each other. I want to go back a couple of years and see when and where any of our current rennies worked the same fairs as the Knights Indivisible."

"How would you even begin?"

"I've got a plan, but we need to pursue Adara and Nicu first."

From his office doorway, the chief waved a piece of paper. "Got the warrant. And you, Ryker, forget about Corbin Foster. Time's running out. Both of you are to focus solely on this case. Now get over there and bring me something I can use."

As Ryker drove, Sara pulled a bag from her pocket. "I got these three turquoise beads from the evidence room before we left. They were found in the swing."

"And could have been left by any visitor."

"Don't steal my fun."

They parked by the outer gate and entered the Roma camp. Yoska was brushing the long tail of a white vanner. The curvature of his back made him appear shorter, perhaps the consequence of age or hard labor before the Roma camp took him in. "Stay here," said Sara, "and let me talk to him."

She approached Yoska and gently ran her fingers along the horse's back. "He's beautiful. Your love for him shows. I'm sorry to bother you again but have one more question. Will that be all right?" She took the slightest movement of his head as a yes. "When I was here before, you said two men were quarreling late Friday night. We think one was the knight who was murdered. Did you recognize the other voice? Could it have been Nicu?"

He picked up a curry comb and made small circular motions on the horse's neck."

"Yoska, it's very important."

He moved to the other side.

A tinge of frustration in her voice. "Please think really hard. Was it Nicu's voice?"

"I don't know."

*That's it? All you're gonna give me. What are you hiding?* Sara shuffled back to Ryker, kicking peanut shells out of the way.

"Get anything?"

"No, he's still not talking and must be protecting someone."

"Could be Nicu who's sitting on yonder porch, watching every move you make."

"Then it's time we spoiled his day." Sara sauntered over and stopped a few feet from him.

He inhaled his cigarette and blew smoke at her. "What're you doing here again? Leave us alone or I'll sue for harassment."

Fingers curled in her palm, Sara tapped her thumb to her lips as if pondering the situation.

"What part of *I'll sue* did you not hear?" he asked.

"Oh, now I remember why we came." She pulled the warrant out, held it open with both hands, and wiggled it in his face.

"How'd you get that?"

"Probable cause. Didn't you *foretell* my coming with one"

He extended his middle finger toward her. "You've got no business—"

Ryker grabbed the offending hand. "If you intend to ever use these fingers again, get the hell out of the lady's way."

"He means it," said Sara.

"All right. Let go, you New York pig."

As they entered the vardo Sara told Ryker, "Look at this place. I've never been in one."

Sun shining through a skylight illuminated a lavish interior decorated with mythological symbols, hand carved birds, flowers, and vines, all brightly painted and accented with gold leaf. At the rear, a chest high bed the width of the wagon lay atop a beautifully carved, wooden cupboard. Cushioned seats along both sides had pull out drawers beneath. Tongue-and-groove oak lined walls encased a large stained glass window. Ceramic tiles shielded a stove across from a small bathroom. The grandeur was beyond anything Sara had envisioned.

Ryker put gloves on. "I'll start with under the mattress and seat cushions, shake out pillow cases and strip the sheets off. Then onto the bathroom."

Sara checked inside the oven and behind the stove, removed utensils from kitchen drawers, pots and pans from a shelf, opened coffee, tea, flour, and sugar containers. "Find anything?"

"Not yet. I'm going over every crack in the wall and around every window."

Sara had left the intimate search of their personal clothing to last. Rummaging through Nicu's turned up nothing. But an elaborate turquoise beaded bra lay hidden in the bottom of Adara's dresser under two belly dancing skirts. She took it out onto the porch for better light. Over time, the sun had faded all but three turquoise beads which had been replaced with shinier ones. The three in her evidence bag had lost their glow. It seemed the Roma queen was saving this bra for other fairs where it wouldn't implicate her in a murder.

"Time to go," she called to Ryker. "I've got what I wanted."

He exited ahead of her. As she descended the stairs, Nicu blocked her. "That's Adara's. You have no right to it."

"Ah, but I do."

"Give it back."

When he grabbed for it, Sara tossed the bra to Ryker who caught it in one hand. Nicu lunged at him but wasn't quick enough to catch the bra flying over his head to Sara. "We're taking this in as exhibit number one," she told Nicu. "See you later."

As Sara and Ryker walked away, he told her, "Scratch was my score. You get this one."

"It's still circumstantial. We need to find Adara and question her about that night."

Shops in the camp were closed except for a candle maker. Sara showed her badge and inquired about the Roma queen.

"Can't talk. I have to work quickly before the wax hardens."

He'd already dipped a candle into coats of colored waxes and only had fifteen minutes to carve layers in blue and green scrolls.

"Dazzling," Sara said, watching him.

"Thank you." He set the candle aside. "Now how can I help?"

"Have any idea where Adara might be?"

"Probably at Merlin's. She and her mother always go to lunch on Friday. They're too busy on the weekend."

"Mother?"

"Yes, Nadya who sews most of the costumes. Her father takes care of the horses." *How could I have been so stupid to miss this?*

"You okay?" Ryker asked.

"No. I'm just too trusting for this job. Yoska lied about his wife dying to throw me off the scent. Family is very important in the Roma community. It seems he and Nadya would say or do anything to protect their daughter."

"Then they must think she's guilty. Do you?"

"I plan to find out."

When Sara and Ryker reached Merlin's, Adara and Nadya had finished eating and put their plates aside. Sara asked Adara, "Can we talk alone a minute?"

Nadya reached across the table to her daughter. "She has no secrets from me."

"It's okay, mum. I'll meet you back in camp."

When Nadya was at a safe distance, Adara asked Sara, "What's so urgent?"

"The DNA results came back and clearly show yours matches that found on Gunnar."

She scoffed. "Impossible. You've made a mistake."

"No, they're quite conclusive and prove you had sex with him shortly before he died."

Adara's confident demeanor waned.

"I also discovered this in your dresser." Sara laid the bra on the table. "As you can see, three of the beads aren't the same." She removed the ones from her evidence bag. "They replaced these found in the bottom of the swing."

"Okay, so we had a little fun. Doesn't mean I killed him unless he died of an orgasmic heart attack."

"How long were you together Friday night?" Ryker asked.

"Hmm, about an hour. And I assure you that man was very much alive when I left him. It's a wonderfully romantic place under the moon and stars, don't you think?"

He frowned. "Did you hear or see anyone else?"

"No."

Sara slid onto the bench across from her. "What I don't get is why you agreed to give a DNA sample."

"I was afraid not giving one would make me look guilty. And I didn't know you could get DNA off him so many hours later."

In an irritated tone, Ryker asked, "Was Nicu aware of your extracurricular activities?"

"Maybe or maybe not. I don't know. He hasn't said anything." A wickedly naughty grin spread across Adara's lips. She toyed with a lock of hair. "We have a kind of arrangement."

"Then you'll have no problem telling him about the DNA?"

"None."

"You're lying. I've seen the bruises," said Sara. "What time did you leave Gunnar?"

Adara circled her left arm in the air over them, displaying her wrist. "Don't wear watches."

"Didn't you check that clock by your bed?"

"You invaded my house?"

"You can answer our questions here or at the police station," said Ryker. "Now what time did you leave Gunnar?"

"Uh . . . I'm not sure. Ten or twelve minutes from the swing to my wagon. Maybe midnight by the time I got home."

"And was Nicu there?"

"No."

"And when did he come in?"

"I don't know. I was sound asleep. An hour of wild sex puts me notoriously out." She gave him a winsome smile. "Doesn't it you?"

Ryker stepped back and told Sara. "You deal with her."

Adara's eyes flitted from one to the other. "Are you arresting me?"

"Not at the moment, but I also want to know if you've worked other fairs with the Knights Invincible?"

Adara picked at her nails. "Maybe."

"Did you ever hear or see anyone confront Gunnar?"

"At the Louisiana fair a few weeks ago, that Viking dared him to meet in the arena at night. We ran to watch. Nobody had ever challenged Gunnar. They were shouting so loud at each other and then started punching and wrestling. The Viking threw Gunnar to the ground and sat on his chest with his knee to Gunnar's throat. But instead of choking him, he shouted, 'Thor has spoken.'"

"And that was it?"

She shrugged. "Far as I know."

"Thank you for your time," said Sara. "Do not leave the village. We'll need to talk again."

As she and Ryker walked back to the car, he said, "Only thing that woman's guilty of is spreading her legs too freely and being ignorant about DNA."

"Why so?"

"Motive. She has none. If you're so damn certain it's a rennie, I'm betting on her fortune teller lover. No man wants to put up with a sexpot regardless of their arrangement. And she admitted he wasn't home when she got back. We don't have enough evidence to bring him or anybody else in." Ryker stopped suddenly, bounced the heel of his hand off his forehead, and grinned. "But wait, we can always go after Foster and topple his empire."

"Yeah right, like that's going to happen in a few days. Are you after Foster to save McBride or to salvage your reputation?"

"Both, and I admit it. And what about you? Are you trying to save McBride or to prove you're a winner to your father?"

*Or just keep my dad out of prison.* We need to get back to the station. McBride's probably pacing a rut in the wood floor."

Neither of them spoke again until they arrived and entered the chief's office. Walking his usual path around the room, he said, "Did you arrest that woman?"

"No, she freely admits to having sex but insists she left him very much alive," said Sara.

"And you believe her?"

"I do," said Ryker. "She has no motive. Her jealous lover's a more likely suspect and has no alibi, but we have no proof."

"Then get it. Both of you find that man and bring him in for immediate questioning."

In the parking lot, Ryker told Sara, "I've watched you handle bigger men than Nicu. I need to go follow up on something before my trail runs cold."

"You honestly have a trail?"

"Trust me. I know what I'm doing."

"You'd better. Now get out of here."

Sara returned to the village. Adara was sitting by a fire with her mother. "Why are you here again?"

"I need to speak to Nicu."

"Haven't seen him since you left."

"Not home Friday night, where would he have been?"

An indifferent, one shoulder shrug. "No idea. We don't spy on each other or ask questions."

"Call when you see him."

Adara had substantiated Ded Bob's story of the fight between the Viking and Gunnar. Stieg wouldn't clarify it but maybe Karina. Sara hoped to find her at Pan's and went to his turret. From outside the curtain, she heard him singing the lyrics he composed for her Friday night. "That's lovely. It's Detective Lansing. May I come in?"

Karina slid the curtain aside. "We're happy to see you."

"I just need a minute. Your father and Gunnar met in the arena at the Louisiana fair and fought. What was that about?"

"I never knew why, but he's been very angry ever since."

"Have you heard your parents quarreling about it?"

"No. My family rarely speaks to each other anymore."

"I'm sorry to hear that." Sara looked at the picture of Pan's mother on the wall. "She has such a beautiful, gentle face. You must have been very close."

He turned, went to a window, and stood with his back to them. Bewildered, Sara glanced at Karina.

She whispered, "He won't talk about her."

Sara paused at the curtain wanting to stay and comfort him for the loss of his mother, but McBride's order to bring Nicu in had priority. She searched the outer shops and all the winding paths in the village center. Clock still running and nothing conclusive to appease the chief, Sara's body tightened in a vice like grip. She had to shut her mind off and loosen the hold this case had on her. She went to the Enchanted Forest and gave herself over to nature, her most constant lover since it demanded nothing emotionally. Lulled by its beauty, her heart slowed and her muscles softened as she walked in the inviting shade of live oaks and magnolias.

Ryker had a lead and couldn't let it go even though speculation at this point wouldn't alter the election. The chief's censure of his Foster investigation denied access to the station's computers. He hated using the phone's small screen but eventually brought up County Records to locate the owner of the abandoned building— Jeff Swanson. Another Google search revealed Jeff owned one of the largest construction companies in Florida, based just north of Miami. What was he doing up here?

Ryker called him. "Hi, Jeff, it's Lee Wright from New York but fresh from completing a multi acre industrial park in Texas."

"Do I know you?"

"I saw you at Foster's luncheon the other day and wanted to discuss solar but had to exit suddenly. Got a text my sister's water had broken and baby was on its way. I couldn't miss that."

"Is everything all right?"

"She had an eight–pound boy, my first nephew. New to the game here, I'd like to meet with you and some of the others about how we'll proceed once Corbin Foster becomes mayor."

"We're planning a major development, but he has to win the election first. The local police chief has a following. If he solves that murder in the Renaissance village, it'll be a tough race." Jeff's voice lowered to barely above a whisper, "But I heard a rumor of some help on the inside is making sure he won't."

"Then Foster wins and so do we," said Ryker.

"He'll welcome your new money."

"And I've got lots of it waiting to invest."

"I'll arrange a Saturday meeting with the largest backers."

"I'm restless to get started down a prosperous new road. But I'm also looking at other exciting opportunities. Couldn't we meet tomorrow? That would work better for me."

"Backers are too busy during the week. There's no rush. We're at a standstill until after the election. Can I reach you at this New York number once I have a time and place?"

"Yes. I'm eager to hear everyone's future ideas."

Ryker hung up and rubbed both temples, thinking, thinking. His only lead were the two New Jersey thugs, but how could they thwart an investigation? Help on the inside bewildered him even more. The answer had to lie in the village even though it was closed to visitors.

Sara had left thirty minutes earlier to fetch Nicu. She'd likely park at the exit shared by the Roma camp and jousting arena. On the off chance he'd spot a car in the elephant enclosure, he drove past there first and saw a New Jersey plate. One or both of those thugs had the guts to return and could be on the grounds with Sara.

Ryker parked next to hers, raced to the Roma camp, and met Adara and her mother. "Have you seen my partner?"

"Not since you and she were here," said Adara, "And no, Nicu hasn't shown his face either."

For Ryker, the village was still a maze of shops, stages, and paths winding through innumerable forests. No sign of anyone. Then he suddenly spotted Sara strolling along the Enchanted Forest Lake. He was about to call out to her when Foster's thugs suddenly got in her face.

"What are you creeps doing here? Move out of my way."

She knows them? Dumbfounded, Ryker stayed out of sight but still within hearing range.

"We're delivering a message from our boss. Questioning too many people instead of slowing the investigation has become very troublesome for him."

"His problem, not mine."

"He gave a simple order, and *bang, bang* you know the cost of not adhering to it."

The man Ryker recognized as Hugo circled her like a hungry wolf. "Where are you going now?"

"None of your business."

Levi blocked her path. "We make *what* you do and *who* you talk to our business. If last night's message wasn't clear enough, I'm warning you to back off or it will be dangerous to your health."

Sara shoved the heel of her hand against the tip of his pointy nose until he begged her to stop. "And I'm warning you that butting into my life will become dangerous to yours."

Ryker wanted to intercept Sara in the parking lot but feared repercussions if the thugs knew he'd witnessed the scene where she deflated their male egos. He'd get the truth out of her later.

With a perverted glee in her step, Sara left before Possum and Grouper regained their macho conceit. She giggled, wondering if they'd report to Foster that a woman had temporarily emasculated them. Nah, they'd be too ashamed.

To simmer down, she went home, nuked frozen mac 'n cheese, and sat on the couch to watch a documentary on the world's second highest mountain, K2.

Seeing climbers die was too depressing. She showered and went to bed, put headphones on, and played the relaxing sounds of a mountain brook while watching the moon behind a live oak through her window. Its leaves made silhouettes like drops of spilled coffee on its face. She tried to sleep, but Michael appeared with tiny snowballs clinging to his brows and lashes on Everest. No more. Thoughts of the past gave her a headache, and tomorrow she'd have to face McBride with nothing new to offer.

# Chapter 19

*B*urr, the phone alarm rang. Sara's hand shot out to silence it. Missed. Her fingers fumbled all over the nightstand. Not there. Where was the damn thing? Propped on one elbow, she yanked the covers off. Her car and house keys lay on the second pillow. Beside them, a note read, "Sweet dreams. By the way, you're low on toilet paper."

*Burr, burr, burr came* from the bathroom. Sara sucked her breath in and held it. Damn Possum and Grouper had been in her bedroom and bathroom, maybe watched her shower. Any doubts about their scrutiny vanished. She grabbed her phone from the vanity and shut the alarm off. Sitting on the edge of the bed, elbows on her knees, she buried her face in her hands. What to do? The slightest hint of their threats meant her dad was dead. His life hung heavily on her shoulders.

She called the nearest locksmith. ETA was forty-five minutes, giving her a chance to make it to the station and back. Fortunately, McBride hadn't come in yet. Sara told the front desk officer she'd forgotten something and slipped into the supply room for the station's bug detecting device. She took a circuitous route home to lose Possum and Grouper if they were tailing her and got back in time to let the locksmith in.

"Thanks for coming on short notice."

"Have to in our business. It's frequently an emergency."

"Somebody broke into my house last night. I want new locks

everywhere plus deadbolts."

He checked the laundry room, patio, and front doors. "All in good condition. Replacing locks is an unnecessary expense. I only need to rekey them and install deadbolts."

"Okay, whatever it takes."

Sara surveyed each room to make sure nothing was out of place. The only thing the goons had messed with was her peace of mind. Next, she swept the entire house with the station's bug device and discovered sound bugs under the coffee and end tables. Both smoke alarms housed tiny cameras. She smashed them all.

The locksmith finished and gave her two sets of keys that fit every door. "Your home is secure again."

"Thank you." She paid and locked the deadbolt behind him.

Ryker phoned. "Where are you? McBride's got that buzzing bee up his butt again and wants us in his office ASAP."

"Leaving now." But wait. The goons might have deciphered the keypad opener. She quickly reprogrammed the code and drove to the station, jaw clenched so tight her teeth hurt.

He was waiting outside. "The chief's losing it."

McBride gave his two finger signal to follow as he shuffled into his office, his body slouched as if all muscles had surrendered, hair disheveled and clothes crumpled.

"When's the last time you slept or ate?" Sara asked.

"Can't remember, but it makes no difference if you don't find the killer. My life's over if I can't protect my city any longer."

"I have suspects but no irrefutable proof," said Sara. "I learned the Viking and Gunnar had an altercation at the recent Louisiana fair. The killer's motive could go back weeks, months, even years. I need to search his trailer."

"Then go. You too, Ryker. You can chase after Foster on your own time, not mine."

Walking to the car, Ryker wagged his finger at her. "And when were you planning to tell me about Foster's thugs whose manhood you destroyed last night?"

"What, how?" All the air whooshed from her body. "Keep your mouth shut." She climbed in and slammed the door. "Have you told anyone else?"

"No."

Sara backed out of the lot, "What were you doing there?"

"Looking for you."

"How'd you make the connection to Foster?"

"On a hunch yesterday, I went back to the elephant compound and waited for the car's owner to show. It was the long nose you shoved. I followed him to an abandoned two story building. And guess who else arrived? Foster."

"They're his henchmen. I named the big nose Possum and the big mouth Grouper after a fish."

"What's the story with them?"

"They've been plaguing me from day one, trying to coerce me into letting the investigation run out until the fair closes. Murder goes unsolved. McBride's labeled an incompetent fool not capable of running a city. Foster becomes mayor."

"Coerce how? You're no push over."

Saturday night, they strong armed their way into my house and threatened to expose my father as an insider trader and have him jailed. They brought proof from his computer."

"But you haven't been slow to act."

"We all took an oath to ensure the safety of our community and the preservation of human life. Choosing between my job and saving my dad has been eating me up inside."

"Why didn't you tell me or the chief about these thugs?"

"If I spoke to anyone, they'd kill my dad. They've been on me twenty-four seven, even while I sleep, making sure I understand the fallout for noncompliance. Last night I found a dagger in my mailbox with a pasted letter saying, *talk to anyone and there will be blood.*"

He ran zipper fingers across his mouth. "My lips are sealed. I need to nab Foster so you don't have to."

"That's impossible before Sunday night."

Sara and Ryker found Gunnar's trailer with the dragon on the front. The place was in shambles. Dirty clothes on the couch and chair, dishes piled in the sink, empty beer bottles, food wrappers.

Whoever ransacked it had opened drawers and dumped contents onto the floor looking for something small. She fished through debris strewn across the floor. "I used to crawl through the tightest hole in a cave, but this makes me claustrophobic."

Sara rummaged through clothing stored under the bed and pulled out a folder with titles to his RV and horse trailer plus three years of tax returns. "Look what I found."

"Seriously, this guy filed?" said Ryker, holding up a lubricant, vibrator, and condoms. "Cleaning lady must have killed him."

"He could have been in trouble with the IRS and decided to wise up. The returns itemize every fair and date, just what I need. Now let's get out of here."

Back at the station, Sara waved her folder at Ryker. "I plan to pursue my theory that the motive for murder may have originated elsewhere. We now have lists going back three years of all the fairs Gunnar worked." She handed him one. "Coffee?"

"Sure, but what am I supposed to do with this?" he called after her. "You know paperwork and I are incompatible."

Sara brought two cups from the breakroom, gave one to him, and sat down at her computer. "Cover the last twelve months. Start with the most recent fair and check every performer and vendor on the Louisiana website against the current personnel roster. Record matching names to interview tomorrow. Then go to the one before that and so on."

She took on the earlier two years. None of the web sites listed past performers and vendors, but they had contact information. She called those with phone numbers and emailed the others. Most provided what she needed. But after staring at the screen for three hours, her vision blurred. She stood up and rubbed her back and shoulders up against the wall.

Ryker laughed. "You look like a bear massaging on a tree. Quit for the day."

She sat back down. "Can't. I have to do all three years."

"And you think *I'm* the obsessed one?"

Two more hours and her body caved. Exhausted and starving, she rolled over to him. "Dinner time. Tonight's the king's birthday party, the biggest bash of the season."

"I'm game."

"I need to tell McBride we're leaving." Sara went to his office and stuck her head inside. "Ryker and I are going to a village party Booze tends to make people less tight lipped. Maybe a suspect will slip up."

"Bring me more than words."

Knowing it would end late, Ryker and Sara drove separate cars and met on the hill to view entertainment in the jousting arena below. Next to him, Sara leaned back on her elbows and fingered the grass. "Look at the king and queen in the grandstand over there. Things can't be too cozy at home."

"Have you eliminated both of them as suspects?"

"I'm still fumbling."

"And I'm still in shock."

She shot a sidelong glance at him. "What's wrong?"

"You were so absorbed in tracking down rennies you didn't notice I left my desk for half an hour."

"I'm not blind. Figured you needed a fix at Franny's Fryery."

"You know me too well. I did go there but only to take care of personal business. I got a text from my New York informant that he located my daughter and to call him."

"You toad. Don't scare me like that." Sara grabbed a handful of grass and threw it at him.

He picked it off and tossed it right back. "Just thought you'd like to know." Shielding his head from another onslaught, he said,

"It's show time."

Men in horse costumes cantered into the arena with papier mache knights on their backs. The person wearing the head and front legs was standing up and could see through the eyes or mouth. The one in back had to bend forward at the waist holding onto his partner's hips.

Ryker laughed. "That gives a whole new meaning to horse's ass. I hope the front guy didn't have beans for lunch."

Sara had noticed Celine sitting by herself. She nudged Ryker in that direction. "The fairy's alone. Go practice chatting again with someone your daughter's age."

Lazzero descended when Ryker left and sat much too close. "Wasn't sure you'd come. Gathering clues on alleged suspects?"

"Just enjoying the celebration." She sat up hugging her knees to her chest to discourage any physical contact.

As the amusements ended, serious drinking began. Knights, Scots, and Stieg stood in a circle, each with a full bottle of beer.

"What're they up to now?" Sara asked.

"It's a speed race where every player starts drinking when the court jester fires a blank. The first to finish signals by holding his bottle upside down over his head. Then the others have to follow suit whether theirs are empty or not."

Soon it was raining beer. Stieg won the first and second round. Warwick yelled, "Hey, Viking catch," and hurled a bottle at his feet.

It burst on impact in a field of glass. Stieg waved an arm at Warwick. "If you can follow me across there walking *exactly* as I do, I'll relinquish my helmet and axe. But fail and your sword and shield are mine."

The strutting cock scanned an insatiable audience. "I accept."

"He had no choice," Lazzero whispered to Sara. "He took over Gunnar's role as the alpha male and can't lose face now."

Stieg stood on his hands and inched forward, picking his way through the glass. When blood spurted from his right hand, he wobbled to the left directly over jagged shards glimmering in the lantern light.

Balgair shouted, "Only heroes go to Valhalla!"

Every muscle in Stieg's arms and shoulders responded, the blood vessels bulging against the skin. He paused as if to summon the strength of his Viking gods, raised one hand, slapped it forward, and followed with the other leaving a trail of blood as he worked his way across to Warwick's feet. He sprang up and stuck lacerated hands in the knight's face.

Sara had read about berserkers—Viking bearskin wearers. Without armor, they fought with the strength of bears and ferocity or wolves, slaying enemies in uncontrollable, suicidal trances. But she'd never been in the presence of one . . . until now.

Everyone awaited the knight's response. He eyed the Viking with a cold, reptilian stare. "You'll soon know what it's like to lose something you care about."

Stieg caught his arm. "Not so fast." He unsheathed Warwick's sword and shield, howled and waved them in the air. Nobody could take their eyes off him. He was Thor, god of thunder, Thor come to earth to battle Jotuns and trolls. He was the invincible one.

Once again, Roma musicians diverted the crowd's attention with rhythmic energy summoning the belly dancers. All attention turned to them except a somber faced Viking watching his wife disappear into the shadows with Warwick.

Sara texted Ryker, "Follow Freya and Warwick."

Then she went in search of a young girl who'd witnessed a crazed father and a mother's shame. She found Karina at the top of the hill under a live oak. "Are you all right? That must have been hard to see."

Tears trickled down her face and fanned out along her chin. Barely audible, she said, "I'm tired of all this."

Sara asked, "Earlier when high, why'd you say, 'It's all over. Nothing matters now?' Were you talking about your dad?"

"I don't remember but wish you could find Gunnar's killer."

Pan climbed up to them, balancing a large cup of soda in each hand. "Here you go." He set them down and gazed at Karina. "Why's there such sadness on your face?"

"I feel bad for the ladies-in-waiting talking about how Gunnar got too personal with them."

The veins in Pan's temples pulsed. "Did he with you?"

She shuddered. "He tried once, but I escaped."

His hands balled into fists. "Then I'm glad he's dead. No man should hurt a woman."

"You're right," said Sara, "but at the same time, nobody has the right to take another's life."

Pan put his arm around Karina, nestled her in the hollow of his shoulder, and whispered something in her hair. A part of Sara envied the closeness she didn't allow herself.

She left them and set out to hone in on a most tenable suspect. Gunnar and the Viking had been at each other's throats for weeks. Had Gunnar come on to Freya too? Stieg referring to her as Hel who ripped a hole in his heart argued so. But a berserker cuckold was an improbable paradox. The more credible premise was a father avenging sexual advances toward his daughter. Both scenarios demanded verification of Stieg's alibi. Sara braced herself for an angry outburst as she approached him and looked directly into the dark, foreboding eyes of a bearskin wearer.

"I'm confirming your statement about being home with Freya and Karina Friday evening and Saturday morning. Would you care to revise that?"

Ignoring her, Stieg strode to a large waste container, pushed Warwick's sword and shield deep inside, and shoved them all the way to the bottom until buried in garbage.

She crammed her voice to the top of her mouth and spit out, "I know you lied. Where were you?"

"With the Scots."

"The entire time?"

"Just ask them."

Her mouth twisted into a contemptuous smile. "I intend to."

Sara immediately sought out Balgair seated at a table. "I need to ask you about the Viking. And before you answer, know that I *will* learn the truth. Any false statement would prompt me to reveal a certain relationship."

He set his plate down hard. "What do you want?"

"He claims to have been with you the night of the murder."

"Same as every night the last few weeks. He came to get drunk over his two faced, snaky wife. He thought up the plan to humiliate those braggadocio knights and helped us make moonshine. That night, we were finishing up our fine brew till three in the morning and sampling as we went along."

"Can anyone else swear to it?"

"All my clansmen over there drinking and singing."

As Sara marched toward their table, they turned their backs as if engaged in conversation.

"To start with, lads, I know how you duped the knights and have no problem with that."

A Scot with a beard as red as Stieg's looked over his shoulder. "Then why are you here?"

"To ask one question. Who prepared your hundred-seventy-proof firewater and when?"

"Started about three weeks ago and bottled it last Friday."

"Who did?"

He waved his arm around the table. "All of us."

"Anyone else?"

Another Scot spoke up. "I don't want trouble. The Viking came up with the plan and made sure we got it right on Friday."

"Then he was there?"

"Till three in the morning."

So why had his adulterous wife also lied? Sara phoned Ryker. "Did you follow Freya?"

"She and Warwick went straight to his place. I'm there now."

"Wait for me and don't let anyone leave."

He was standing outside the trailer. "It's been a rocking and rolling ever since I got here. And I'll wager my favorite dish from Franny's Fryery that Stieg's known about them all along."

"An even greater question is whether she and Gunnar ever got it on." Sara grinned. "Shall I knock and cause coitus interruptus?"

That prompted a wide smile on Ryker's face. "Do it."

Knock. Knock. Knock. "Detective Sara Lansing. Open up."

"Come back tomorrow morning," said Warwick. "I've already gone to bed."

Hands in her pockets, Sara rocked back on her heels. "Hmm, so it would seem. I need to speak to both of you."

Warwick opened the door an inch and inspected them from inside a trailer illuminated by a single candle. "I'm alone."

"I don't *think* so. Shall we talk here or down at the station. I'm not going away."

He took a step backward, opened the door, and turned on a light as Sara and Ryker entered. Freya was seated at a table in one of his long shirts, tousled hair, mascara smudged. Rumpled sheets lay in disarray on the bed.

Sara slid onto the bench opposite her. "Balgair and the Scots support your husband's contention that he was in their camp the night of the murder and not with you as previously claimed. Would you care to amend your story?"

Warwick sat beside Freya and took her hand. "She was here with me all night."

"Then why lie about being home with Stieg and Karina?"

Freya sagged as if she'd sprung a slow leak. "To protect him."

"Who you thought killed Gunnar?" said Ryker.

She shuddered. "Yes."

"What about your relationship with good ol' Warwick here?"

"I'm planning to tell Stieg after closing on Sunday night." She put her other hand on top of his. "We've tried to be discreet."

"Leaving the party with him isn't exactly discreet," said Sara. "You as well as stamped adulteress on your forehead. What kind of message does that send to your daughter?"

Freya's eyes shied away. "She understands."

"No, she doesn't. Thirty minutes ago, she watched the bottom of her world drop out." Sara bit her lips to keep from adding *You're a worthless scumbag who should have never given birth.* "What time did you go home on Friday?"

She picked at her thumb cuticle. "Eleven forty."

"You always record your departure so precisely?"

"The late news and weather had just ended," said Warwick.

"Were your husband and daughter home?"

"Karina was asleep, and he hadn't come in yet. I found him passed out on the hood the next morning."

Sara slapped the table to get Warwick's attention. "Somebody saw a light in here Saturday at one fifteen a.m."

"I must have gotten up to use the toilet."

Ryker's nostrils flared. "Enough bullshit. Tell the truth."

"I have been. My relationship with Freya has nothing to do with Gunnar's death."

"Were either of you aware of his advances to Karina?"

The color drained from Freya's face. "She's an innocent child and would have told me."

Sara carefully measured each word to insert a speed bump between her brain and mouth. "Wrong. You're so far emotionally removed from her that she can't come to you." Sara slid off the bench. "We'll continue this conversation at the station."

"Is that really necessary?" Warwick said.

"I can haul you both in."

He backpedaled, waving his hands. "No, no don't need to."

Ryker took Freya's arm and escorted her out the door. "You're coming with me to the station."

"Not now," said Sara. "I'll explain later. I want to conclude this conversation woman to woman."

After he left, she told Freya, "I think there's more to the story and it has to do with something you're not telling Warwick."

She squirmed as if uncomfortable in an overly tight blouse. "I was young when I fell in love with a strong, handsome Norseman, but he's gone. His grandfather's gods robbed his soul." She made helpless gestures with her hands. "I need someone to be here for *me*, to take care of *me*."

"And your baby."

"What? How . . . how'd you know?"

"Lucky guess . . . and also that it's not Stieg's."

"It couldn't be. He got fixed right after Karina was born, said being on the road was no life for a child."

"Yet you did just that."

"Travel was in his blood."

"Is it Warwick's baby?"

"No, Gunnar's. And it was only once nine weeks ago after Stieg and I'd had a big falling out." Freya blinked, masking tears. "Gunnar and I were so drunk after a party we stumbled into the woods and did it on the grass under a romantic Louisiana moon."

"Did he know he was to become a father?"

"I'd missed my period and was nauseous but not certain. The queen gave me a ride from here into town after a Sunday party. I couldn't take our bus without Stieg noticing."

*Whoa.* "Did you tell her what for?"

"No way. I took the pregnancy test when Stieg left for his shop in the morning. I was sitting there bawling, the strip lying in plain sight on the dining table, when he walked back in." The skin around Freya's mouth rippled. "He wasn't supposed to see it. He had three pairs of custom boots to make before the weekend and shouldn't have been home until dinner."

Sara found a bench. "Sit here and tell me what happened."

"He . . . he . . . went crazy, out of his mind, screaming at me."

"Did he threaten you physically?"

Her shoulders slumped. "No, he would never lay a hand on me but demanded to know who the father was."

"And you told him."

"Had to."

"What about Gunnar?"

"I went to his trailer the next day and told him I was pregnant. He looked so pitiful I almost felt sorry for him, but that sentiment quickly changed."

"Why?"

"He said it was a consensual one night stand, and he wasn't cut out to be a father. He wouldn't even know where to begin and would screw the kid up. I was married and already had another child. My husband and I could raise the baby as our own."

"He didn't know Stieg was impotent."

"Of course not. Nobody knows that."

"You must have hated him with every fiber of your being."

Freya's chest filled and let the air out in a staggering breath. "Yes, I wanted to kill him but didn't have the courage."

"Where does Warwick fit into this infernal mix?"

"I suspected I was pregnant the first weekend here and then knew I couldn't remain with Stieg once he found out."

"So, Warwick was an easy mark. Does he know the reality of what he's getting into?"

Freya chewed a piece of loose skin on her thumb, causing it to bleed. "I'm not showing yet. When I do, I'll lead him to believe it's his. We're leaving together on Sunday."

Freya had drawn him in like a Venus fly trap. Sara tried to remain neutral, but her traitor body showed disdain by hardening like the blacksmith's steel. "Why'd you refuse a DNA sample?"

"I was afraid of you naming me a suspect if it came out I'd been with Gunnar."

"It casts a shroud of guilt over you and Stieg. You both lied to me. Does Karina know about this? Are you taking her with you?"

"No to both. I'm starting a new life with Warwick. She's

better off without me."

This woman deserved no mercy, abandoning her daughter to an unfit father just as Sara's dad deserted her to an abusive mother. Sara left Freya slumped over, head in her hands, weeping.

She met Ryker at her car. "What was all that about?" he asked.

"Listening to that feckless liar made me gag. Gunnar got her pregnant and dumped her. Now she's pawning the baby off on that unwitting, power hungry Warwick. And guess who drove her into town to buy a pregnancy test."

He opened his hands, questioning.

"The queen."

He howled. "So, two scorned women with motives."

"I feel waist deep in mud and can't wriggle out." She opened her car door and got in. "See you in the morning."

# Chapter 20

Early Saturday morning, Ryker munched on day old donuts and sipped coffee with cream and sugar as he reviewed his notes on Foster's backers. The meeting was in the abandoned warehouse at eleven. Not knowing who'd show up, he left thirty minutes early and parked out of sight to gauge attendees as they entered. Let the games begin. He turned his phone off to silence calls or texts from Sara or McBride that could jeopardize his identity.

Jeff greeted him at the door. "I apologize for the venue. With so much at stake, we can't risk any exposure."

"I agree. You can never be too safe."

Ryker took a seat at the table with six backers. Jeff introduced each man, all in the construction industry.

"Why have you come to us?" one asked.

"Some influential financiers knew I was seeking a new project and referred me to Foster. I vetted him and was quite impressed by his creative approach to business and the savvy to accomplish what he sets out to do."

"But you must understand we're not in a position to discuss details until after the election in three weeks."

"TV ads show Foster's campaign is based on his opponent's inability to solve that murder in your Renaissance village. I saw posters with tomorrow night as the closing date."

Jeff spoke, "The fair people will pack up and move on like they do every year."

"Thwarting the police and Foster wins. Right?"

Several of them squirmed in their seats. "That's our plan."

Ryker checked his watch twice as if time was of the essence. "Gentlemen, thank you for meeting with me on such short notice. Since you're not able to discuss details at this point, I'm under the gun to make a decision. The financiers also recommended another project head who is waiting to hear from me by end of day." He strode across the room like a lawyer giving his final summation. "So, if you'll kindly excuse me, I need to go."

"Wait," said Jeff. "We'll order in pizza and then discuss this further. What would you like?"

Ryker stroked his chin. "Hmm, deep dish with pepperoni, sausage, and extra cheese."

Jeff snapped his finger at the man across from him. "Call in for three large. We'll pick them up." He nudged the man next to him. "Go get several six packs of beer."

Two men gone to pick up lunch, Ryker spoke to the elder of the other backers, "What type of construction are you in?"

"Commercial. I've developed two shopping centers."

"And you're looking to put one here?"

"If everything works out."

"And you?" Ryker asked another.

He hesitated and looked to Jeff as if seeking approval. He got the nod. "I own a demolition company."

"Razing buildings sounds like fun," said Ryker. "My mother would never let me wreck my Lego castles until the entire neighborhood saw them. I wanted to use the Legos to build something new."

Lunch arrived forty minutes later. As Ryker lifted a piece of pepperoni pizza dripping with cheese, he heard Sara harping in his head about the worst possible meal. And beer too. He wiped grease off his chin and asked the demolition man, "If all goes as planned, which buildings will you be knocking down and replacing?"

Total silence.

"Did I say something wrong?" Ryker asked.

Skittish looks darted back and forth.

Ryker reached for another slice. "Hmm?"

Jeff finally spoke. "Anything you hear must never be repeated to anyone, not a single sole. Is that understood?"

Ryker took a bite and spoke with his mouth full. "I'd have it no other way."

Shopping center man leaned across the table to divulge their secret, "The Ren village may cease to exist."

A piece of thick crust caught in Ryker's throat. Did he hear that correctly? He swallowed hard. "How's that possible?"

"Reunion Heights owns the land," said Jeff. "Their lease is up, and Corbin won't renew it. Then we can do whatever we please and charge excessive costs."

Ryker grinned. "The perfect money laundering scheme."

"So are you in?" Jeff asked.

"Only a buffoon would pass this up. I'm with you one hundred percent. Now all we have to do is get through Sunday night and the election in three weeks." He ate two more slices and washed them down with beer. "Now I really must go communicate my decision to the other projects."

Saturday morning, Sara wrapped both arms around a pillow and waited for the misty rays of dawn to steal across the floor. It arrived much too soon, its pale light filtering through the leaves of a black cherry tree. She set the snooze alarm for another fifteen minutes. It would be a tiresome day questioning rennies who'd previously worked with the Knights Invincible.

With less than forty-eight hours before everything fell apart, she gathered her notes and left for the village. She noticed a much too familiar car parked across the street and leaned on the horn in passing. "Wake up boys. Early day."

Sara arrived as gates opened for the Pirate Invasion weekend. Visitors streamed in dressed as Captain Hook and Blackbeard. A boom sent a wave of them to the Enchanted Forest where a three-masted, pirate ship had been anchored the night before. With loud sound effects, four cannons shot powder making it appear as if real balls had been fired.

The demons of a sea faring life lowered a boat and rowed to shore with the captain in the rear shouting orders to plunder silver and kidnap wenches for ransom. They landed at the dock and ran into the village brandishing swords and firing blank pistols. Visitors pretended to flee in terror. The invasion spread through the fairgrounds with mock sword fights and the pillaging of hats and backpacks which were quickly and secretly returned. Kids wearing painted pirate faces went on treasure hunts in search of Blackbeard's gold. It all looked like great fun, but Sara had to attend to more important matters.

She questioned every rennie who'd work with the knights at previous fairs if they'd observed Gunnar in any kind of verbal or physical confrontations with other rennies? Her usual suspects— the Roma camp, Scots, and Viking—had all worked with the knights before and offered nothing new. She interviewed Irish dancers, singers, a magician, juggler, and numerous comedy acts. Stories infused with gossip barraged her with details of everyone's love life, who got drunk too many times, who argued with whom. She extracted the most plausible and relevant, much of which she'd already surmised.

The sword swallower had worked two fairs with the knights. She'd needed to question him, but his act had already begun.

"For those of you in disbelief," he said, "I'd like a volunteer."

A man in his twenties immediately jumped up onto the stage. The sword swallower asked him to verify the authenticity of a solid, steel blade. Then he explained to the audience, "When you swallow food, your muscles contract as it passes from your throat to your esophagus to your stomach. I have to deliberately relax those muscles to cram a twenty-two-inch, cold, rigid blade down the same path. When I have completed this, I'll signal our brave volunteer to carefully extract it." He then tilted his head back and slowly inserted the sword. Eyes widened and jaws dropped. A minute later, his fingers beckoned the young man. Gaping mouths in the audience turned to an outburst of cheering.

Sara spoke with him afterward. "That's pretty impressive how your GI tract acts like a living scabbard." She displayed her ID. "I'm investigating the knight's murder. You worked with them twice in the last three years. Did you ever witness any verbal or physical disputes?"

"Amongst themselves and once with that Viking but nothing that would incite murder."

"Thank you."

Few things had challenged her convictions as much as he just did. His act required an emotional and mental transformation from disbelief to acceptance that swallowing a long, steel blade was real.

Shows were staggered to accommodate audiences. Between performances, Sara talked to shop owners at Leather by Lancelot, Mud Fellows Facials, Face Painting by Zerona, and Lionheart Hat Shoppe.

The woman in M'Lady's Braids substantiated Adara's and Ded Bob's account of the arena fight. "I first saw the Viking about three years ago. He dressed the same as now to attract customers. But since then, he's gotten more and more into it like last night. He scared me."

"It was very unsettling to be sure."

Next stop, Mythological Jewelry. Pan was playing a sprightly tune on his flute and dancing around three teenage girls. "Good morrow, sweet lasses. Verily, thou art as comely as spring morns. Perchance thou wouldst enjoy a pair of these most beauteous ceramic horns or other uncommon adornments."

Giggling, they tapped his horns and tugged the goat tail

before entering his uncle's shop.

"Congratulations on attracting customers," said Sara. "You're good at it. I've been talking to everyone who worked the same fairs as Knights Invincible, hoping they heard or saw something that could help us." She climbed onto the boulder he sprang from that first day and sat with her feet braced to keep from sliding off. "Mythological Jewelry was at the same venue three years ago as were the Scots, Roma camp, and knights. Remember everyone?"

"Think so, but I'd just turned fourteen. My mom was overly protective and didn't want me around drugs or alcohol. I wasn't allowed to go to the evening parties and only knew people in the booths next to ours."

"Karina says she met you eighteen months ago at the Texas Renaissance Festival."

"It's the largest one in the country, open two months. We had a lot of time together."

"Since then also, I hear. She has quite a crush on you."

"And I love her. We're going to stay together forever."

"Even though you're both still teenagers, I truly believe that's your destiny. If I had children, I'd want them to be just like you."

"You'd be a good mom."

"Thanks. I like to think so but just never had the chance."

Sara hopped down and glanced inside Mythological Jewelry. "The girls have left and your uncle's not too busy. I need to chat with him before you charm more customers. I hope he can fill in a couple of blanks in the stories I've heard."

"He probably won't be able to remember. He's pretty forgetful and confuses things that happened only a month ago. I kinda take care of him."

"That's quite a burden on you."

"I owe it to him. He's been good to me."

Sara stepped inside the shop. Pan's uncle was all angles and bones. The knobs in his spine poked through his shirt like a chain of miniature hills. A web of fine wrinkles framed the outside of alert, bright eyes that showed no indication of a failing mind.

"You have a fine place here and a very sweet nephew."

"He's a good boy. I like having him travel with me."

"I'm talking to performers and shop owners who've worked fairs with the Knights Invincible. I think you did three years ago."

"I remember only too well. It was a very somber time for us. My sister died in a hiking accident just six weeks afterward."

Sara spotted Pan lingering outside the door as she said to his uncle, "Not of cancer nineteen months ago?"

"Oh, no. She was a beautiful, healthy woman. Arriving three days early for the Colorado Festival, I had enough time to set up by myself. She and Pan had been in such low spirits for weeks that I wanted to cheer them up. He'd never been to the Rocky Mountains, so I suggested they go on a picnic hike."

"Why were they in low spirits?"

"Not sure. Thinking back, I figured it must have been the high altitude. We'd come straight from sea level to 6,900 feet. I read that a quick change in elevation can tire you out and affect decision making. I should have known better than to send them even higher, but I wanted them to have fun. I packed a lunch and got a trail map." His eyes filmed over. "Off they went but she never returned."

Sara glanced back at Pan, but he'd disappeared. She leaned against the edge of a display table to steady herself in this seismic shift about his mother. "How'd she die?"

"It had rained earlier making those rocks wet and slick. They climbed to over ten thousand feet and didn't pay attention on a narrow trail. My sister slipped and fell five hundred feet down a boulder field."

"And Pan?"

The uncle quivered like an autumn leaf. "Paralyzed with fear at first. He was fourteen and didn't know what to do. He skidded and fell all the way back to my car and drove to the ranger station for help. A rescue team pulled his mother out two hours later."

A sickish lump in her stomach, Sara said, "How did both of you ever get past this?"

"Painfully. His mother's death traumatized him. He shut down and wouldn't speak to me or anyone. This went on for months until a woman finally got through to him using art therapy. She told him to draw everything that happened. She interpreted dozens of his pictures to help him understand what he was experiencing."

"Have you seen them?"

"He wouldn't let me."

Wisps of uncertainty swarmed like gnats in Sara's brain. Pan could cope with the idea of his mother dying of cancer easier than a hiking accident? Bewildering. After thanking his uncle, she left for the Mail Works. At the base of the stairs, involuntary tremors in her legs caused her to stop and get control before climbing. She finally stood outside the curtain. "You there, Pan?"

Silence.

"Can you hear me?"

Still nothing.

She cautiously drew the curtain and saw the iPad, backpack, and picture of his mother were missing. The satyr's shaggy legs and hoofs lay on the floor. Lots of brown hair. It had never occurred to her that his costume would come into play. Not Pan. She compared the single strand in her pocket. It matched. Couldn't. There had to be some mistake.

She remembered pieces of paper stuffed in wall cracks and hoped they wouldn't reveal untold secret drawings. Tentatively, she withdrew the first and unrolled a picture of aspen, spruce, and pine viewed from a high point, perhaps from the trail they'd hiked. The second was his mother wearing a backpack and sitting on a boulder facing away from him. Next showed a chipmunk nibbling sunflower seeds from Pan's hand. In the fifth, he was jamming his heels against the boulder and trying to pull his mother back from the edge. The sixth drawing laid bare the horrific scene of his mother's broken body on a mound of jagged rocks. Then a series of pictures: Pan running down the mountain, the car, the rangers, a rescue team carrying his mother past him, her body torn.

Sara slid the last paper out, a picture of the tattoo identified by Rudd as having been done for Gunnar years ago. She'd picked up the pieces and connected the dots, but it required an emotional and mental transformation from disbelief to acceptance that this was real. It felt as though her stomach and been shoved all the way to her spine.

She called Ryker and got only his voice mail. "I know . . . I know who murdered Gunnar." She shook the phone. "Dammit, answer my call. Speak to me." Struggling to digest the indigestible, she continued, "Pan, the boy dressed as a satyr. There has to be a reason, but I can't imagine what it is." She hung up, took several long deep breaths, and called once more. "I need to find him before police become involved and accidently hurt him. I'll update when you answer your damn phone."

Pan could have taken a short cut back to the Mail Works that night. Sara walked the route in reverse past the swing. Under a full moon, he would have seen Gunnar and Adara together.

Sara reached the bus. The ferocity of Stieg's precious Gokstad ship had been obliterated by white paint smeared over thirty-two oarsmen. Axe blows had slain the dragon masthead glaring from the prow, splintering its blazing eyes and bony snout. Karina had jumped ship, mutinied. But where would she and Pan go? Naira might know.

Sara felt like a squirrel in traffic scurrying in and out among thousands of visitors clad in multicolored Renaissance garb and myriad swashbuckling pirates. She blustered her way through an audience gathered for spontaneous banter between a pirate and peasant visitor.

"Put thy toad spotted body in yon cart and bring it hither," a pirate yelled, "and I shall give thee one pint of grog in return."

Sara pushed through a crowd chanting. "Grog, more grog."

She ran past the magician and juggler. "Have you seen the boy satyr or flower cart girl?"

Not them, not the tree man on stilts, not the mud wrestlers, not the beggar—nobody.

Her pulse banged in her ears as she squeezed among another crowd watching pirates hanging on each other's shoulders. "Here's to rum and tobacco. For I spent all me tin with the lassies drinking gin and across the ocean I must wander."

Too many visitors in the way.

Noise.

Confusion.

Then the sweet song of a girl pushing a cart overflowing with gay flowers. "Buy a garland for thy maid. And tonight, thou might get . . . dinner if thou art lucky."

"Naira," Sara cried, trying to keep her stomach down. "Where are Karina and Pan? I think something's gone terribly wrong and must help them before it's too late."

Naira's body went limp. "Gone wrong? What happened?"

"No time to explain. I must find them quickly."

"I haven't seen either of them today."

"You're the only one who might know where they'd hide."

Naira hesitated.

"Please, I beg of you."

Fingers on her temples, eyes closed. "I remember telling them about my ancestors hiding in the Everglades."

"Thank you, but those are much too far away."

But Possum and Grouper weren't. During her frantic search, they'd given up all pretenses of staying out of sight. Their proximity added confusion to Sara's already addled brain. Something Pan had said about animals bounced around in her head. It was right there, just out of reach. *Think. Think.* Wild boars. The veterinary student fascinated by animals from chipmunks to whales wanted to see wild boars in the swamp north of here. *Oh, my God, they're heading for the Okefenokee.*

# Chapter 21

Possum and Grouper were visibly on her tail now as Sara darted between visitors and behind stages. She hustled through a crowd gathered along the parade route and beat the goons by seconds across the path to lose them among the royal court and more than forty other rennies in full attire.

She raced to Mythological Jewelry and asked Pan's uncle, "Do you know where Pan is?"

"Out in front somewhere drumming up business."

She shook her head. "No, no, no. He's gone and may have taken your car. I need your model and license number."

"What's going on?"

"Don't have time to explain. Please, just write it down."

Sara couldn't bear to tell him a truth as implausible as a man sliding a twenty-two-inch blade down his throat. She ran to her car and drove away from the village to elude Possum and Grouper. She parked in a narrow alley and googled the nearest border to the Okefenokee—estimated time of arrival forty minutes. Heading north, she called Ryker and got his voice mail again. "Where the hell are you?" she screamed into the phone. "Answer me! Pan and Karina are headed to the Okefenokee Swamp in his uncle's car. I'm going after them."

They had at least an hour's head start. To make up time, Sara sped around long haul trucks on a straight stretch of highway, checking every car and license plate she passed. No sign of them. She finally reached the outer edge of the swamp and took three obscure dirt roads that led to dead ends. She drove down a fourth narrow road hidden between dense groves of oak, magnolia, and cypress. A car was parked twenty yards ahead at a dead end.

Sara phoned Ryker and got nowhere again. "I may have found them." She turned the engine off to avoid startling Pan and Karina and walked toward the car with Ryker's phone still on the line. "His uncle's number matches the plate, but the car's empty. They must have gone into the swamp an hour ahead of me. I've gotta go in after them while there's still three or four hours of daylight. I'll call when I know something more. Bye."

Sara searched the road for signs where Pan and Karina may have entered. The oak forest on the right was less intimidating than cypress sitting on massive bottle shaped trunks to the left. Their limbs draped in eerie, gray clusters of Spanish moss became ghosts in tattered clothing. A shaft of pale light broke through the dense canopy, a perfect place for hump-backed gnomes with long beards.

She had navigated through jungles in adventure racing and recognized how nature always reaches for the sun. People shove obstacles aside or plow through them, leaving bent and broken brush. A trail of crushed undergrowth signaled they had come in among the cypress, perhaps to discourage followers.

No bars on her cell, she stepped from under the forest cover to phone Ryker but spotted a familiar car coming down the road. *Damn.* Still speaking to voice mail, she said, "I'm at the swamp but Foster's goons must have planted a GPS tracker on my car. They'll soon be within feet of me and will follow. Gotta duck out of sight into the forest and go after the kids. I'll lose cell coverage."

Ryker exited the warehouse proud of his undercover work but couldn't prove Foster guilty of a crime, only of evil intentions. Was it enough to smear Foster's name before the election? He took the phone from his pocket and turned it back on. There were several messages from Sara. Something must have really riled her up. He tapped the first one left at 11:05 a.m. saying the boy who dressed as a satyr was the murderer. He chuckled at her attempt to make up for not being able to find the true killer. But the third message about knocked him off his feet. Her voice conveyed foreboding not humor. She was heading into the Okefenokee Swamp after the boy and Viking's daughter. Dreading the 12:50 message, he steadied himself against the hood of his car and tapped the screen. Foster's thugs had tracked her car and would follow. She'd lose cell service.

She had tried contacting him within minutes of his clicking *Do not Disturb*. Why'd he stay for pizza? He phoned Sara but got voice mail. Ryker slammed his fist on the hood. "Are you insane, woman, rushing into a swamp alone with two murderous goons after you. Remember chastising me for not calling for backup?"

Next, he got hold of McBride and briefed him. "Foster's thugs will kill Sara. Tell me what to do. I'm at a loss on how to help her."

"Most of the Okefenokee is in Georgia. We have no jurisdiction except for the area in northern Florida."

"But you could call Georgia for help."

"I'll do my best but don't know where to send them. It's a very large swamp."

"I'm going up there to locate her car."

Ryker googled the swamp on his phone and pulled up a map indicating main entry points. Suwannee Canal Recreational Area was the closest and most likely to have rangers available. The drive was interminable with visions of his partner hunted by goons, snakes, and gators. An hour and ten minutes later, he pulled into the parking lot and checked every row of cars for Sara's. Not there. He ran into the visitor center and pushed ahead of others at the counter. "I need to talk to the person in charge here right now."

The clerk said, "Wait in line, like everybody else."

Ryker whipped out his badge. "Police. This is an emergency. I demand immediate service with someone in authority."

The clerk gestured to a young woman in a service uniform. A moment later, a man with a sun weathered face emerged from a back office. "What's so urgent?"

He extended his hand. "Ryker Harris, detective. My partner is somewhere in the swamp pursuing a killer while being chased by two henchmen who don't want her alive. I've got to find her."

"Any idea where she is?"

Ryker's heart was beating so fast he thought it would break a rib. "None. I desperately need your help."

"I'll alert all the rangers to keep a lookout but can't afford to assign anyone to a blind search in such a vast area. My budget's been cut to a minimum. I have to take care of the tourists on hand. Coming up from Florida, she may have entered from the south on one of the dirt back roads used by gator and rattlesnake hunters." He drew a diagram of possible access and gave Ryker a card. "If you locate the car, text me the GPS and I'll bring rangers myself."

Ryker forced an enthusiastic, "Thank you."

All the way back to the mapped area, Ryker kept his window rolled down listening for sounds as he explored all possible routes. He stopped suddenly before a large, black bear, its long brown nose sniffing the air. Once on a nature show, Ryker had learned bears can smell seven times better than bloodhounds and can tear the entire side of a car down like opening a sardine can. He reeked of nervous sweat as the bear stood on its hind legs and clawed a tree ten feet from the car. Marking its territory?

He rolled his windows up and slowly moved forward. "Place is yours, buddy."

Transfixed on the bear, he hadn't noticed Sara's car fifty yards ahead. Why had she parked there? He reached it and understood she'd stayed behind to not spook Pan. His uncle's car stood in front of a Jersey plate. Ground zero. He immediately texted his position to the head ranger.

A minute later, Ryker's phone rang. "Good work. I know right where you are and will be there first thing in the morning."

The skin on the back of Ryker's neck prickled. "No, you have to come now."

"Impossible. Your partner has several hours head start. It will be dark by the time we get there. She won't be moving in the night. Nor will we. And you certainly should nix any crazy ideas of your own about entering. I promise we'll be there by twilight. There's nothing more you can do tonight. Go to a nearby motel and remain on call in case she finds cell service."

# Chapter 22

Parked behind Pan's car, the Jersey boys stood in front of theirs with a vacant look on their faces. They mumbled something Sara couldn't hear and began checking both sides of the road.

*Take the easy path into the woods. You'd be headless chickens running around here in the cypress.*

Grouper stopped in the middle and heaved his shoulders as if in total resignation. He reached into his pocket and had just taken his phone out presumably to call Foster when suddenly from the oak forest came hoarse grunts. A deer zigzagged through the trees hounded by large animals covered head to foot with thick, stiff bristles. Vicious eyes gleamed in the underbrush as the lead boar thrust its heavy head at the deer. Large, curved tusks cut into its flank and thrust the prey onto its side. The doomed animal's high pitched squeals trailed off and died as the boars ripped its flesh apart and gorged themselves in a bloody feast.

Possum's knees buckled. The crotch of Grouper's pants grew increasingly moist.

Sara laughed to herself. *Welcome to hell, boys. What'cha gonna do now?*

Grouper paced, yelling and flailing his arms, before making a short call. When he hung up, terror replaced the vacant expression. Sara guessed they'd been ordered to come in after her but had no freaking idea where to start. It would be amusing to watch them muddling about, but she needed to move on.

Pan and Karina had chosen a remote, isolated path away from tourist boat rides and boardwalks. No longer able to contact Ryker, Sara quietly slunk into a labyrinth of deep and mysterious gloom. Mossy branches blocked the sky. Shrubs and grasses fought for every inch of space and littered the ground with their decaying bodies. She picked her way through nearly impenetrable, twisted growth among a web of tangled roots and fallen branches. Thick vines dangling in long chains threatened to entangle her.

She tracked flattened leaves here, a broken branch there, and wandered deeper onto a floating peat bog formed by a mix of decaying moss and woody heather shrubs. The land was so soggy trees didn't have a stable hold on the ground. Although it appeared solid, it was more like walking on a giant, mud soaked sponge. Sara jumped to make the ground quiver. Native Americans had named it Okefenokee, Land of the Trembling Earth.

She spotted what looked like a row of small lights and crept toward them. Turtles lined up on a log with sunlight reflecting off their shells plopped into the water one by one. Her movement had signaled danger to a sandhill crane. A great flapping of wings and the bird took flight, soaring a moment before spiraling down to roost on a tree. She knew the piercing cries of the watchmen of the swamp could send distress calls two and a half miles.

A single, sharp gunshot suddenly rang through the air and brought down one of the graceful birds bearing gray plumage and a red crown. A scream escaped Sara before she could clap her hand over her mouth. Foster hadn't ordered them to intimidate her. He wanted her dead. They must have told him she solved the murder. There was no turning back now. She feared Foster would stop at nothing to get elected even if it meant killing Pan and Karina too and disposing of all three in a surreal graveyard.

A voice as rough as bark yelled, "We know where you are."

Her startled cry had given away her location. She stood on a soggy mound and had to choose between fleeing on the peat bog or wading into coffee water darkened by decades of the tannic acid of the decaying vegetation. Water ruled the swamp, and water belonged to the thousands of gators that considered it home. She could wade in making it impossible for Possum and Grouper to track her, but gators and five viper species waited.

Sara chose to remain on the peat island even though following her would be easier but not *that* easy. With layers of muck beneath the peat, her feet sank and her footprints filled in the second she withdrew a leg before it went too deep. Hearing rustling behind her, she spun around. "Which way did the kids go?" she whispered to a possum perched in a black gum tree, its long, bare tail wrapped around the trunk.

It blinked as if to say, *Quiet, you're disturbing my Z's.*

Sara searched for signs of Pan and Karina among dead trees and twisted branches. To conceal her path from the goons, she gently pulled back long, matted clusters of Spanish moss without disturbing it. She had just passed under a colony of bats hanging upside down when something cold and wet brushed against her face. She tried to sweep it off and surprised a glossy, iridescent, blue–black snake. It reared, swaying side to side, flattened its head, and flicked its tongue. She sucked in a rapid breath but exhaled slowly recognizing only a harmless eastern indigo. But a sudden encounter with the largest native snake in the US would panic anyone, especially two city boys. She backtracked creating an obvious trail to a snake large enough to take on small mammals and hatchling alligators. Even the swamp's eastern diamondback rattler wasn't safe from an indigo.

Minutes later, she found a clump of fur snarled in a cluster of tiny branches. She lightly pressed it between her fingers, trying to fathom what swamp creature bore this texture and color. None that she could envision. Then it hit her. On Saturday, Karina would have been wearing her Viking long sleeved dress trimmed in fur at the collar. The swamp gods had spoken. Karina came this way.

Sara couldn't risk revealing her location by calling to Pan and Karina. She needed to find them before dark and stood on a peat bog listening to the clattering sound of a flock of wood ibis as their powerful curved bills gathered frogs and insects in water. A plan brewed in her brain. She ripped off a small piece of her sleeve and placed it in an obvious place to lure Possum and Grouper into gator territory. Then for breadcrumbs, she hung a few strands of hair shoulder height in plain view and strewed broken carnivorous pitcher plants on the path. As she neared a large pond, Sara spotted numerous snouts. The gators' heads rose out of the water like scaly, prehistoric stepping stones, and their rough skin looked like floating logs. For the finale, she scuffed up the shore as if there'd been a struggle and left Karina's fur at the water's edge. The goons had stalked her enough to recognize it. If they assumed Karina and Pan were dead, maybe they'd clear out.

From behind trees, Sara watched the path she'd set to make sure the hired guns who killed a sandhill crane took the bait.

*Speed it up, you worthless piss ants. I have to find two lost kids before dark.*

A blue heron stood immobile in shallow water near the bank, waiting for its prey to come within range. Using its long neck and head, it thrust a sharp, dagger-like bill and impaled a fish. After shaking it to break up the spines, the heron swallowed the catch whole and then slowly waded a couple of feet before assuming its statue pose again.

A chorus of frogs croaked unearthly noises when Possum and Grouper arrived in brown–stained pants. Sara chuckled to herself. *Way to go, indigo, you spooked these dumb-witted city boys.* They inched closer to the bank and retrieved the piece of Karina's fur. As they appeared to be assessing the find, the heron suddenly made hoarse croaking sounds and beat its wings hard while taking off. The dark water mirrored the bird's flight before it disappeared into a tangle of trees.

Sara as well as the goons saw the cause of its alarm emerge from a dark pool hidden by reeds and grasses only a few feet away. A gator used its tail as a catapult and sprang onto the shore, water dripping from its armor of bony plates. Paralyzed, Possum and Grouper watched the long, black body move on stunted legs, the head swinging and mouth open revealing rows of yellow fangs. Then the grisly crunch of breaking bone and shell as blood and water rushed from the gator's mouth and a cloud of vapor shot from its nostrils. A desperate snapping turtle thrashed back and forth as the gator submerged again leaving only the head of its victim above.

Sara stifled a smile as intense shaking began in the men's legs and rippled up their torsos into their shoulders. Possum shouted, "My bloody head's not gonna hang out of some gator's mouth."

Grouper shoved him hard. "Get yourself together. We don't know if those kids are dead or where that damn detective is. Foster said not to return until we got rid of all three."

Possum reeled backwards and stumbled. "Call him like you did before. Ask what to do."

"I tried. There's no service in here."

"I'm leaving."

Grouper fired a scathing look. "The hell you are."

Sara left them screaming at each other. She needed to do some calling of her own without leading them to her. They wouldn't dare follow in gator infested water now. She broke off a dead branch and made a sturdy pole to test the depth before wading in up to her thighs. She probed the solidity of the ground before each step to avoid getting entangled in submerged holes or roots as she wound through trees, shrubs, and plants. She drove her legs forward but couldn't escape feeling watched by gator eyes glistening above the black surface as furtive creatures swam below, largely unseen.

One came near her. Slender and about twenty inches long, it

had the red, yellow, and black bands of a coral snake—the second most deadly in the world. Sara's heart raced as she quickly checked the coloration, repeating the rhyme, Red on yellow kill a fellow. Red on black friend of Jack. The red bands touched black on both sides. She expelled a large gulp of air. It was an imposter scarlet kingsnake mimicking a coral one to deter predators.

The lowering sun cast a pale haze. Sara had to find the kids soon. The goons likely hadn't followed her in the water. She cupped her hands to her mouth. "Pan, Karina, it's Detective Lansing. I only want to help." Her voice was lost among the birdcalls and acrobatic dragonflies catching insects on the wing.

Prodding for hazards, she stirred up bubbles of methane gas produced by decaying organic matter trapped below the surface. The flatulent wetland burped swamp farts. Sara continued calling to Pan and Karina but heard only the steady hum of buzzing flies, twigs snapping, the unearthly noises of animals and birds hunting and being hunted.

At twilight, inky silhouettes infused the sky. Gaunt trees were zombies draped in cobwebs rising from their graves. Sara exited the water and called again, but the clamor of singing frogs muffled her. As she approached them, the croaking concerts ceased. They must have felt the vibrations and stopped to see what's up. When they hushed, she yelled in anguished cries every two minutes.

From the unbearable silence came a high, thin, "Over here."

"Karina?" *Forget about gators, snakes, and goons. Go find her.* In the deepening shadows, thousands of brown bats introduced the nightlife of the swamp, flitting and whirling about her head. She flailed at them, lost her balance and staggered to her feet again, calling with such urgency her throat was raw.

She found her sitting under a tree like a newly hatched robin with its wings and feet tucked against its body. Sara bent down and took Karina in her arms. "It's all right. I'm here. I'm here." She swept the girl's hair back from her face. "Are you alone?"

"Yes."

"I can't believe Pan would leave you."

She sniffled so hard her nostrils caved. "My left side hurt so bad I was slowing him down. We heard you calling and knew you were close, that you'd find me and help. We'll meet again later."

Sara was stunned "How'd you hurt yourself?"

"It's not important now."

Sara wiped moisture off her face. "You okay otherwise?"

"Yeah."

"Where will you meet Pan?"

"He said not to tell anyone."

"Sweetheart, two very unpleasant men are looking for us. We have to keep moving and find him first. Can you walk?"

"I think so."

"Which direction did he go?"

Karina pointed toward a dense forest to the left of a pond. "I watched him disappear into those trees."

Sara draped Karina's arm over her shoulder and rose slowly helping her to stand. "Now lean on me. We've got to reach safety wherever that might be."

Long arms of gray moss brushed their faces and snagged in their hair as they slogged forward. Suddenly, a thick, black mass of mosquitoes attacked every inch of exposed skin and through pants and shirts. As light glimmered on a pond, Karina stumbled toward it, swinging her arms wildly at the unremittent onslaught.

Sara screamed, "Stop! It's not safe."

But ruthless mozzies called in reinforcements. Karina threw herself in water up to her chest, making her shirt balloon.

"Get out of there. What're you doing?"

The water lapped at Karina's shoulders. She tipped her head back, her long hair fanning out and floating on the surface. Then she slowly disappeared leaving only a swirl. Sara waited for her to bob back up, but the concentric circles grew wider. She emptied her phone, gun, and wallet and dived in. Holding her breath so long her head pounded, she blindly groped and was about give up when her hand caught Karina's sleeve. Sara hooked her arm under the girl and pulled her to the surface gasping.

As they crawled onto the bank, she swatted the lead bombers of the next squad, keeping them off Karina so she wouldn't go nuts again. Mosquitos couldn't get through mud. She dug into muck and plastered it over every inch of bare skin. Karina shivered under the cold. Sara ripped Spanish moss off trees and packed it around her for warmth before covering herself too.

She held Karina. "Don't worry. Everything will be all right. I've spent many nights in swamps and never contended with more than itchy bites. Pan's alone out there and certainly not moving in the dark. We'll find him first thing in the morning."

"Please just let him be. We'll disappear and never be seen or heard from again."

"I want to for reasons you can't possibly imagine. I know he's not a bad person." The next words slipped out before she dared to release them. "I love you both as if you were my own children."

Still shivering, Karina tucked her arms and legs tighter against her body. "You don't understand. He's done something really awful and could go to jail forever."

"Maybe not. I know what he did but not why. Do you?"

"He wanted me to understand before I chose to go with him."

"Then tell me."

Karina's hands knotted in her lap. "Three years ago, they were working the same fair as the Knights Invincible. One of them was always coming around and touching his mother in private places."

"Gunnar."

Karina nodded. "That swine bullied everybody and preyed on women. One day, Pan warned him to not go near his mother again. Gunnar shoved him against a brick wall and asked, 'Or what, you sniveling little weasel'"?

"Those were Gunnar's exact words?"

"Pan never forgot them."

"By the end of the faire, most of the rennies had already left. Pan's uncle went into town to buy provisions for the road, leaving his sister and nephew alone in the trailer."

Sara's throat tightened. She didn't like where this was going.

"Gunnar forced his way inside and locked the door. He held a knife to their faces and shushed them to keep quiet. He stripped down to his waist, knocked Pan onto a chair, tied his arms behind his back. Then he knelt, his tattooed chest right in Pan's face."

"And forever etched in his mind."

"When Pan dropped his head and squeezed his eyes, Gunnar slapped him until his nose and lips bled all over his face and down his shirt." Karina's breathing grew irregular and stopped as if her body had forgotten how. Then she added, "Pan was crying so hard he could barely continue. I told him no more details. I didn't want to hear."

"Of course not."

"Gunnar . . . he . . . raped Pan's mother right in front of him and threatened to hunt them down and kill them if they told anyone. Then he tore a necklace off her throat and left."

The one in the photo. Sara's stomach burned. It was all coming together. Pan had raided Gunnar's trailer to recover his mother's necklace. "Didn't they report it to the police or tell Pan's uncle?"

She shook her head. "Too scared of what he'd do. His mother was ashamed and couldn't live with the memory of her son seeing her like that."

"And the hiking accident?"

"Six weeks later, they worked the Colorado faire. His mom had been lost inside herself and rarely spoken since the attack. Pan's uncle was worried about them. He packed a picnic lunch and told them to take the day off and go to the mountains."

"The uncle still didn't know?"

Karina continued in a low, dwindling voice, "No, he stayed to set up the shop. Pan and his mom hiked up a very steep trail and stopped for lunch on a large boulder. From that high, they could see peaks for miles and miles. She seemed to be taking in the view." Karina looked at Sara. "You know how much he loves animals?"

"Yes, and I tried getting close to him by narrating a brief tale about water-holding frogs in Australia."

"He liked you sharing your story. He thinks you're cool."

Sara gave her a little hug. "And both of you are too."

"Feeding pumpkin seeds to a chipmunk out of his hand was the first time he'd had fun since it happened. He looked up to tell his mom to watch and noticed she'd moved too close to the edge. He yelled it wasn't safe. She ignored him. When he crawled forward and grabbed her rucksack, she slipped her arms free of the straps and fell hundreds of feet onto a pile of rocks."

Tears formed tiny rivulets in the caked mud on Karina's face, and Sara's sinuses tingled meaning tears weren't far behind. "So it wasn't the accident Pan told to his uncle. She wanted to die."

"Yes. He blames himself for not realizing how much she was suffering, feels she couldn't have done it if he'd paid attention, if he hadn't been feeding seeds to a chipmunk, if he hadn't been thinking of his own happiness."

Sara placed her hand under the girl's chin and gently tipped her head to meet hers. "He was only fourteen and not responsible for the actions of a rapist. Guilt is a cannibal that devours souls."

"So is vengeance. Three years Pan searched for Gunnar and almost didn't recognize him wearing a full beard now. But he saw the tattoo one morning when the knights practiced shirtless in the heat. After walking me home that night, he passed the swing and saw Gunnar with the belly dancer. He took a dagger from the Mail Works, waited for her to leave, and, well, you know the rest."

Sara wiped salty tears from Karina's face, wanting to protect these children. "Why did you go so far out into the pond like that?"

"I'm dead inside and have a huge empty space like yours that can never be filled. I've lost the most important person in my life and am all alone. Can't go back home. Mother left to be with Warwick. My father's gone berserk and will never forgive me."

Sara wrapped her arms around and held her tight. "I saw the bus. But why?"

"Viking gods possessed his spirit. I had to release him. The kind man who runs the petting zoo had painted his buildings just before opening day. I got two cans of white from him and smeared it with my hands all over my dad's precious Gokstad ship. Then I stood there covered in paint, expecting to feel relieved but didn't because a Viking demon still glared at me from the prow. My dad wouldn't be free until I slew the dragon. I hauled one of his axes to the front of the bus, raised it high, and whacked that ugly head. Crying so hard I could hardly see, I hit it harder and harder until the prow fell and slammed into my side." Karina picked at her nails. "Some paint flecks are still under here."

Sara cuddled Karina in her arms. "I promise we'll find Pan in the morning. Now go to sleep."

In a cocoon of mud and silvery-gray moss, they sat like dead trees watching and listening as darkness consumed the swamp. Macabre voices shrieked and wailed: the steady hum of mosquitos, an owl's plaintive hooting, the fluttering of bat wings. A red glow loomed on the pond—the eyes of an army of submerged gators reflecting light. When most of the birds fell silent, frogs croaked, chirped, and clicked—some in piercing cries as if aware they were the main course for everything else in the swamp.

For Sara, there was something irresistible about the fusion of danger and the primeval beauty of a place so quiet and yet so loud. She welcomed the dark. To get a sense of her place in the universe, it had become more difficult to find skies unblemished by artificial light. She and Michael had lain in the Everest base camp gazing at these same stars during the same month but 17,600 feet higher.

# Chapter 23

As the ranger suggested, Ryker found a motel near the swamp's southern border. His phone at 100% for an emergency call or text, he sat on the edge of the bed. *You brave, ignorant fool. What dark rabbit hole have you run down? Where will you sleep? What will you eat? Have you found the boy and girl? Have Foster's thugs already caught, tortured, or killed you?*

He turned on the TV as a distraction but couldn't get Sara out of his head. He googled Okefenokee on his phone. Horrors. She could be surrounded by venomous snakes, wild boars, black bears, and 10,000 to 13,000 alligators. Add in two bloodthirsty stooges, and she might not make it through the night.

Instead of perched like a bulbous lump, he should be out there protecting her. He crawled into bed and felt guilty lying in comfort while she was trapped in his worst nightmare. He lay awake trying to convince himself this woman was an international adventure racer who'd been in swamps before and knew how to survive. She'd definitely be alive and well in the morning and call him first thing with good news. Or she, the boy, and girl could already be dead fodder for gators.


The quiet woke Sara just before dawn. Not even the flutter of a leaf broke the silence. It was as if the swamp held its breath waiting for day creatures to stir. A queer green mist seeped into the clearing and everything shimmered with the excitement of a new morning.

Sara gently released Karina and rose to her feet. She pried the remaining mud off her face and cast an eagle eye left and right—no imminent attack. She whipped the moss out of her hair and puffed a gray thread from her upper lip. Two feet away, a dusky colored frog made a peculiar whistling sound blowing up the sack beneath its chin. "Shhh," she whispered, "Don't wake Karina."

Sunlight burned through the mist, and a teal-blue sky looked down on the green and black world. No knobbed snouts or bulging eyes skimmed the surface of the water. Gators must have crawled onto land as the sun's warmth touched what was left of the cool darkness. Sara studied the bank for drag marks and bear or bobcat prints. When all seemed clear, she slowly waded in to wash mud off, hearing *plop, plop, plop, plop* as more turtles queued on a log dived into the water. She chuckled. Imagine anything in the swamp being afraid of her.

A gunshot woke Karina with a start. "What was that?"

Sara quickly waded back. "Those two men following us are in a world completely alien to theirs. They probably panicked at a gator or snake and fired. That's all they know how to do."

"Why are they after us?"

"It's a long story. Trust me. We have to get out of here now and find Pan. He'll be on the move again in daylight."

Sara broke two branches off a tree to use as hiking poles for balance through a mesh of gnarled roots threatening to pitch them headfirst into the mire. She fought a relentless battle with vines swiping at Karina's face. At this rate, Pan would slip beyond reach. An urgent message came in the bugling alarm of more cranes, perhaps warning of a two-legged intruder.

"Pan may have startled those birds," said Sara. "I can't judge the distance of their calls, but they appear to be coming from the other side of that slow moving river ahead." Sara had hesitated taking Karina into the water, but it was the best means of throwing Possum and Grouper off the trail. "Always keep the pole in front of you to check the ground and not step in a deep hole or trip over hidden, slippery roots."

To the sound of their feet squishing in mud, they floundered through murky water unable to see the bottom. Karina jumped and screamed when something touched her leg.

"Probably only a fish."

"Barracuda?"

"No, not the kind that swims. But the predators stalking us are just as dangerous and not far behind. I heard them grumbling."

Karina shuddered as if jolted by an electric shock. "Are they going to kill us?"

"I promise not to let that happen," Sara said, "but we must keep moving."

Half an hour after entering the water, Sara finally spotted a flock of the long-legged birds take to the air and fly on a thermal with their necks outstretched. If Pan's presence had alerted them, he probably wasn't too far ahead.

She and Karina passed a raccoon on the bank using its long, slender fingers to search for frogs or fish. With a defiant stare, it shuffled a few feet toward them as if to say *this is my space*.

Amused by its boldness, Sara said, "They eat alligator eggs. In retaliation, gators devour raccoons they catch when swimming."

In a dense grove of cypress trees, they wandered among the massive bottle-shaped trunks and conical knees until Sara located on their left the only feasible exit onto firmer ground. Thirty feet across on the right bank behind them, a congregation of gators basked in sunlight.

"They may look like statues sunning themselves along the swamp edge," she warned, "but they can react lightning fast."

Karina clutched Sara's arm. "Will they come after us?"

"Not if we're smart and stay at least fifteen feet away. If they hiss or show those god awful sharp teeth, we'll back off even more. If attacked, fight 'em. A gator once bit a guy I know. He escaped by boxing it on the snout and jamming fingers into its eyes."

Karina still held her injured side and winced. Sara needed to get her to safety. As they made it onto a shoreline covered in leaf litter, she noticed a dark–colored, banded snake sunning itself. First impression—venomous—but it didn't have the wide body and blocky head of a cottonmouth. A master of disguise, the non venomous, banded water snake flattened its body and head to appear more threatening as they passed.

*I mean you no harm. Enjoy the warmth.* She didn't alert Karina to the snake and spook her. They'd make better time if she weren't so despondent and scared.

"What will become of me? I can't go back to either parent. If I lose Pan too, I might as well just give up and die." Karina crossed her arms over her chest and scuffed at a gator drag mark. "And what will happen if you catch Pan?"

That question had gnawed at Sara from the first moment she withdrew pictures from his turret wall. "One option is to let him go free once he's safely out of the swamp and take you with him."

"Will you?"

"I honestly don't know what to do. It's complicated."

Karina abruptly turned her back on Sara and marched to the water's edge. The air grew heavy between them.

"We can talk about it later," Sara called to her. "But we have to go now. I heard the men behind us after we passed the racoon."

"I'm too tired."

As if the swamp's orchestra had tuned up to ease the tension, nature played a symphony with wind sighing in the tallest trees as an overture. Bullfrogs croaking their strange songs formed the bass; a cardinal trilled a solo with a chorus of chirping crickets; a cuckoo and a woodpecker drumming on a rotten tree made up the percussion.

But the music stopped when Possum came around a corner bent forward and swinging his entire weight left and right with each step, gun in hand. He didn't see the gators until one hurtled toward him. A horrific scream as he fired three rapid shots at its head forcing the razor-sharp teeth to release their hold. Thrashing wildly, the gator retreated underwater. Possum clawed his way onto the shore and lay there, his right thigh bleeding and his face mottled with swollen, red, mosquito bites. He'd lost his pistol.

"You putrid pond scum." Sara whipped the gun from her belt and held it at his head. "You'll bleed out if you don't put pressure on that bite using the weight of both arms."

The muscles in his jaw bunched as he uttered a mournful plea for her help.

"Hah, don't look at me. Where's your buddy?"

"Right here," shouted an unmistakable voice. "Drop your gun or the girl's dead."

Sara spun around and saw Grouper standing at the shore's edge where she and Karina had come aground. He gripped a pistol with both hands and aimed directly at Karina.

"Your cohort's going to die," said Sara, "if you don't stop the hemorrhaging by applying full pressure at least twenty minutes. Ease up and the bleeding will start all over again."

Grouper glowered at her. "We gave you every chance to just back off, but the job was more important than your own father. The New York cop got it right. Nobody will come to your funeral."

*You despicable weasels listening with your planted bugs.*

"We know you're chasing the satyr boy. By the time the gators are done feeding on the three of you, there won't be anything left to bury." He raised his arms to shoulder height, aimed, and wrapped his finger around the trigger.

"Wait, wait!" Sara screamed and lowered her gun. "Don't hurt her. I'll drop mine. Do what you must with me but let these kids go. Pan won't turn himself in. Case unsolved. Foster wins the election."

"And you turn us over to the police on some bogus charge."

"It's called blackmail."

"Well, that ain't happening. The girl's not getting out of here either. She knows too much." He turned his pistol on Sara. "Drop your gun."

She tossed it slightly to his left onto the leaf litter. Pointing his gun and keeping an eye on her, he reached down and hurled hers across the water at the gators.

"Aaaaahh!"

He leaped sideways, lifted his pant leg, and shrieked. The high pitched, nasal screams flushed hundreds of grackles from the trees, a whoosh of air as the iridescent birds swept into the sky.

Sara snickered to herself. "Snake bite you? I know the ways of a swamp. Let me take a look at it."

Grouper shook all over as if riding on a washboard road and pointed to an agitated snake.

"Appears you pissed off a cottonmouth, one of the deadliest vipers on the planet, but your death will come slower than from other species. You won't notice anything for quite a while, but the venom is already beginning to destroy the lining of your red blood cells making your blood unable to clot. First you'll bleed from the ankle bite, then the mucus membranes in your mouth and eyes. As your insides liquefy, your kidneys can't filter that many dead cells. They'll fail. Muddled and woozy, you'll puke all over yourself."

His face turned the color of a shammy skin. "Isn't there a kind of medicine for snake bites?"

"Some venomous species have no antivenom. Fortunately, the cottonmouth does, but you need the injection before it's too late. Even then, the venom is so strong you'll have to go back many times for blood tests to make sure your blood is clotting properly. Could be for years."

"I saw a guy in a movie who sucked the venom out and then

tied a tourniquet above it."

She laughed. "Old cowboy tales. Wrap your ankle and entire leg to immobilize it. Then stay put. Movement spreads the venom faster. And you with the gator bite will lose that leg if you don't get antibiotics soon. Gators carry bacteria in their mouths from eating rotten meat."

Grouper pointed his gun at Karina. "You'll help us get out of here or the girl's dead."

"And what am I supposed to do? Neither of you can walk, and we can't carry two gorillas through a swap."

He waved the gun back and forth between Karina and Sara. "Come up with something now or I shoot you both."

"Hmm, well then, I choose bullets over gators. Their powerful jaws break bones to get chunks of meat the right size to fit down their throats. And they digest anything they swallow, not leaving a trace you ever existed."

Possum cried out, "My leg's killing me. Do something."

"Shut up!" Grouper shouted back. "I'm the one who could die."

"You're both disgustingly pathetic," said Sara, "so here's the deal. You sit still while I make it to a nearby town in forty minutes. I've lived and worked in these parts five years and know my way out of here and the outlying area."

"Put your damn gun down," said Possum, "and let them go."

"Smart man," said Sara. "But, oh, there's the question whether I'll send help back or just serve you up as gator fodder. What's in it for me?"

"My not killing you both."

"You're a moron but not that stupid. I'm your only chance of staying alive."

Sara took Karina's hand. "Come on, sweetheart, let's go into town and get you something to eat and drink."

"You can't leave us here to die."

"And why is that?"

"It's . . . it's inhuman . . . sadistic."

"And against the law," Possum shouted angrily.

She turned her back on them and waved goodbye. "Enjoy your last few hours, boys."

An anguished cry from Grouper. "Stop. We can pay or make a deal. Whatever it takes."

Sara kept walking. "Not interested."

"Something that will sway the election."

"Don't need it. I've solved the case and will turn the killer in."

"I trusted you," Karina said, trying to pull her hand free.

Sara squeezed it and picked up her pace. "I'm negotiating."

"Is there antivenom in that town?" Grouper asked.

"This close to a swamp with venomous snakes? Of course, as well as antibiotics for your buddy's leg."

"We have information," said Possum.

Sara turned with a gaping yawn and rubbed her eyelids. "I'm too tired to play games. I need more."

"We're dead men if we talk."

"You're dead if you don't. Your choice. I leave you alone here with no chance of getting out alive. Or give me what I want, and I'll send medical help back."

Grouper said, "What do you want to know?"

"Foster's agenda. I've got your mug shots on my phone and the recorder is on. Your time's running out. Talk fast."

The goons exchanged glances before Grouper spoke, "Foster becomes mayor and the village lease runs out a few months later."

"Sorry, nothing new or illegal." Sara backed away and turned. "So long, fellows."

"He hired an arsonist," Possum screamed after her.

Sara halted. "Go on."

"He's planning to set fire to the village."

She spun around. "You bastards. When's this taking place?"

"That's our trump card. If help arrives, we'll tell you when."

She curled both hands into fists and demanded he repeat

that Foster ordered their deaths and planned a village fire."

Neither of them would make eye contact.

"I will only ask one more time."

Their silence said it all, but she wanted it on record. "It's a yes or no answer. My sending help back here to save your pitiful lives depends on a truthful one."

Empty faces.

She filled her lungs and let the air seep out. "Deal's off. Even if you could walk, you'd be miserably lost and easy prey. Good luck. You've got one pistol between you to use on gators or yourselves."

An irritating voice yelled, "Yes, yes, yes."

"Okay." She turned her phone toward them. "We know your names but state them for the record, confess to blackmailing me, and then give the dirt on your boss."

As his prize henchmen ratted Foster out, Sara wore a gleeful smile and did a little victory dance before sauntering off.

"You agreed to send help for us," Grouper yelled after her.

Karina looked up at Sara. "Are you leaving them to die?"

She snickered. "Of course not. I lied about the snake being poisonous but had to make them want our help or they would have shot us on the spot. Story of the other guy and antibiotics is true. I need them stay put until police arrive. I have GPS coordinates."

"So you have been in here before and can find our way out?"

"No, but I've navigated enough other swamps to understand the flora and fauna."

While racing, Sara endured thirst and hunger and went days without sleep. For Karina this was a terrifying experience much in need of the anomaly lying ahead—a snake with a strange upturned snout. Sara knew it was an eastern hognose but let the scene play. It flattened its body, raised its head like a cobra, hissed, and struck at Karina. But strangely, it didn't reach her or open its mouth. Sara defended her by tapping it with her stick, but not too hard. It jerked convulsively, twisted onto its back, and remained motionless with its tongue hanging out and expelling small drops of blood. A foul-smelling musk mixed with feces dribbled from its rear.

"You killed it," Karina shouted in a kind of euphoria.

"It's not dangerous and only pretending to be dead. Watch."

Sara gently turned it over with her stick. It promptly rolled onto its back again as if to make sure they knew it was dead. They skirted around it and had gone about ten feet when Karina was attacked by an uncontrollable fit of laughter. The snake had raised its head, looked around, rolled onto its belly, and begun slithering away. She stomped her foot, and it flipped onto its back, mouth open, tongue hanging out, more stinking musk.

Sara finally couldn't contain herself. "It's a hilarious hognose and will keep playing dead until we're gone." As with telling Pan about water holding frogs, she lamented not having children to share her wonderful, adventurous world.

The hognose was a necessary diversion, but Sara's heart beat painfully in her chest as she agonized about which way Pan had gone and what to do when she found him. The threat to her father's life still loomed heavily over her if she turned the boy in.

"What happens if police catch Pan?"

"I can't say for sure. It depends on the court. Being seventeen with such a compelling story, he may not be judged too harshly. But the brutality of the murder will argue against him. He'll serve time. The question is how long and where. What about you?"

"I won't give up on him."

"You'd wait through what could be many years?"

"Yes."

"In the meantime, what will you do when we get back?"

A single shoulder shrug.

Intent on their conversation, Sara hadn't noticed a rustling in the brush until a wild boar crashed through a thicket and bolted toward them, grunting and tusks raised.

# Chapter 24

Sara knew boars weighing hundreds of pounds could charge at short speeds with no provocation. Instinctively she reached for her gun. *Damn. It's gator trash.* The only means of escape was climbing the nearest tree. She dragged Karina to a pine. "Grab a branch and pull yourself up."

"I can't. My side hurts too much."

Grunts only a few yards away.

"Grab anything you can find."

Helpless sobbing.

Sara squatted and ordered, "Quick, get on my shoulders and I'll boost you onto the lowest branch."

Then with a surge of adrenalin, Sara hoisted herself up just as razor-sharp tusks nicked the bottom of her shoe. "Move higher. It's growling and walking up the trunk with its front legs."

When Karina's limb bent under her weight, she shrieked.

"Quiet. You'll anger it even more."

Sara found small toe holds on the trunk and stood clinging to a slender, overhead branch.

"Why'd it come after us?" said Karina.

"They don't usually attack humans but get pretty aggressive during rutting season. We must have invaded its territory."

"I didn't see them."

The testy boar was still going at it, standing on its back legs, the front hooves scraping the bark. Five-inch tusks on its lower jaw jabbed at her. Smaller upper ones sheared them like a whetstone to sharpen weapons capable of stabbing prey.

Pressing hard on the tenuous toe holds made Sara's foot go to sleep. Her calves burned. Her arms ached.

"My butt's sore and needles are poking me in the face," said Karina. "What'll we do?"

"Be patient and wait it out. It'll either get bored or lured away by a luscious porcine passing by."

For no apparent reason, the boar suddenly sniffed the air.

"What's going on?" Karina asked.

"No idea. Maybe the scent of a male rival."

Pan emerged from the dense forest wielding a knife. The boar moved toward him for a better look. The hackles on its shoulders raised. The boar swung its head, displaying the menacing tusks.

Pan turned slightly with his weight even on both feet, one in front of the other facing his opponent . . . blade ready.

The boar charged and thrust its head upward, gouging Pan's thigh and groin. It retreated a foot and then attacked again, butting and flipping him over.

Sara screamed, "Go for the throat!"

Vulnerable on his back beneath the boar, Pan drove his knife deep into its neck. Squealing, it foamed at the mouth. When Pan struck again, it spewed slobber and fell onto its side, gushing blood.

Pan withdrew the blade, pushed himself onto his feet, and just stood there, immobile, his arm hanging at his side.

Karina cried, "Get me down! Get me down!"

Her foot still asleep, Sara carefully dropped to the ground on the other leg and held her arms up to lower Karina.

She rushed to Pan. "How'd you find us?"

"I never left you far behind. I watched what Sara did with the mosquitos and covered myself in mud too. This morning, I startled those birds to let you know I was near. But when you screamed, my heart stopped. I couldn't let you die too."

Sara knew the next words out of her mouth had to reassure Pan, not frighten him into fleeing. She recalled the training on how to talk to suspects under stress, but it blurred as her mind tried to construct a scenario where everything turned out all right.

She went over to him. "That was remarkably brave, but you could have been killed."

"I put you in danger."

"We've all made it this far." Sara reached for her phone to get the coordinates. Gone. "Karina, my phone must have fallen out my pocket when I dropped from the tree. Find it while I look at Pan."

"Let me see that leg." Sara knelt before he could take off again. "You're lucky the tusks didn't go deeper, but you still need medical attention to avoid infection. Boars carry dangerous bacteria." She spoke softly out of Karina's earshot. "Why'd you leave her alone?"

"I knew she'd be safe with you. I panicked and wasn't thinking straight when I even agreed to let her come. I'll end up in jail and don't want her throwing her life away waiting for me."

"But you love each other, and it may not be too long."

Karina came up behind her and handed Sara the phone. "What may not be too long?"

Sara got back on her feet. "The jail sentence. Hopefully, courts will take into consideration Pan came back to rescue us and turned himself in."

"But you have to help us escape."

"Believe me, my heart wants to." Tears welled in Sara's eyes. "Because I care about you both so very much, but you'd never be free. Always on the run, always looking over your shoulder. You'd never have a life together. Right now, we have to focus on getting out of here before two city boy idiots realize they've been conned."

"I saw a canal ahead on the left," said Pan. "Maybe they won't follow us in there."

He led and Sara took up the rear, noting landmarks for police. They reached slow moving water with moss-laced trees reflecting off its black mirror top. Water lilies with aromatic white flowers swayed side to side carpeting the sunny areas but also the swamp's murky depths that concealed both the dangerous and benign.

They entered up to their thighs. Sara cautioned, "Water hides pitfalls like slippery mud that sucks you in over your head before you know it." As their legs fought to push through the water, gator eyes peered above its eerie, black surface and from behind cypress.

"You can't escape feeling you're being watched," said Sara, "because you are." She asked Pan, "Where's your mother's picture and the iPad?"

"I slipped in muddy water and lost my bag with everything in it. Gun shots shifted me into fast gear without looking back."

Suddenly, a man's voice yelling, "Whut're ya doin' thar?" sent a shock wave through Sara. Had Foster hired a local mercenary?

An old man in a flat-bottomed boat, pole in hand, said, "Ain't safe out hur in this mean ol' swamp."

Reluctant to tell the truth in case he was an armed bounty hunter eager to turn Pan over for his reward, Sara stammered, "We . . . we were—"

"Spik up." His head tilted as if listening with only one ear.

She spotted a fishing line hanging over the stern. "Yesterday, we . . . uh . . . were fishing and a gator knocked a hole right through our boat and came after us." She showed the blood-stained knife. "This brave young man stabbed it in the eye."

"Thun whut happen?"

"Gator swam away," said Pan.

"Ya poor things. But whar's yer boat?"

"Sank."

"Ain't no use look' fer it then."

Standing in the stern, he poled the boat in closer to them. He wore overalls with a green flannel shirt and a tattered hat that bent his ears down under its weight. His wrinkled, gray face reminded her of the potato head she'd carved as a kid and let dry. His nose almost touched his chin over a toothless mouth that kept moving in a sucking motion. A brown dog with sloppy jowls and long ears leaned over the prow to sniff the strangers.

"Git in," he said offering a hand. "Shun't nuver go out if'n ya don't know the swamp. Waters always a changin'. Way ya cum in the mornin' might be covered with peat an' gone that night."

He seemed as harmless as the banded water snake and their sole chance of escaping and finding medical help for Pan. "Go ahead and climb in," she told Pan and Karina.

All three securely seated, the old man edged them away from the bank. "Hear all that gargling in the night? It's the male gators callin' fur a mate." Bending beneath low lying boughs, he poled through a tunnel of dense interlocking branches into water that was like wine-colored glass reflecting giant cypress and sweetgum trees in mirror images. For Sara, their solitude and beauty helped diminish the terror of the past two days.

The boat slid between cypress rising from massive bottle shaped trunks like the splayed out feet of giants. Their dark roots poked up through the water in twisted, deformed knees. A large, olive-brown snake basked on one within a few inches of the boat. It stared at them, eyes green-slitted and cold, and drew back its broad head, its open mouth displaying a creamy–white lining.

"Cottonmouth," said the old man as it slid into the water and swam off leaving only the high, sweet smell of parsley.

Sara watched the shadow his stooped body cast on the water as he talked about growing up in this strange world of eerie light. "Ain't nuver had no schoolin' like city folks, but I knows the ways of the swamp. Callin' of a tree frog means rain. An' snake eggs is a sure cure fer stutters."

The dog stood with its paws on the bow, head and shoulders

straining forward to point the way. It had too much skin for its body. Pan pulled it up over the dog's forehead in folds and watched it slowly roll down again. "What's his name?"

"Brown Dog."

Sara's heart ached knowing Pan might not share such a bond for many years to come, if ever again. The old man's anecdotes had momentarily deflected the inevitable anguish of turning him over to McBride. What if she was wrong about the courts and they put him away for the majority of his adult life for a crime committed when he was fourteen and traumatized by the vulgar rape of his mother? A fiery vengeance had smoldered within him for three years. What would prison do to his soul? He might not survive.

They reached the pier of a gas station on a deserted dirt road. Sara asked the old man where to find the nearest medical center and police station.

"Ya needin' help fur the boy?"

"Yes, and I'm sorry for bothering you."

"Shucks, t'ain't nothin' gittin' thar. Folks hur help each other. I knows the owner of that thar truck. He be lendin' it to us."

The old man borrowed an old pickup with rusted sides and frayed upholstery. Sara climbed into the cab and let Pan and Karina share time alone together in the bed. Both had been robbed of their childhoods and faced dark, uncertain futures. She felt like giving them a credit card to buy what they need and disappear.

As soon as they entered a small town with cell service, Ryker's ringtone announced five text messages, all asking what was going on. Her stomach was too gnarled up to talk now. She checked her location. Thankfully, they'd come out in northern Florida and the same county as Reunion Heights.

The truck stopped at a police station. "This what yer needin'?"

"Yes, there's one more favor to ask. Two men are still in the swamp close to where you picked us up. I'm very happy to pay you to show the police where that was."

"Sure 'nuf. But got no need fer yer money."

"You're too kind. I'll forever owe you." Sara got out and closed the cab door with an extra push to make sure it shut tight. "I'll be right back."

She displayed her badge to the desk sergeant and explained the urgency of the situation. She wrote down the coordinates and landmarks noted in her phone. "The old man out front knows the swamp and will recognize these. You should be able to go by water most of the way. The men are dangerous and armed, but they're seriously rattled. I convinced the taller one that he was bitten by a cottonmouth and will soon experience an excruciating death. The other one had a run-in with a gator and needs antibiotics."

A grin spread across the officer's face. "How'd you get away with that?"

"They're ignorant New Yorkers, totally out of their element."

"If we reach these guys, then what?"

"Cuff them and immediately confiscate their cell phones. Say you don't stock antivenom because most visitors take guided tours, rather than risk entering a perilous swamp on their own. Use your siren to convince them of the gravity of their situation. They must  get to the ER at St Joseph's hospital in Reunion Heights We'll take over from there."

Sara returned to the truck. Brown Dog barked and wagged his tail, jowls slobbering. Pan scratched his ears. "Take care, fella."

She lowered the tail gate for Karina and him to climb down, his face evincing pain.

"Ya got summun helpin'?"

"Police will follow you. I can take care of the rest."

"Yer sartin?"

"Positive. Thank you again."

Three minutes later, the truck disappeared in a whirl of dust followed by two cars. No one had eaten since early yesterday. They walked along what appeared to be main street to an outdoor café. While Pan and Karina scarfed down burgers and fries, she stepped away to phone Ryker.

"Where in the world are you?" he said.

"In some small town. Why was your phone off? I desperately needed help?"

"Meeting with Foster's backers, I couldn't blow my cover."

Sara crossed the street to a sign. "I'm in Boxerville, Florida, population thirty–five hundred."

"You alone?"

"No, with Karina and Pan."

"You tracked them down in a swamp?"

"Long story. Now this is only between you and me." She lowered her voice. "It's hard for me to bring this boy in."

"He killed the guy. Made a bloody mess out of him."

"I know, believe me I do. But Gunnar forced Pan to witness the rape of his mother."

"Then I would have chopped that prick into pieces, one inch at a time with him alive and screaming."

*Whoa.* Sara was taken aback. Ryker was a bit short on mouth control. Clearly, abusive men were a sensitive subject, but he needed to hear the rest. "Pan's mother was so despondent she committed suicide right in front of him a few weeks later. That's why I'm struggling with the arrest." She watched Pan and Karina sitting close and holding onto each other. Choking up, she had to turn away. "It's time we disclosed the details of the blackmail and coercion to McBride so he'll know why the local police are bringing in two goons."

The pain of her last two days dissolved into a smile. "I played these fools into believing they faced imminent death. I took mug shots and taped both of them admitting Foster hired an arsonist to set a village fire and ordered our death. With what I've got on my phone, he's done for. So far, he thinks his thugs killed me and the kids. Case goes unsolved and he wins the election. If Foster learns I solved it before we're done here, my father's still at risk."

"You're not the only one on the job. I'm in tight with Foster's backers planning a massive money laundering scheme but have no verifiable proof. Now that you've got me, what do you need?"

"A ride to St Joseph's. Text me when you arrive."

Sara cleared the tears in her throat and returned to the café. "Time to take care of you two. A town this size should have some kind of medical center. Pan, you did the right thing by turning yourself in. Swear you won't do anything foolish."

"We've talked it over and understand yours is the only way."

The love in his face and eyes as he gazed at Karina convinced Sara that he sincerely cared about her and could be trusted. Three blocks down main street, they found a walk–in medical center. She registered them both and took responsibility for all charges. Sara didn't accompany Pan to the exam room. The groin injury would require an intimate diagnosis and treatment that could embarrass him. She did go with Karina to help soothe her nerves as the girl glanced about the room anxiously.

A doctor gently pressed her rib cage and listened to her lungs as she took deep breaths. "Feels like two bruised ribs."

"Can you take an x-ray?" said Sara.

"Yes, but it may not tell much if it's a fresh injury or if they're only cracked. I don't have CAT or MRI machines. You'd have to go down to St Joseph's for that. This type of injury generally heals itself in about six weeks. She should ice it and go easy until then."

Sara glanced at Karina. "I'm sure you'll do whatever it takes."

The canal had washed most of the mud and blood off, but Sara didn't want the kids to enter the police station looking like riff raff. She took Karina to a woman's restroom to wash her face, arms, and hands with soap and warm water.

"Have you and Pan really thought this whole thing through and talked about how and where you'll stay while he's in jail?"

Karina's eyes moistened. "Pan said his uncle's very kind and will understand what happened. He'll also be lonely with both his sister and nephew gone. Or maybe I can stay with Naira's family until we know where they'll send him."

Sara splashed water over her own face and pulled a paper towel down from the dispenser. "His uncle seems like a good man, but at some point, you have to be able to feed and clothe yourself."

"My mother taught me how to make jewelry, and I learned how to sell goods from both parents. I'll find work near Pan and see him on visiting days." She wiped tears clinging to the sides of her hair. "I have to hope they won't hold him too many years."

Sara and Karina went back into the lobby and waited for Pan. A minute later, a nurse entered. "The young man will be fine and is in the restroom. We cleaned the wound and stitched it, but he still needs to take antibiotics and should start on them now. Here's a prescription for the pharmacy next door."

"I'll go fill it. Stay here, Karina and tell him I'll be right back."

A woman unable to control two rambunctious children was in line ahead of Sara. The ever present question. Had mom not raised them well, or did they pop out of the womb that way? *How would I contend with such unruly kids? Moot question. Late thirties would be pushing it.*

Gone ten minutes, she expected Pan to be waiting with Karina. "He's not done yet?"

"I listened at the door and still heard running water. I think he wants a few moments alone before the police."

A wisp of doubt. Surely, he wasn't dumb enough to screw this up. She knocked on the restroom door. "Pan, time to go now."

Nothing but a steady flow of water.

Sara tried the knob. Locked.

"Does this bathroom have a window?" she asked the nurse.

"Yes. Is something wrong?"

"Please take care of the girl." Sara ran onto the street but go in which direction? She asked an elderly couple outside an ice cream parlor, "Did a teenage boy about this tall," she gestured with one hand, "and wearing blood stained pants come by here?"

The man said, "He wanted to know where the bus station is."

"And?"

His wife pointed. "I told him about a mile up the highway."

Pan could have a fifteen-minute head start and board a bus before she caught him. Sara took off with the burst of energy at the start of every race. Only she wasn't running for glory this time but to save the life of a boy she cared deeply about.

The soles of her shoes slapping the asphalt highway echoed in her ears, but Sara's mind raced faster than her feet. If he made it onto a bus, she'd have to call for road blocks. If he got off before the next stop, police would go after him with dogs and show no mercy. She had to reach him first. The wind whipping her face, she sped past a blur of parked cars, shop windows, children playing.

No sign of Pan. *Where are you?* He knew she'd come after him and might have veered from the path. A former world class runner should be able to overtake an injured boy. Beads of sweat dripped from her forehead. She'd never given up no matter how dangerous a climb or difficult a race and wouldn't in this most crucial one.

Still no sign of him. The old couple could have been confused and sent her in the opposite direction. Too late to turn back. At a truck stop, she reached a complex of parked semis as daunting as the swamp.

She charged into the restaurant. "Police. Has anyone seen a teenage boy this tall with blood on his pants."

Not a word, only stark silence.

She raced back out. He could be hiding among the trucks or have already hitched a ride and be twenty miles away. Sara darted between them, climbed onto running boards to check inside, and dropped to her knees to peer underneath each row. She'd caught that biker in a parking lot and was determined to find her satyr.

Spotting a familiar pair of sneakers and pant legs fifteen feet ahead, she crept behind a Walmart trailer. "Pan, it's Sara. Don't do this. Come with me."

"I can't."

"Yes, you can. It's the only way. Think of Karina."

"I am thinking of her." His voice waned. He was moving away and had bailed on her.

She ran from behind the trailer and saw him on the highway shoulder. "You couldn't leave her in the swamp."

"Because she was in danger. I know she's safe with you now."

"But you never will be. They'll hunt you down like an animal."

His feet pounded the asphalt harder and faster.

She followed. "Pan, you have to turn yourself in."

"Stay back!"

Panting, she slowed, both hands up in defensive mode. "Okay, okay. Stop and let's talk this over."

He halted and turned to face her.

"Please, I beg you. Come with me. It's the only way you'll have a life. " Sara took a few steps forward.

"I told you to stay back."

"All right. Sorry. Karina loves you will wait as long as it takes."

"That's my point. I love her too much to let her do that for me."

Sara moved a foot closer. "It may not be too long. You're young and have such a compelling story to tell. Gunnar assaulted other women too. A jury will listen."

"And if it doesn't? This is my only chance to set Karina free."

He took off again across the highway just as a red SUV came around a blind curve.

"Stop!" Sara screamed.

# Chapter 25

Horn blaring. Brakes squealing. SUV swerving. The thud of metal striking flesh.

A shrill cry pierced the air as Sara raced across the highway to Pan lying on his side in fetal position. Fingertips to his neck, she found a pulse. "Help! Somebody call an ambulance!"

The driver ran to her, visibly shaken, his voice trembling. "I didn't see him and couldn't stop fast enough."

"I know. I know. Not your fault."

Sara felt as if cut glass under her skin had shredded every part of her being. "Why didn't you come with me?" Sobbing, she pressed Pan's hand to her cheek. "Please forgive me. I should have listened, understood, not pushed you to the brink. You could have boarded a bus and soared like an eagle until a thunderstorm came." She sniffled to clear the tears. "You deserved moments of freedom. I robbed you of them."

Two emergency personnel arrived within three minutes, the benefit of a small town. Sara wiped her eyes and displayed her ID. "He'd given himself up. I was bringing him in."

They checked his vitals and placed him on a stretcher to load into the ambulance, procedures she'd witnessed many times. But this was different. This was the son she never had, the Greek god Pan—protector of shepherds, goatherds, and their flocks.

"Miss, he's still unconscious and may have internal injuries. To which hospital?"

"Huh?" His words pulled her out of a fog. "Oh, St Joseph's in Reunion Heights is the closest. I'll call ahead for someone from our station to meet you."

Sara phoned McBride who blew up before she could even get a word out. "Where've you been? The fair closes tonight, and I don't have a goddamn suspect."

She exhaled a long, staggered breath to create some air space between them. "I found the killer, a seventeen-year-old kid who was forced to watch his mother being raped. He's injured and on his way to St Joseph's. Meet the ambulance." She could hear him collapse in his chair. "There's more. The Boxerville police will bring two of Foster's henchmen. Put them in a private room. They think they're dying. Call me the instant they arrive. I have leverage to use against Foster."

"Who, how—?"

"Quiet, listen to me. Don't arrest Foster yet. He must not know they failed to murder and dispose of two kids and me or that his men are in custody."

Sara hung up, entered the truck stop restaurant, and went to the restroom. She leaned on the sink with both hands and stared at a face as gray as an old headstone. Karina shouldn't see her like this. She washed off the sweat and tears and finger combed her hair. From an order of iced tea, she wrapped the cubes in paper napkins and pressed them against her lids to reduce the redness and puffiness from crying.

Sara called Ryker. "How close are you?"

"Fifteen minutes according to Google Maps. Something's not right. What's going on?"

Air didn't seem to reach her lungs. Her lips were moving but no sound came out.

"Talk to me, Sara."

"Pan did a runner to protect Karina. He's been hit by an SUV and is unconscious with possible internal injuries." She paused to steady herself. "Paramedics are taking him to St Joseph's. McBride will meet the ambulance. Karina's waiting at the medical center on main street and doesn't know about the accident."

"Where are you?"

"At a truck stop a mile up the highway. Stay with her and say I'm on my way, but don't let on you know anything. That onus falls on me."

Walking back along the road, Sara felt as though someone had thrown the OFF switch and shut her entire system down. In her job, she'd broken news to family members of the death of loved ones, but nothing wrenched her gut like this.

When Sara entered the lobby, Karina rushed to her. "Did you find him? Is he okay?"

Truth lay in a deep, dark place. She couldn't bear to unearth it yet. "We'll talk on the way back to the village."

"Why? Did something happen?"

"Let's start home. Ryker's car is outside. He'll drive us back. Come sit with me in the rear seat."

"I don't understand what's going on. Where's Pan and why'd he leave me?"

Sara chose the words carefully so no regrettable ones would slip from her tongue. "Because he loved you too much to let you put your life on hold."

"Then you talked to him?" A smile hung around the edges of Karina's mouth. "So you let him go?"

"I couldn't, sweetheart."

"Yes, you could."

"No, always on the run, he'd never be free with you or himself. I begged him to come back, pleaded with him to stop."

"Then where is he?"

"On his way back to town."

"Why not with us?"

"He was injured in an accident. An ambulance is taking him to the hospital."

Water streaming down her face, she pummeled Sara. "You

did this to him."

As insoluble lump in Sara's throat. "He was running away to save you from ruining your life and didn't see an SUV."

Karina's heart chilling screams broke through the final layer of Sara's isolation and defenses erected as a child. She cradled the inconsolable girl until her tears ran dry. Karina laid her head in Sara's lap, so stuffed up she could barely breathe.

Sara stroked her hair. "He stayed in the swamp until you were safe. Regardless of what happens, you'll carry his love with you forever. Few of us ever experience one so everlasting and selfless."

Sara gently fluttered her fingertips along the girl's face and arms in butterfly kisses until she fell asleep. "I don't know what will happen to her now," Sara whispered to Ryker. "Neither parent is there for her."

"You could be wrong. My daughter felt I didn't care when in truth I loved her with all my heart. Maybe we men aren't so good at expressing it."

She noticed him watching her in the mirror. "What? Do you have something else to say?"

"We had several suspects: a jealous Viking, king, Nicu, or the blacksmith. Power hungry Warwick, vindictive queen. From all of them, how'd you come up with this boy?"

"Everything was circumstantial. We had no proof. And the tattoo obliteration puzzled me. There had to be a darker motive. If I hadn't checked past engagements with the Knights Invincible, I wouldn't have gone to the boy's uncle and discovered Pan lied to me. He claimed his mother died of cancer nineteen months ago, but his uncle said she died in a hiking accident three years ago. Why do that? And why run if innocent?"

Sara lightly touched Karina's cheek to ensure she was asleep. "The single brown hair forensics found on Gunnar matched Pan's satyr legs. And a drawing of Gunnar's tattoo was stuffed in the wall of his turret. There's no other way he could have known what it looked like. As to motive, I presumed it had to do with his mother. He would never talk about her and had an emotional breakdown when she died. As for means, I bagged two matching daggers from the Mail Works. He could have wiped one clean or disposed of it some other way."

"Opportunity?"

"After taking Karina home Friday night, he could have walked past the swing under a full moon about the time Gunnar and Adara were going at it."

"I get it now and am truly sorry. I know how much he and the girl mean to you."

As they neared Reunion Heights, Sara phoned McBride. "Are you at the hospital?"

"The boy's in surgery now. They don't know anything yet."

"Ryker and I are bringing Karina in."

"I'll meet you at the station and have a female officer ready."

"Thanks. We're only a few minutes out."

Sara gently woke Karina. "We're at the police station."

She held her side, whimpering, "I don't want to go in there."

"It's okay. Someone's waiting to help you."

"Am I in trouble?"

"Oh, no, they'll simply ask a few questions."

"When can I see Pan? I know you said he doesn't want me to put my life on hold, but I need to see it in his face and hear it from his lips. I want to tell him how much I love him and that my life would be nothing without him."

"He's still in surgery now and will take a while to come out of recovery. Even then, he'll be a little groggy." Sara put her arm around Karina and walked her into the station. "I promise someone will take you to him as soon as he's allowed to have a visitor."

McBride gave Sara a telling look as he told the female officer to take Karina to the break room for something to eat and a place to rest. Then he spoke to her privately in the hallway. "You look like a mildewed dishrag someone wrung out."

She wiped the back of her sleeve across her eyes. "I admit this one tore me up. I got too emotionally involved."

"Does she have family we can call? We'll watch over her until arrangements can be made, but she'll need someone here when the doctor tells her about the boy. His injuries were more extensive than was first thought. He's not likely to make it through the night."

McBride's words struck the air with a hollow sound. This couldn't be true. Sara fell back against the wall and slid down to the floor. She sat slouched, unable to see through the tears clouding her eyes. "I would have fought in court for him with every part of my being and never given up. He's so young. I should have set him free."

"But you couldn't."

"I know. But now Karina's lost everything and has nowhere to turn. I must help her."

"Do what you need to," said McBride. "I'll greet Foster's men at the hospital."

Sara pushed back onto her legs. "Turn up the heat and make them sweat."

"Where are you going?"

"To convince a derelict mother to nurture her daughter. I've already sent Ryker to fetch Pan's uncle."

Sara took a patrol car to the village hoping she can control her captious tongue. Late afternoon on closing day, Freya had already shuttered her jewelry shop. Assuming she no longer resided in the bus, Sara sought her out at the arena and found her on the grassy hill watching the final joust—Warwick's bravado.

"What now?" piped the goddess of love and beauty.

*Take a deep breath. Be civil. You need to win this woman over.* Sara sat next to her. "Do you know where your daughter is?"

"What business is that of yours?"

"It's kind of what I do."

Freya's chest swelled when Warwick galloped onto the field, a lance tucked under his arm.

"I repeat, do you know or even care where she is?"

"Why? Are you her baby sitter?" Freya didn't take her eyes off Warwick. "Daddy's little girl, his treasure, is probably with him."

"Were you aware of her boyfriend?"

"She's too young for that."

"No, she's not. The young man she loves was critically injured in an accident today. Your daughter's endured a tragic ordeal and desperately needs support. It's time you stepped up."

"I live with Warwick now. His place is barely large enough for two. I was on my own at Karina's age and turned out just fine."

"As a lying adulteress? Is that the morality you wish to bestow on your only child?"

"I learned life's lessons the hard way and have spent the last eighteen years as a good mother. Now it's time for me. When the fair closes, Warwick and I will go west. Karina can stay with that Seminole friend of hers."

"How and when did you lose your soul?"

"Life betrayed me with false hopes of who I am and what I could become."

"Is that what you want for Karina?"

"She has to find her own way. I can't do that for her."

*You feckless wretch. Even the most primitive animal species care more for their young than you do.*

Sara fought to chain her loathing of the woman and walked away before she did something that could get her in serious legal trouble. She remembered a little girl standing beneath a waterfall with a man who felt Thor's hammer crackling through him. Karina couldn't imagine anything better in this world than being there.

Leery of him, Sara approached his booth expecting Stieg to be foaming at the mouth like a rabid dog over the destruction of his hallowed ship. The instant he saw her, he rushed from behind his counter. She was in no mood for this. Every muscle in her body tensed preparing for a fight.

His brows rose in the middle, and his mouth curled down. "Do you have news of my daughter?"

Sara did a quick double take and had to revise her reaction to the berserker standing before her. "Ah . . . yes I do."

He wheeled around and signaled her to follow him to the back room. Stieg moved leather pieces off a box to create a seat. "Is she all right?"

"She has a couple of bruised ribs suffered when she whacked the dragon prow."

He sat across from her. "I thought it might have been Karina and can't blame her. I drank too much and went crazy after finding out Freya was pregnant. Can she ever forgive me?"

"Your daughter needs you right now."

He rolled his shoulders forward and hunched over staring at the floor with his hands clasped between his knees. "Your being here tells me something's gone wrong."

"Were you aware of her friendship with the boy who dresses as a satyr?"

"I guessed there was someone but didn't know who. And I may have been too strict trying to protect her heart." He wiped a hand down over his face as if to erase fatigue. "It destroys your soul when someone breaks it."

"And makes it so difficult to mend or trust again," she agreed.

Sara watched the flicker of emotion in the eyes of an ironic confidant as she told the story of Karina's love for Pan, the murder, their escape, the swamp, his accident and uncertain future. "She's lost and alone. Her entire world has disintegrated around her."

"Why didn't she ask me for help?"

"She was scared of what you'd become and destroyed the

bus to set you free."

"That was my Ragnarok. Thor's dead and can't take control of me again."

"I'm curious. Why'd you lie about where you were the night of the murder? You must have surmised it cast suspicion on you."

"In Louisiana, I learned Freya had been with Gunnar."

"You challenged him in the arena."

He nodded. "And I thought that ended it until the knights were at this fair too. I followed her to his trailer. They spoke but he didn't let her in. She was used to men fawning over her, not shutting the door in her face. When I heard he was dead, I thought her ego had sought retribution. I lied rather than lose my family."

"Then you discovered she was with someone else here."

He closed his fingers tight until the knuckles turned white. "Yes, Warwick the Black. I'm done fighting for my goddess. I need to be the father my daughter deserves. Where is she?"

"At the police station. Bring her a cherry malt."

The hand that had gripped Sara in a fist all day loosened its hold. She returned to the station. Ryker was pacing outside. "Climb into my car. McBride's screaming for you to get to the hospital."

"Why?"

He hit the accelerator as soon as she cleared the door. "Two musclemen are whining for antivenom and antibiotics." He looked over at her. "Pretty proud of yourself, aren't you."

"Yeah, I loved sticking it to those bullies." A tear crawled onto her chin. "Did McBride tell you about Pan?"

"Uh, huh." He reached for her hand. "You must be in shock."

"With so much else going on, I haven't fully processed it yet. Karina's been my priority."

"Is her mother coming?"

"No, her father."

Ryker crowed and slapped the steering wheel. "You mean the Viking who's going take a seat in the halls of Valhalla and spend eternity eating, drinking, and fighting? That guy?"

"The very same, and you won't believe the conversation we had." She feigned a serious tone. "We bonded."

He threw his head back as if in disbelief. "Ah, woman, you constantly surprise me."

When they arrived at the hospital, McBride met Sara at the door, his face pinched so tight the muscles twitched. He led her down the hall. "Staff rushed your two guys to a toasty room as directed. I don't know what you have on them, but it had better be good. They're threatening to lawyer up."

Sara smiled. "You won't believe *how* good, and it's all recorded on my phone with mug shots."

She instructed the hall nurse on what to say and told her to follow her in. She did exactly as ordered while pretending to read from the goons' charts. "Looks as though they may have gotten you here in time, but we won't know until we get the lab results."

Grouper spat out, "What lab results? They haven't done any fucking lab work yet."

"We need to do a blood draw to check the lining of your cells and see if it still clots and to determine if you might have an allergic reaction to the antivenom. Some people do."

Grouper rolled up his sleeve and held his arm out. "Take it."

The nurse turned to Possum. "And the doctor should be here soon to prescribe antibiotics."

"I'm burning up," he said. "Get them in here now."

Sara gripped the footboard rail of Grouper's bed and gave it a shake. "You reneged on our deal. I was to send someone to take you out of the swamp and you'd tell me when the village fire is."

"Bringing us out isn't worth shit without the antivenom and antibiotics. Where are they?"

"I promised evacuation, not drugs." She leaned forward on both arms. "Telling me your boss is going to set fire to the village is empty noise without knowing when. So you see, we're faced with a bit of a dilemma here."

"You go first," Grouper grumbled. "Ours is more critical."

"Indeed it is." She lifted the bandage to inspect the fang marks. "Every minute you delay, internal bleeding liquifies more of your innards." She covered the marks. "You make the call."

"And if we tell you, how do we know you'll come through."

"You have my word. If I were you, I wouldn't waste any time."

Sweat glistening on his face. Griper glanced at Ryker. "You're our witness."

He gave the nod.

"Okay then, the fire's set for near closing on the final day."

Another gut punch. "But that's today in less than two hours!" said Sara. "You should have told us earlier."

"And you should have forked over what we wanted."

You don't need any. It was a harmless banded water snake imitating a cottonmouth."

"You bitch." He bounded off the bed and lunged for Sara's throat. It took Ryker and McBride to pull him off and cuff him. He shook his arms. "What are these things for?"

"You're both under arrest for blackmail," McBride said and read them their Miranda rights.

"You can't charge us with blackmail because there was none," Possum said. "It was a grand hoax, a fake printout on his letterhead and a flash drive as empty as the snake venom. He had pictures of her everywhere. It was easy taking one."

Unaware of the relationship with her estranged father, Sara knew McBride had no inkling of the tsunami sweeping over her. His sole aim was solving the murder and beating Foster. He cuffed Possum. "Sorry, boys but under Florida statute 836.05 for threats and extortion you're guilty of a second degree felony and are going to jail."

"We're allowed one call to our lawyer."

"Not until we avert the fire," said Sara. A bone chilling dread echoed through her. "And we have less than two hours to find an arsonist in a thirty-five-acre village."

# Chapter 26

Ryker drove since Sara's car was still parked at the swamp. "You need to help find me better living quarters," he told her.

We got Foster. "You can go home to a hero's parade."

"My daughter won't visit if I'm in New York."

"What? You talked to her?"

He'd always been the tough cop. To admit vulnerability was not in his play book. He took the deep breath Sara preached. "Last night I was agonizing over your situation and couldn't sleep. If you didn't make it back, I'd be left all alone and couldn't face that. Still terrified of being rejected again, I finally got the courage to call my daughter's number the informant had given me, and we chatted. She's willing to come here in two weeks."

"So you need a cool crib. Great news."

"Now back to work. This is insane. Bad news is trying to spot an arsonist hidden among visitors dressed in costumes and playing roles. No one is who he appears to be."

"Good news is the numbers are thinning. Stages are empty. Performers who've done their last show are already packing up. Only shops and concessions will stay open until closing to ring up the last dollar of the season."

He parked in the rennie camping lot. "I've worked many bomb threats. Worst thing to do is create panic. We should split up and avoid doing anything out of the ordinary. I'll search the perimeter. You know that labyrinth in the middle better than me."

"Stay in touch."

Ryker went directly to the elephant compound. The private gate gave an easy escape route for an arsonist torching bales of hay. Flames would engulf everything. He crept along the barn wall and entered. Bo's odor lingered everywhere. Absolute quiet and then a thud as something hit the concrete floor. Muffled sounds.

"This is Detective Ryker of the Reunion Heights police. You're trespassing on private property. Show yourself."

A teenage boy and girl stepped from behind a storage cabinet, their hands in the air, clothing in disarray, lipstick smeared.

He chuckled at their adolescent lust. "Lower your arms and scram. The fair's closing." After they hightailed it, he did a quick search and found no hint of a planned arson.

Next stop, the zoo. Eight kids were petting goats and holding bunnies. He couldn't allow anything to happen to them. "I'm sorry," he told the mothers. "The weather station announced a rain storm with possible lightning, so we're closing a few minutes early." No time for idle conversation, Ryker then ordered the keeper to move the animals out immediately.

Sara phoned. "I found no incendiary devices. Heading to the blacksmith now. He's got a fire in his gut as well as the forge."

"Good luck with that. I just entered the Roma camp and will check the back gate."

The fortune teller intercepted him. "You people are like the cockroaches I keep stomping on and can't get rid of."

Ryker waved him off. "Not now."

He assumed the arsonist was a man and scrutinized every male visitor for telltale signs of nervousness. A man in his thirties holding a bag close to his chest was bouncing up and down on the balls of his feet, clenching and unclenching his free hand. He took a quick look around as if to ensure there were no cops. Time was too short for the usual prolonged surveyance. Ryker identified himself and asked what was inside.

Flustered, the man said, "Just some items my wife bought today."

"Where is she?"

"Getting a henna tattoo in that booth over there."

"Open it please," Ryker said.

"I already told you just a few—"

"Now."

Fingers trembling, the man unzipped a bag full of items with tags from Vitelli's Gold, the camp's most expensive shop.

"Receipts?"

His chest collapsed.

"Hey, Nicu," Ryker shouted, "Want this lowly shoplifter? He's all yours."

On his way out of the camp, he called Sara. "I just wasted ten minutes tagging some guy an arsonist who was a mere thief."

"I told Lazzero to get himself and his birds out of here ASAP, but he said he won't budge until we discuss Argentina."

"Did you?"

"Now's not the time. I shoved him away."

"Keep moving."

The herald walked past Ryker ringing a bell. "Hear ye, hear ye, me fair lords and ladies, the fair will close in fifteen minutes. Please hasten thee to the front entrance."

Ryker spotted a man wearing a Friar Tuck robe loose enough to conceal a device. The bag of flabby skin below his chin looked like a pelican pouch. "You there, I need you to open your robe."

"I will not, sire, for I wear no clothing beneath."

"You *will* open it."

"Nay."

"Then we're about to become real intimate friends." Ryker patted down every inch under there and found only blubber. He glanced at his own belly. Sara was right. Women wouldn't find that appealing.

A man on the path ahead kept checking his cell phone and

touching his face in masking behavior used to hide discomfort. He quickly turned away. Ryker was about to move in on him when a little girl exited the Royal Flush, took his hand, and looked up at daddy with a sweet smile.

Ryker's eyes moistened remembering Dulce as a kid that age. More time wasted. He'd focused too much on catching the arsonist rather than identifying the location. He called Sara. "I think we're going about this all wrong. I'm skipping the jousting arena. Sand and grass won't accelerate a fire. And a burned camping area won't justify not renewing the lease. Foster needs to destroy village real estate and make it appear to be an accident to clear himself of any  wrong doing. Think about where most home fires start."

"In the kitchen," she moaned. "I'm off to the food court now."

Ryker headed there too and smelled smoke. Knowing how many visitors could die, he felt his stomach climb into his throat. Waving his arms, he yelled, "Emergency. Get out of here. Go. Run!"

Nervous sweat ran down his body. His breathing quickened. His pulse pounded in his ears, pumping extra blood to his legs. Sara wasn't the only savior. He was Sir Galahad.

A loud boom, blinding flash, and then smoke billowed from Franny's Fryery. She was standing in front, paralyzed. A fiery ball burst in hot golden flames like a great famished beast devouring all in its path and belching thick gray smoke that burned Ryker's eyes. He hurled himself at her, dropped them both to the ground, and shielded Franny.

Her body heaved and fell beneath him in sobs. He choked on the thick acrid smell of smoke but kept telling her, "We're gonna be all right. Don't give up. I won't leave you." He wrapped tighter to cover her as tiny pieces of shattered wood rained down on them. Blaring sirens grew silent The fire department had arrived. "Help is here," said Ryker. "Just hang in there a little longer."

Minutes later, firemen doused them in water and lifted Ryker to his feet. "Go to your friend over there. We'll take care of the lady."

A fireman carried Franny to safety. Ryker hobbled behind and saw Sara rushing toward him. Two bystanders held her back as orange and yellow flames shot fifty feet high between them.

When he got through to her, Sara cried, "You're hurt."

"Nothing more than the usual minor scratches when you dive onto the ground and the sky falls down. I'll live but Franny's pretty shaken up."

Her face was ghastly white. She pointed to the Fryery. "Two of my workers are still in there. Please get them out."

Two firemen sprayed the front while a third ducked a falling timber to gain entrance. Ryker exhaled deeply to clear smoke from his lungs and hoped for the best but knew the odds weren't good. The building was too far gone. The fireman returned minutes later, his face downcast. "I'm afraid one didn't make it."

In a stupor, Franny asked, "What about the other?"

"I only saw one."

"How tall?"

"About your height."

"My nephew." She crumpled to the ground as if her bones had turned to liquid. She opened her mouth wide and wailed.

Sara went to Franny and held her until remains of the wooden shop smoldered and the fire died out leaving only ashes in its wake and a deathlike grayness floating in the smoky air.

The captain spoke with Franny afterward. "How did it start?"

"I have large commercial fryers. I was busy out in front getting ready to close down for the season and told the new man, Jason, to turn all three off as he'd done the last two weeks. Seconds later my nephew hollered the fryers were burning. I trained him. He should have known better but was young and panicked. He threw water on it. A loud blast, flash of light, and being pulled to the ground is all I remember."

Ryker asked the captain, "You're positive, no signs of Jason?"

"My men did a thorough search. What are you implying?"

"I'm not at liberty to say."

Ryker motioned Sara to join him and speak to Franny. "I know this is a very difficult time, but we have to ask a few questions. Will that be all right?"

She wiped her face on a sleeve and nodded.

"You said Jason turned the fryers off the last two weeks. Who did it before then?"

"His brother Ron."

All the muscles in Ryker's jaw hardened. "You're certain they were brothers?"

"He had a picture of them together as kids and said Ron had finally been hired for a high paying job he applied for a year ago." Franny rubbed her fingers nervously. "Jason said he came to fulfill his brother's contract."

Sara cupped both hands over Franny's. "It's okay. You've done nothing wrong. Did Ron come by to pick up his last paycheck?"

"No. And I thought it strange a faithful worker for two seasons didn't even say goodbye."

"Have an address or phone number for Jason?" Ryker asked.

"Inside on my cell phone, but everything's been destroyed."

Sara said, "Will you come to the station, repeat what you've told us, and help our sketch artist with a picture of him?"

Franny nodded. "Anything to help."

"Is there anyone you can stay with?" Ryker asked.

"A friend in that trailer right over there next to mine."

"Get a good night's sleep. An officer will come by to pick you up in the morning."

This was Franny whom Ryker had grown fond of stopping at her Fryery every day. He called McBride with details and then told him, "Place a guard at the trailer where she's staying tonight in case Foster tries to tie up any loose ends."

With a gentle hip bump, Sara said, "Let's go get those *minor* scratches taken care of."

That little bit of playfulness masked her grief and softened the lines in his face. "Taking your car, are we?"

She smirked. "Give me your keys."

McBride met them at the hospital. "How are you doing?"

"This old bull isn't ready to be put out to pasture quite yet."

"Shielding her was beyond the call of duty."

"The poor woman lost her entire livelihood," said Ryker.

"And a boy died trying to be a hero for his aunt," Sara added.

"We've got Foster guilty for her nephew's death," said Ryker. "He had to plan the fire several weeks ago in order to get rid of Ron and plant his arsonist in the Fryery. Jason ignited it, slipped out the back, and disappeared Scot free."

"Or so he thinks," said Sara. "Franny will make a full statement tomorrow and meet with the sketch artist. We'll get him."

Ryker was restless, shifting his weight left to right. "We need to nail Foster before he learns his thugs didn't finish the job."

"I've got his address and a beautifully signed arrest warrant." The corners of McBride's mouth twitched with an unleashed smile. "Let's go get the bastard."

McBride and a couple of uniforms in squad cars were already there when Sara and Ryker arrived at a large contemporary house hidden behind tall junipers and elms. They entered a covered lanai. Sara and Ryker waited out of sight to the side of the door while McBride rang the bell, warrant in hand.

Foster answered and spoke through the screen. "If it isn't our second-rate police chief who bungled a murder investigation right under his nose. Inept fool ran out of time." His voice rose in grating laughter. "And look, he even brought a letter." With a cocky stance, he added, "Your woeful resignation, and I fully support your desire to move down to the bush league where you're better suited."

"I'd like you to step out on the porch, please," said McBride.

"And why should I?"

Ryker stepped in front, opened the screen door, and yanked Foster out. "Because he told you to and very politely, I might add."

Sara moved into the light from the silver globe above his door. She relished the look of horror on his face.

"What . . . who . . . I thought you—"

"Were dead? No, I'm very much alive as are the boy and girl you ordered murdered and disposed of."

"Turn and put your hands behind your back," said McBride.

Foster resisted until Sara and Ryker each grabbed an arm and forced him to face the house. McBride pulled cuffs from his belt, clicked them around his prisoner's wrists, and turned him to the front again. "Corbin Foster, I have a warrant for your arrest."

"On what grounds?"

"Conspiracy to commit murder, first degree arson, and drug trafficking. You have the right to remain silent. Anything you say can and will be used against you in a court of law. You have the right to an attorney. If you cannot afford an attorney, one will be appointed for you."

A smile worked its way across McBride's face as he walked Foster to the squad car and opened the rear door. "Crawl in there, NYPD's most wanted criminal. You're a nothing but a has been."

"My lawyers will free me within forty-eight hours."

Ryker slapped the roof. "Not this time. We've got you dead to rights. Your two thugs are in custody with signed affidavits."

After the car left, McBride turned to Ryker and Sara. His body relaxed as if a marionette had loosened the strings. "This is the first time in nine days that I haven't felt my life was over. And the city owes immense gratitude to you. Foster and his cronies would have destroyed it."

"I wanted to get him as much as you did," said Ryker.

"Does that mean your stint here is over and you'll be heading back to New York?"

"Not sure. Thinking of staying if I can find work."

McBride burst out laughing. "You're hired, but I don't want

to see your hide for two days. And you, Sara, are to take the next week off to recover from your little swamp antic."

"Thanks, I won't balk at the offer. My physical and emotional selves need mending."

Ryker took Sara's arm and walked her to his car. "I'll stay on your couch tonight and drive you to the swamp in the morning."

Her forehead against the passenger window, she stared at the passing city lights without seeing them.

"Do you want to talk?"

"Not now. I still haven't come to grips with Pan's imminent death yet."

"You will in time. And it will get easier. Do you regret opening your virtual door to Pan and Karina?"

"No. Those two kids facing almost impossible hurdles weren't afraid to love. They taught me that staying in my closet, I was just marking time. With her father's strength to hold onto, Karina will get through this. I've been flying solo with no parachute all my life and don't want to be alone anymore."

"You need to go to your father."

"Agreed, but I'm too emotionally and physically bankrupt to face him yet." Sara turned to Ryker. "And what about you? Are you staying here?"

He gave her hand a little squeeze. "Well, it appears I have no choice. My daughter will have nothing to do with dear old dad if he's in New York."

"Good for her. I think we'll make a good team."

"But only if you stop hiding behind a locked door."

"I promise to leave it ajar."

The End

# About the Author

Linda's favorite university classes were in cultural anthropology. They kindled her desire to travel the world and explore different societies. She's visited 69 countries as of 2024 and is not done yet. She immersed herself in Sherpa culture, helped them found the first lodge system in Nepal, and later led treks to the Everest base camp. *Beyond the Summit: Everest Adventure & Romance* published by Pilgrims Publishing is a fictional account of this endemic tribe Working one summer at a Renaissance fair, she lived in the village. The color, costuming, and mandated Elizabethan speech of rennie artisans and performers who travel the US circuit intrigued her. In her free time, Linda plays pickleball six days a week and hikes.

Other books by Linda LeBlanc. *No Summit out of Sight: The True Story of the Youngest Person to Climb the Seven Summits* published by Simon and Schuster 2014. Linda is the sole author.

*Four Teens on Everest* 2014 YA fiction

If you enjoyed *A Fair Knight Slain*, please tell your friends and write a review on Amazon.

Linda will meet with book clubs at any time or place, in person if within driving distance or via Zoom.

Email:maa07yaa@gmail.com www.facebook.com/nepalwriter/